Hold You Close

The Seattle Sound Series
Book 3

Alexa Padgett

Hold You Close © 2016 by Alexa Padgett

Edited by Bev Katz Rosenbaum and Nicole Pomeroy
Cover Art by Sarah Hansen of Okay Creations

ISBN: 978-1-945090-11-0

CHAPTER ONE
Mila

Fourteen months ago, I tossed away my entire life. For him. Murphy. He didn't know any of it, and, finally, I was coming to terms with the fact he probably never would.

He didn't want to see me, never would again. His song, "She's So Bad," reinforced my opinion—hard.

I walked down the narrow, hard-packed dirt path, ducking under the thick limb of a gnarled tree. The last few days proved more difficult than I anticipated—wasn't the first year supposed to be the hardest?—but the visit to Me-Kwa-Mooks Park was nonnegotiable. I needed the soft sound of water to ground me, give me a reason to move forward. Problem was, water, the beach, reminded me of Murphy. Even this gray Seattle version, so different from our Sydney favorite with its soft, white sand and surfers dotting the water.

I settled in on the narrow strip of sand, gazing out over the tumbled gray boulders and the fog-riddled green-gray water. I patted my other pocket. Thank goodness for my trusty little bottle of Xanax, the only reason I'd get through these next few days.

Pulling out the ticket, I read the date. He'd be here in Seattle tomorrow, performing sold-out shows at Key Arena and the more intimate Tractor Tavern. That's the ticket I held now. Probably a complete waste of the $80, but I needed to see him.

My phone range.

"Mila!"

Mum's voice sent me back into a tailspin. I might love my mother, but that didn't mean I trusted her. She'd let me down too many times. She was part of the reason I'd moved.

1

"I'm thinking of coming for a visit. I've never been to America."

And my stomach tanked even further. "That's okay, mum. I'll get out to visit you." Lie, lie, lie. I'd never set foot in Australia again. I'd made that promise on my last trip to the cemetery to visit my son.

She made a disgruntled sound. "You've said that for the last year. And last time we Skyped, you were so thin! It's those crazy hours you work."

"I like my job," I said, standing. No point in sitting here enjoying a view when my mum's criticism had already destroyed the moment. "Sure, I work a lot but that's because I have to go through a second residency to be licensed in the States." I'd completed the certification but still had more than two years left on my accredited residency. The good news was I was able to work in my preferred field.

"I don't know how you could. You haven't been home for a visit in ages. I barely know what you do."

"Because you're not interested."

"Of course I am. Jordan asks me all the time."

At the sound of his name, I stumbled. The phone slid from my fingers but I managed to catch it before it hit the dirt.

"You didn't tell him I was here, did you?"

"Now, why would you worry about that?" Her voice was all innocent. She'd blinked her eyes, I'd bet. I hated that expression because it meant she'd done something royally stupid. Or insane. Like the time she'd married a man fifteen years older than she was. The bloke was a rancher with a cattle station out in the Western Territory. Their affair lasted long enough for us to travel to his godforsaken stretch of red, dusty land before my mum dug in her heels, insisting he take us back to "civilization." He'd dropped us in Sydney, disgust shining from his eyes.

That summed up my childhood—one flighty mistake after another. At least the mistakes didn't hurt anyone. Until Jordan. But he wasn't my mum's mistake. More like *her* mum's.

"Mum," I said. I backed away, planning to dart back into my car and…what? Hyperventilate? Call the police because I was scared?

"Don't be like that, Mila." Impatience laced her tone. Her mouth must be puckering in that annoyed moue she tried hard not to let settle over her still-perfect skin. "Jordan loves you. And anyway, why would he care about your boring old doctor job in the Pacific Northwest?"

"You told him I live here?" My voice went from too loud to too quiet. I couldn't breathe. I clutched my keys and purse like they could hold me erect.

Allowing my mum to visit was the *worst* idea. Danger smeared this situation. At least she only knew I was in the Northwest, not the name of my hospital, and I refused to have my photo taken for the website and used my initials for my bio, intentionally sounding as masculine as possible in any and all professional documentation. I'd never given my mother my precise location, fearing she'd rat me out. I glanced around the deserted Seattle beach. My private sanctuary destroyed with fears of being accosted. Dragged from the safety of my life. I'd already lost my boyfriend, my baby, my future because my mother didn't believe me.

"It's been *years* since you made up those silly accusations, Mila. Nothing came of it and Jordan's forgiven you. Let it go."

Fourteen months and four days since I left her house for good. Twelve months and twenty-one days since my last run-in with Jordan Jones when he mowed me down on that bicycle. I dropped a small pill into my open mouth and swallowed. Thirty-one minutes and the relief would begin to trickle through my system. I closed my eyes.

"See? A lifetime. I'll make the flight arrangements today. Should I fly into Seattle or Spokane? Vancouver? Portland?"

Sweat burst across my skin. Subtlety wasn't my mother's strong suit. It was obvious Jordan had asked her to fish for more information. I grabbed a tree branch as I passed by, holding it tight in my hand as my knees weakened.

"Oops! I'm late for my next appointment. I'll touch base with you soon." I hung up the phone before my mum could respond. I'd turn it off completely but I needed the reassurance of being able to call 911 in under five seconds. My legs gave out completely and I plopped onto the ground, my breathing ragged and my eyes stinging with the tears I wouldn't shed.

My mum hadn't believed me then. Not when I was eighteen and scared. Not when I was twenty-one and jaded. And definitely not when I was twenty-seven and so broken, I never would have been able to put myself back together if my best friend, Noelle, hadn't collected my sorry self and forced me onto that airplane.

That my mother would actively help Jordan seek me out again, even after I'd moved halfway around the world, told me how little she'd ever cared for me.

But she didn't know where I lived, and I wasn't about to tell her.

Anyway, I was being silly. Jordan was in Sydney. I kept tabs on him through social media. Well, actually, Noelle was the face of the accounts. I couldn't be that close to him, not even via the binary code of computers.

I released a shaking breath and forced my legs under me. No way my mum would bring him here. I sucked in a breath and released it slowly. My legs were stiff, but I managed to stand and walk to the car. I settled into the supple leather seat. Immediately, I locked the doors and slid the key into the ignition. Shoving the car into reverse, I refused to acknowledge that my hands trembled or my breath came in shallow pants.

I was safe. Thousands of miles away from Jordan Jones. There was no reason to panic. No reason to worry.

I pulled over onto a side street and let the shivers take hold of my body. Finally, the medication kicked in and I leaned my head back against the seat, closing my eyes as I forced my tensed muscles to relax.

My mum's phone call brought it all back. All the ugliness I'd been trying so hard to put behind me.

I'd wanted to go back to Perth for the first anniversary, but I couldn't gather enough courage. Plus, I'd reasoned, Murphy was touring through the American Northeast at the time. Not much chance of me running into him in Perth if he was in the States. And that's what I needed: a chance meeting.

To tell him the truth.

To apologize for killing his child.

———◆———

I parked in my normal spot behind the hospital, gaze flicking faster than a startled bird. My mum's call shattered my peaceful life. Even so, even with the added protection of my security system and the anonymity that came with eschewing social media, the old memories slithered out of the box I locked them in, gripping me by the throat long before I could push them aside.

"Mila, love. Roll down the window. There's a doll."

I shook my head, pulse racing. Jordan tried the car door, slammed his palm into the glass separating us when he found it locked. I always locked my doors. My windows, too. I knew what would stalk in if I didn't. I had the nightmares to prove it. When Jordan's hand slammed the glass for a second time, I flinched but managed to get the car into reverse.

"Jordan, what are you doing? Mila, where are you going?" Mum raised her voice.

I pulled out of the drive, trying to contain my shivers. Didn't work. Where to go? I had no one here who believed me. I was so alone.

I huddled deeper into my sweater, half-expecting to see his face, florid with anger and lust, mere inches from mine. No, that incident occurred almost a decade ago—when I was twenty. Half the world away, too. But for weeks thereafter, I lived on the streets until I finally found a place to stay near my university. Even then, I wasn't safe enough to stay in one place long.

Because I knew Jordan wasn't going to stop harassing me until he got what he wanted. He'd changed his tactics now, using my mum as the intermediary. Not surprising, really, because Mum loved Jordan.

"He takes such good care of me," Mum would singsong into the phone. Like the time he'd bought her a new car right after I graduated from high school. Or the time he brought her favorite meat pies before she left for work, and she told him to stay, get comfortable. He took that to mean kiss and cuddle me, willingness be damned. I shuddered hard, hating the memory, hating *him*. Jordan used money and gifts as a form of manipulation, but my mother refused to see that. Didn't want to see my low-life scum of a step-relative for what he truly was.

He lived with her now, she'd said. After the *incident* in Perth that cost me my child and almost my life, she'd let him into her house, my old bedroom. That's when I decided to leave the country for good.

I clicked my phone on and pulled up Noelle's number. Anything to keep myself from reaching into my pocket and pulling out the bottle of pills.

Want to go for drinks tonight?

I forced my hand to open and withdrew it from my pocket.

I wasn't going to give in. I wasn't going to abuse my pills anymore.

Sure. I'll text Maura. Noelle responded A moment later my text app beeped again. *You up for a girls' night?*

Noelle knew all about Jordan and his sick obsession. She knew about my mother's disbelief. She'd been the one to get me the position here after I'd called her to tell her I'd lost my baby. Noelle was my best friend, the woman who saved me from myself—as I would for her if she ever needed me to.

Much as I wanted to, I'd never told Noelle about Murphy. I wasn't willing to share my stupid fantasy where Murphy slid his pointer finger down my nose and over my lips like he used to. Even after his lyrics, his womanizing, I wanted nothing more than to be tucked into his side in his bed. We'd rarely shared a bed because our moments together were few and much further between than either of us would have liked.

What was *wrong* with me?

Heading into the building, I took deep, even breaths. Time to let him go. He'd moved on—I had to, too.

I blinked back the building headache and swallowed down the tension-relieving and refreshing herbal tea in one suffering gulp. I double-checked my larger tote, which held my work ID, my wallet, and a variety of other important details, including my lunch, my passport, and the ring Murphy gave me just days before our relationship ended.

I pulled the slim silver band out and slid it on my finger. It wasn't an engagement ring, but it was delicate and beautiful. Murphy had seen it from a shop window while we were strolling through Darling Harbor one of those long-summer afternoons.

He'd popped in and dashed back out, sliding the platinum band on my ring finger as he kissed me.

"It'll feel even better when I do that officially."

"What?" I'd breathed against his lips.

"You're mine, love." He'd raised my hand and kissed the ring and someone snapped a picture of us, there, so happy.

The picture changed my life forever.

I sighed, my throat convulsing as I tried to keep the memory fresh, hold on to the warmth in his eyes just another moment. Whatever. Time to move on.

Maura's text back to both Noelle and me was immediate: *If you're buying, I'm drinking. Like a fish.*

She would, too. Maura's break from her last boyfriend a few weeks before still made me wince. She'd hoped to get married and he'd decided to move out and onward with an older woman. Not the stuff fairy tales were made of. Unless they were the original Grimm stories. I'd always hated those.

The day passed smoothly. I ate at my desk, as was my habit. I spent the afternoon eyeballs-deep in patients. It's one of the things I loved best about my job, the ability to focus on their problems, their ailments, and block out all the messy emotions trying to pour over me. I jerked when Siggie, another resident in my program, told me he was leaving.

"What time is it?" I asked, blinking at the computer screen where I'd been finishing up some notes.

"Crap! It's after seven. Gotta go, Siggie. See you tomorrow."

I saved my work and grabbed my bag, sprinting from the building. I sped down the sidewalk, weaving in between late-evening commuters. One man tried to engage me in conversation for all of the four seconds it took to shove my earbuds into my ears. Greatest invention ever.

If the earbuds didn't work, I'd fish out Murphy's ring again. The band surrounding my finger was comforting, a lightweight tether. No—a bridge between this reality and my previous one.

I wasn't sure how Murphy came up with the money for it. Cash was always short in those days, and I'd loved him most for his willingness to work hard and do without some of the youthful fun so that his mum was secure. He'd shared a tiny flat with his brother Jake, who was often sitting on the small, sagging couch, fiddling with some new bass beat.

Because both Murphy and I valued privacy, we'd spent hours walking on the beach. Our best dates included a visit to a small diner to share fish and chips. He'd talked about taking me out some place fancy. Like that mattered more than the attention he gave me. After growing up as I did, spending more time taking care of my mother than the other way around, I cherished Murphy's

9

desire to coddle me. He made me feel special, safe. I missed that.

I didn't bother to turn on my music or even plug the earbuds into my phone as I hurried down the sidewalk. The point: getting people to ignore me so I could continue to ignore them. The man's eyes lingered on my face before shifting down to my figure, trying to take my measurements through my sweater and long skirt.

Noelle wouldn't let me dress in anything too baggy or form-concealing, stating my need for professional attire even at the hospital—though I did prefer a size-too-large scrubs and a knee-length lab coat over anything formfitting. She always frowned, pointing out I deserved to wear clothes that gave me confidence. She was both right and wrong.

I reached the door to the bar, my mind spinning, when someone called my name. A man. My heart began to pound and my hands shook. I turned my head in cautious increments, the need to be sure outweighing my desire to flee. I glanced up and down the street, quickly sifting through the men to find one with a similar build to Jordan, but didn't see anyone I knew.

I exhaled in a harsh gust of frustration and fear. Mum couldn't tell him where to find me because I wouldn't tell her. She remained stubbornly stupid—if it didn't fit in with the reality she wanted to live in, then it didn't exist. Like Jordan's stalking. Never mind the many times I told her about my discomfort or fear. I even went to my school counselor, but my mum simply waved it away, explaining my fatherless childhood led to this ridiculous need for attention.

So no one believed me, and Murphy's mum was accosted because of it. All in the past. I was in Seattle—granted the population was much smaller than in Sydney—but no way Jordan could've found me so quickly. It was unlikely he'd find me at all.

After another long glance around, still unnerved, I stepped into the bar.

Maura waved me over to a table in the middle of the room. I slid into the booth and muttered an apology. She shook her head, smirking.

"Please. It's all good." She sipped from her gin and tonic and winked. "Some nice gentleman at the bar got me all settled in."

"And how do you plan to pay him back?" I asked.

Her grin widened. "With a smile and a kiss."

I rolled my eyes. Maura was my opposite—tall, with a model's lean figure, heaps of natural blond hair spilling down her back, and piercing green eyes. The woman knew how to flirt and she knew how to work every inch of her long-limbed figure. I was her petite, dark-haired friend who preferred to remain unnoticed and dressed somewhere between a librarian and a church granny.

"Sorry I'm late," Noelle said, bumping me with her hip. Her brown ringlets bounced around her head in a halo of thick corkscrews. She wore her hair long to keep the curls tamed—her words—but I'd never seen those ringlets as anything other than wild. A man glanced over, his eyes dipping to Noelle's hair. Yep, his thoughts skewed to holding all that glorious hair in a fist while he did naughty things to her lush curves.

I smirked at the guy, whose cheeks brightened. He smiled, a bit sheepish to have been caught, and turned back to his date. Hell, I got it. I was a straight woman and understood Noelle's appeal.

With a single glance, she pulled me tight against her side. I rested my head on her shoulder, thankful for my friend's continued support. We'd met nearly seven years earlier when she'd spent a year at my uni in Sydney. She ran into me one morning, late to class. After doubling back to make sure I was okay, she'd bought me coffee. Since she'd missed her class, I made up for it by showing her around Sydney—the good parts tourists didn't see. Years later, when I'd needed a place to land after escaping Perth, I'd called Noelle. She'd invited me to come stay with her without asking any questions, waiting until I was ready to spill the rest of my sordid secrets. Well, most of them anyway.

After a few shuddering breaths, I pulled back.

Noelle tucked my lank hair behind my ear. "You look terrible."

"Been a rough couple of days."

"The meds aren't helping?"

I sucked in my lip. "I just started the script." This *bottle*. I'd been on the meds before I even moved here, but I'd been too embarrassed to tell Noelle. As another health care professional, she understood the pills' purpose, and she'd know that, over time, the effect from the original dosage could wear off. Still, I'd used the pills as a crutch this week, and that couldn't be healthy.

"Alpie's not helping?" The question was rhetorical and Noelle continued. "You'll feel better after the show. Alpie's been learning new soothing sayings."

Alpie was my bird, a beautiful rose-colored Galah cockatoo. I'd connected with her at a bird sanctuary Noelle dragged me to a few months before when I refused more intense therapy. While Alpie wasn't a service animal, she did provide emotional support, and she made coming home easier. I'd never liked the idea of living alone.

"What did you teach her?" I asked, narrowing my eyes.

"You'll have to ask her," Noelle said with a smug grin. "Good news is you'll be much better able to sleep after the concert tomorrow. You can cocoon in that big bed of yours for a couple of days."

There was a time, after I lost the baby, I wasn't sure I'd ever leave my bed again. But eventually, after my depression abated enough, I craved the company of others. Problem was I couldn't stand the idea of another man touching me intimately. A mistake, that. I should have tried harder to find someone, especially after I settled into my job with one of Seattle's top OB/GYNs.

"You're probably right," I said with a sigh.

"What's got you so peppy?" Maura asked, smirking at Noelle. She leaned forward and sucked on her straw.

"You won't believe who I met today!" Noelle said. "Briar Moore. You know. The one who's dating super-hottie Hayden Crewe from Jackaroo."

I jerked, knocking Noelle in the leg, unable to control my body at the mention of Murphy's band. Why did everything lead me back to thoughts of him?

Noelle pulled my hand up onto the table and patted it.

"No need to hate all things Aussie, Mil. Sure, you're easier to understand now that you speak American, but even you have to admit those Jackaroo guys are talented *and* hot."

They were. All of them. I only really knew Murphy and Jake, but Hayden and Flip appealed to the female population, too. After leaving Perth—and Australia—for the last time, I'd become a closet Jackaroo gossip junkie. Correction: a Murphy Etsam gossip junkie.

During way too many late nights spent crushed by Murphy's man-whore ways, I'd learned interesting new tidbits about Hayden. He was an introverted man, but now he was stuck with the job of leading a band.

Best not left to Murphy anyway. He lacked the ability to organize and hated schedules. I frowned. Or he had. I used to be the one who prodded Murphy, getting him to work and his gigs on time, thrilled to be useful. But I hadn't been there to help in a long time, and clearly, Murphy had changed.

The waitress appeared, asking, "Your pleasure?" which irritated me. Why did everything have to be sexual?

Maybe it wasn't. Didn't matter, though because Murphy didn't want me. I was going to die, unsexed, unloved, still paying the price for trying to protect the only family that ever mattered.

"Vodka martini," I said.

"Whoa! Bringing out the heavy guns, aren't we?" Noelle said. "No need to go nuclear this early in the evening. I'll have a gin and tonic. Light on the gin, real heavy on the tonic."

I shrugged as the waitress left, unwilling to share my inner turmoil. Maura ordered another drink before she asked Noelle to dish on her meeting today. She wrapped her pretty pink lips around her straw as she made eye contact with a guy across the bar. She winked before turning back to us.

"So Briar Moore wants to start a counseling program for families of cancer patients. Especially those with low chances of recovery. She received some private grant from a patient and met with the cancer chief to discuss possibilities. She's super nice. Not at all what I expected."

"What did you expect?" Maura asked. "And is she pretty? Some of those pictures the paparazzi took when Hayden ditched her weren't flattering."

"She's gorgeous. She has these blue eyes that just kind of catch you up in them. She's taller than me and in extremely good shape.

And, *man*, can she listen. Like all her focus is on you. It's intense."

Maura snickered as the waitress set down our drinks. I snagged mine, taking a big gulp.

"You're a little in love with her," Maura said.

Noelle shrugged. "I might've been if Hayden hadn't shown up. That guy rocks. In every sense of the word. He oozes music and raw sex appeal."

I took another gulp and motioned to the waitress to bring me another. She nodded.

"What's up, Mil? You're quiet and slurping down liquor faster than Maura."

"Hey!"

"What?" Noelle said. "You know you drink too much."

Maura glared, pushing back her drink.

"I thought I heard Jordan calling my name just as I came into the bar." I shivered. To cover it up, I downed the last of my drink.

"You're coming home with me tonight, shug," Noelle said, eyes filled with concern.

"Tell me more about Crewe. I want to hear about his intense hotness," Maura said, throwing her straw across the table at Noelle. It hit me in the hand and I picked it up.

"He's the front-liner of the band," I said. "He and Murphy used to split singing duties, but the fans like Hayden's voice better so he's taken on the front-man spot. From the current reports, that's caused tension in the ranks. My guess is Murphy feels threatened, especially since his song catapulted them into super-stardom."

Both Noelle and Maura gaped at me for a long moment. The waitress dropped off my drink, eyeing us with concern, before either of them shut their mouths.

"You *know* the members of Jackaroo?" Maura asked.

My gaze fell to the table top. "No, I knew Murphy Etsam. He was my boyfriend."

"Holy fucking shit!" Noelle's eyes were wide. "How didn't I know this? He's the Murphy you left because of Jordan?"

I snatched up my fresh glass. I nodded, miserable. I sipped my drink. The vodka felt like gasoline as it slid down to my stomach.

"Wait! Oh my god!" Noelle shrieked, and all the heads in the bar turned toward us. "You're the girl. You're 'She's So Bad.'"

I set my glass down with exquisite care. I both hated and loved that song. I hated that Murphy thought that of me. I loved that he'd loved me enough to pour all his feelings into a song.

Noelle wrapped her arm around my shoulder. "I wasn't thinking. I'm sorry, Mila. You're nothing like the girl in that song."

"But I am. As far as Murphy's concerned, I *am* that girl. Some of the lyrics are from the note I left him. He wanted me to be sure I knew he'd written that song about me."

"I'm missing something," Maura said, leaning in. "You dated Murphy Etsam from Jackaroo? The super-hot, broody, man-whore lead guitarist?"

I nodded.

"And his song, the one that made the band an international phenomenon, is about you?"

Again, I nodded, my throat too clogged with emotion to speak. Noelle petted my head.

"Give me more than that," Maura moaned.

I licked my lips. "He loved me," I sighed, willing my eyes not to tear. "But then Jordan…" I pulled the ring from my pocket where I placed it earlier, needing the false sense of security it gave me. I slid it on and off my finger, debating whether I wanted to wear it or just hold it.

Noelle gripped my hand, her eyes focused on the simple silver band. "I've never seen you wear a ring. Wait, Murphy gave you this?" she asked, her voice full of sympathy.

"Yeah, about a week before I broke up with him."

I didn't drink often. My experience with Jordan taught me to be ever-vigilant.

Only with Murphy did I ever give over and have more than one drink. I knew he'd keep me safe. And he did. Until I let him go.

"Why?" Maura prompted.

Noelle squeezed my arm. She knew what came next. I placed my other hand on top of hers, watching it shake.

"The stalker found me again."

"Step-uncle," Noelle said.

I shrugged, dropping my hand away. "He'd lived with us for a while when I was in my last year of high school and my mum insisted I call him Uncle Jordan."

Maura shook her head, her eyes never leaving my face. "I'm confused."

"Jordan has an obsession with Mila," Noelle said. "A very unhealthy sexual one."

The worst of the tension drifted from the back of my neck, easing the pounding in my skull as I finished the last of the liquid in my glass. There wasn't enough. I still hurt. The fear clawed through me, ripping at my insides; I needed to be numb.

I looked at the ring on my finger, my chest aching with the need to scream building there, my mind clouded with memories of that horrible night that altered the trajectory of my life. The fear was

17

overpowering, especially when Jordan held that knife and threatened to use it on Murphy, his brother, and mother. So, after leaving Murphy with the note, a note I'd struggled to write, I let Jordan pull me into his car and take me back to my mother's house. I let the letch touch me, kiss me, pet me on that sagging couch. And because he still held the bloody knife, I kissed him and touched him, too.

When Jordan fell asleep, a sated smile on his face, I took all the cash in his wallet—over two thousand dollars. The bastard owed me, I reckoned. I walked to a bus stop. From there, I called the police with an anonymous tip, stating the Etsam brothers and their mum were in danger from a rabid fan. Sure enough, I read the police picked Jordan up in front of Susan's house the next day. He'd threatened her with the big knife the night before in his car but no charges were filed.

I traveled aimlessly until I got short on funds. I ended up in Perth working at the hospital because it's what I knew. For a month, I spent most of my time glancing over my shoulder.

One time, I hadn't looked for Jordan fast enough.

CHAPTER TWO
Murphy

The song's lyrics were a poison in my gut, and typically they were just waiting to burst out of my mouth. Tonight, though, the words felt thick and clunky on my tongue. I hated performing this song, always had. Sure, I should be thrilled with its success— this angsty rip into a girl's character catapulted my band, Jackaroo, into the stratosphere.

But this wasn't a girl. No, the woman I railed against was Mila. I sang the hell out of the next line because she *was* bad. She'd left me, not caring I still loved her, and never bothered to come back. And I'd proven I didn't need her or her love. I made lots of points to prove it.

I missed my next cue, catching it a moment too late. To cover up the mistake, I bent down to do some fan hand-touching. The sheilas lapped that sappy tripe up. I would have my pick at the end of the night as I did every night.

I didn't much care. Not about the women. Worse, though, I no longer cared about myself either.

Not since I near-ruined my best mate's chances with his girl. I glanced over, but Hayden avoided meeting my eyes, just as he had every time we were in the same vicinity. Since that night in Amsterdam.

I finished the song on the building growl the fans seemed to love. I held my arms out wide, breathing hard, as I finished the last song of the second-to-last stop on what could very well be our first and only world tour. The audience screamed their love, a few sets of panties appeared on the stage and a girl just in

19

front of me flashed her tits.

I glanced over in time to see Jake rolling his eyes. He expected me to take the girl back to the bus because I usually did. I didn't know how to tell him what I was just beginning to understand myself: the sex couldn't solve the problem. *I* was the problem—my hurt at Mila's actions. But *my* actions caused the rift in my band.

Hayden walked over to stand next to me. He bowed and the decibel level went up, way past eleven. The girls preferred him. I smirked at him, my eyes dropping to the growing pile of ladies' undies. His lip curled in distaste and he shook his head in an almost imperceptible negation.

The reason why stood not ten feet from him just in the stage wings. She and Hayden were pretty much surgically attached— either via hand, hip, or lips.

Briar's eyes slid from Hayden's back and caught mine. She crossed her arm over her chest and clutched her opposite elbow but she didn't relinquish my gaze. Instead, she raised a brow. I'd made a point to stay out of her way—neither she nor Hayden were much interested in my apology even though I'd tried to give it multiple times. I tipped my chin to her, an acknowledgment of her status. Hayden stiffened, his hands fisting. Not wanting to push our tenuous peace any further, I turned back to the crowd and took my bow.

Jake stood on my other side. No one touched me. Just the women who didn't know how deep my rottenness delved. Flip joined us. My gaze flicked down to the girl who'd flashed me. She was pretty. They all were. But I didn't have much interest in her.

Fuck all, I wanted Mila. Stupid though it was, I *missed* her. At least, the woman I'd thought she was. Until she ripped my heart to shreds.

Might as well make the most of the tail end of the tour and try to forget my driving need for the one woman I couldn't find, let alone have. Only the gig at the Tractor Tavern left. Flip was desperate to get back to Cynthia and his two-month-old son, John. But Harry'd added these shows in Seattle to the end of the tour so Hayden could spend more time with Briar, get her settled in her new counseling program and help her sort out some of her friend Rosie's last wishes. At least, that's what Harry said. More like, he and the rest of the record label knew as soon as we split, we weren't going to get back together any time soon. If ever.

Probably to the guys' surprise, I hadn't argued the point. In fact, I was glad for the four days in one place. Key Arena was huge, but not one of the biggest venues we'd played. After the Tractor Tavern gig tomorrow night, I was at loose ends. Seven months on the road, pretty much a show every night. We were burned out from the constancy of seeing each other and working, sure, but I'd burnt too many bridges with my bandmates to call them my mates. Or us much of a band. Our chemistry had been sliding for weeks. Even before I made the fatal mistake of trying to keep Hayden away from Briar. Not my place, and I'd known it then, but I hadn't wanted my best mate to fall into the same angry trap I couldn't crawl out of—all because of a woman who wasn't what he needed. I'd been wrong about them. Much as I shouldn't feel it, under my anger with Mila and my shame for how I'd treated Hayden and especially Briar, was grief. Hayden got his girl in the end, and I... Bollocks. I hated feeling this lonely.

I slid the mic back into its stand and made my way off stage.

I asked the roadie to find the girl who'd flashed me. If not her, then another pretty one as long as she didn't have brown hair and brown eyes. I steered clear of any woman with features or coloring similar to Mila. Screwing a look-alike was too pathetic, even for me.

I made it to the dressing room and swiped at my sweaty forehead. No one joined me. Not that I expected them to. Sure, it hurt, Jake's defection the most. My younger brother had long viewed me as his hero. Until I stepped so far over the line even he couldn't defend me.

The girl entered.

"You eighteen?" I barked. I might be a complete arse, but I wasn't going to jail.

"Yes. Of course," she stuttered.

"Let me see your ID." I held out my hand while she fumbled through her bag. "The real one," I sighed.

Flustered, she managed to pull out a driver's license with her actual picture. Pretty. Fresh. And too damn young.

Handing it back, I snagged my pen and a bottle of water. "What can I sign for you, sweetheart?"

Relieved, and angry because I was relieved, I pulled out one of our band tees and scribbled my name on it. I thrust it toward her as I called, "Harry!"

Our manager strolled in. He pretended to ignore me in favor of pulling a piece of lint on his bespoke suit. I scowled as I nodded to the girl and he moved toward her, cupping her elbow and leaning toward her. If he wanted her, fine. But I wouldn't be the one written up on a gossip site for screwing an underage Yank.

Jake sauntered into the room. "Glad to see you aren't a complete dissipate."

"Not yet," I said, sighing as I slid onto the couch.

"I'm going back to the bus. Might grab a bite." He hesitated. "You want to come?"

I glanced up, wondering if he wanted to offer or if he felt like he should. "No worries, Jakey. Do your thing."

"Murphy, it's just…you seem unsettled. Want to talk about it?" he asked.

I chugged the rest of my bottle before I threw it, hard, toward the rubbish bin. I missed but didn't have the energy to pick it up. Not that I needed to worry about cleaning anything. Someone was happy to fix my—our—messes. Like the girl, our roadies and even the stadium staff thought of us as gods.

"I'm fine. Enjoy your night."

Jake stepped farther into the room as if he planned to start the first real convo since he'd told me he planned to quit the band. Back in Europe. These last few weeks had been some of the longest and loneliest of my life.

"What's the worry?" he asked.

"Not sure I want to go back to Sydney."

"You haven't been, have you? Since you wrote 'She's so Bad?'"

"Just the venues. Not to our old stomping ground," I sighed. And I didn't want to go back now. Mila shattered me, but staying away wouldn't help. I needed to find her. I'd asked around. Mila disappeared the night she dumped me.

She left me and everyone who knew her, up and quitting her job with no notice. Totally out of character. At the time, I'd reckoned she'd been too ashamed of her cheating and the fact she'd left me to face the rabid bunch of journos, desperate to hear all the dirty secrets as to why she dumped me just days after that photo hit the Sydney paper.

Those sick, slimy bastards questioned me about her affair. I wouldn't believe the allegations until I read in the papers a few weeks later that Mila Trask, ex-girlfriend of up-and-coming indie rocker yours truly, was in a car accident. Every instinct told me to go to Perth and see for myself if she'd survive. To find out why she was in Perth of all places. Couldn't get much farther away from Sydney, which worried me further. I'd been about to hop on a plane when I opened another gossip site and found out she'd miscarried a baby.

And I'd hated her since.

I never did meet the bloke who stole and impregnated my girl. In fact, his name never went public. Probably for the best she'd managed to slip away with her new man. If she hadn't, I might well have spent these months locked up for ripping him apart instead of turning to my guitar with a kind of singular focus that got me to the highest level of rock stardom possible. Multiplatinum levels, thanks to the song "She's So Bad" and Hayden Crewe's formidable talent.

Not my talent. After writing that song, I hadn't completed any new material. "She's So Bad" sold nearly as many copies as Adele's "Hello" but our album sold over three million copies—and was still selling. We were being compared to the big guns—Pink Floyd, The Rolling Stones, and the biggest thrill: The Beatles. I might have written the song that caught the world's attention, but Hayden carried the band now. I was a one-hit wonder—the sad, pathetic former bandmate who would eventually star in reality TV shows and lose all his hair.

I flicked the tip of my tongue through my lip ring. I wasn't quite thirty. I didn't need to worry about aging yet, but I should slow down on the partying and booze. Too little sleep and too much alcohol weren't as much fun as it used to be and didn't help me focus on my goals. I needed another song to bring to the table, especially now that the label requested I consider a solo project.

In a month, I'd meet with the execs to hash out the agreement, but next week, I was scheduled to be back here in Seattle for a charity concert. I'd signed on as soon as I found out the proceeds were earmarked for battered women and children. I'd aligned myself with the cause early on, before we were famous, and I was pleased to have helped so many families.

But I didn't want to go to the meeting with the record execs. I didn't have anything worthwhile to show them. Worse, Jake didn't know about the offer. I'd lied to my brother. By omission, sure, but didn't change the fact. He and I weren't in the best place, and our relationship wouldn't take many more blows.

Since Mila left, everything I'd worked for skyrocketed into the stratosphere before I began the long and painful descent back to Earth. I hated feeling this unsure of my next step.

CHAPTER THREE
Mila

"Mila."

"Wha—"

"Sweetie, it's after seven. Are you going to work?"

"Leave me alone."

The bed dipped, causing the worst sensation ever—somewhere between seasickness and death. I clamped my teeth shut, refusing to vomit. I hated being sick. Not like a normal, *ick!, that's gross* feeling. No, more of a *there's no way in hell I'm letting that come up my throat* feeling. Because I didn't vomit. No matter what.

I'd powered through three months of morning sickness, and I could power through this as well.

"You are so hungover," Noelle giggled.

"I hate my life. I hate you."

"Aw, sweetie. No you don't. I'm the reason you didn't go to the hospital."

I cracked open an eye, angry when it immediately swelled too large for the socket. I took the ibuprofen Noelle handed me and swallowed it quickly. "I hate being a patient at the hospital most."

"I know. That's why you're thrilled with me right now."

"What do you mean?"

"You wanted a third drink. Considering you never drink and those martinis were doubled, I think you owe me a huge thank you."

I closed my eye and groaned again.

"I want to hear the words."

"Thank you," I mumbled.

"You're welcome," Noelle chirped.

"Wait. Did I cry?"

"Buckets," Noelle said, hopping off the bed. "But you've held those tears in for way too long. We're going to talk again about the fact you dated Murphy Etsam and you didn't tell me. Now are you going to work?"

"I never knew him when he was famous."

"You knew him."

I knew him *then*. I didn't know the man he'd become now. I'd read everything I could find on him once I discharged from the Perth hospital. The pictures splashed all over the Internet showed the progression: each week, his eyes hardened more and his features tightened with disgust.

I'd done that to him. He'd loved me as much as I'd loved him. It wasn't as though I could forget the expression on his face when I told him we were over. He would have pleaded with me, his pride be damned—that's how much he'd wanted me—or kissed me until I told him the truth. So I gave him as much truth as I could while backing from the room.

I scrubbed my cheeks with the sheet, reveling in the slight scratch.

"Later. Please?"

"Has to be. I'm running late right now as it is."

"I guess I'm going to take a sick day."

"No, you aren't. I refuse to let you sit around and stew."

"I'll work from home."

"You aren't home."

"My office doesn't know that."

"You see patients. Can't do that via Internet connection."

"Fine. I'll text them I'm coming in a little late because I'm recovering from a stomach bug."

Noelle snorted. "College code for hangover."

"I'm too old for this," I moaned.

"'Kay. Well, I'm off. Hop in the shower, will you? You smell like the bar."

"I feel worse. Why did I think going out for drinks was a good idea?"

"Because it was. You talked about all that crap you've been suppressing. Just wait. The whole world will seem better."

"Not right now it doesn't."

Noelle patted my shoulder, and I squeezed my eyes and jaw shut. "Bye, sweetie. See you tonight!"

"Do we have plans?"

She tucked her mass of hair up inside a black cap and tugged down her cute pink scrubs top. Must be raining outside. Noelle's hair was even more out of control in the rain. "Course we do. You're spilling the rest of your life secrets. Maura's coming, too."

"Can't," I rasped. "I have to go to the Tractor Tavern. I need to see Murphy, to finally let him go."

Noelle smiled gently as she took my hand. "I know, sweetie. We're going with you."

"You are? How'd you get tickets?"

"Friend at work. I told him it was an emergency. You owe me two-fifty for the tix, by the way. He wouldn't let them go easily."

I crawled out of the bed, trying not to gag. I didn't believe Noelle's statement about an improved world, but she planned to be there for me tonight when I'd finally see Murphy again. She had hugged me while I cried, and she'd gotten me back to her place.

I wrapped my arms around her, pulling her in tight. "Thanks, Noelle. I appreciate your support. You are a great friend."

"I'm an amazing friend. Now, I have to go to work. If I'm lucky Briar will be there." She waggled her brows. "And where there's a Briar, Hayden Crewe isn't far behind." She winked and waved before heading out the door.

I made it to the bathroom, my stomach still rolling higher than the waves at Bondi Beach. I glared at my reflection, hating my puffy, red eyes, the mascara streaks over my hollowed cheekbones. Fine, my gaunt features were because I didn't eat much or often; I'd struggled with meals since I broke up with Murphy. Just the thought of Jordan finding me gave me chills and twisted my insides into a mass of emotions I was too tired to try to untangle.

I took a long, long shower. If Noelle paid for her water, she would have cursed me seven ways to Sunday. Thankfully, I knew the utilities were included in her monthly rent.

Stepping out, confidence built in me. I would survive the day.

I wandered back into the bedroom's closet, wrapped in a towel, and pulled out some clean clothes I kept here. Noelle moved nearer her new job at a large clinic late last year—nearly an hour from my residency at the hospital in Federal Way. Because of the distance, we left a few outfits at the others' homes for just this type of occurrence. The slacks and blouse were loose, courtesy of my difficulty eating a decent meal these days, and the only shoes in the closet were the low-heeled sandals from yesterday. I shrugged. The brown shoes weren't ideal but I had much bigger issues to deal with. Like getting through the day. And the night.

The day at work proved long. An emergency cesarean kept Dr. Cahill in surgery all morning, so I managed her caseload as well as my own. At five o'clock, I headed home for some cuddle time with Alpie, hoping she'd ease my fears.

She snuggled onto my shoulder and shushed me, rubbing her feathered cheek along mine.

"What would I do without you?" I asked.

Alpie fluttered her wings before hopping onto the back of a kitchen chair to preen. "Love-oo."

I smiled, tears in my eyes, as I caressed her head feathers. "I love you, too, darling girl. Noelle's taught you right."

"No-elle. Love-oo," Alpie called before clicking her tongue against the roof of her beak. "Ca-shoo. Ca-shoo."

I laughed. I tossed a handful of nuts into Alpie's cage, ensured she had water and that the latch was locked. Now, an hour later, I'd changed into jeans and a pretty knit top but was too nervous to consider going to the show. I pulled out the ticket and fingered the edge.

No way I'd get to see Murphy, and if I did, what would I say?

As if they were able to read my mind, Noelle texted me right then to let me know she and Maura were already at the Tractor Tavern. The selfie showed them, cheeks pressed together, with margaritas out front. I stared at the picture for many minutes, debating with myself. I should go. I didn't have to see Murphy. I could hang back, leave as soon as it ended. Better yet, I'd walk out right after he sang "She's so Bad," leaving him and his anger where it belonged—in the past.

My chest was tight as I exited my house and into the Uber I'd called. I desperately wanted to see him, be in the same room as him. Hear his voice sing those lyrics—throw my words back at me. Then, finally, then I'd get the closure I needed and more on.

I could do this—I *needed* to do this. The driver dropped me off out front and I walked slowly toward the entrance. Once again, I thought I heard someone call my name.

I turned, and this time I saw him. About five foot ten, with well-styled salt-and-pepper hair. A large nose and a slight pot belly. Typical middle-aged Westerner. His spectacles made it impossible to see his eyes, but they were brown, a few shades darker than my own. I shoved my way through the door, panic building in my chest. I stumbled up to the table where Noelle and Maura were laughing.

"The band just took the stage so you're just in time! This is going to be so much fun…What's wrong?" Noelle asked, eyes darting from my face to the swelling crowd.

"Jordan," I panted.

The people around us quieted and a man's voice came over the microphone. Aussie accent, baritone. Hayden.

"He's here?" Maura asked. She narrowed her eyes as she stood on the rungs of her bar chair. "That no-good piece of shit. Where?"

"Outside." My teeth started to chatter. "I can't stay here. He'll know I came to see Murphy. He'll try to hurt him." The words stopped, and I sobbed into the napkin Maura handed me.

"What's done is done," she said, her voice practical. "He knows you're here."

A thick, heavy hand dropped on my shoulder. I wasn't quite able to stifle the scream as he spun me around to face him.

"Mila, darling. It's been too long."

His blunt fingers wrapped around my wrist, and he tugged me toward him. This time, I screamed long and loud, clawing at his fingers, the fright of him being there, touching me, overpowered everything else.

Pandemonium erupted around me, and I didn't care. I *needed* Jordan's fingers off my skin. Away from me.

Maura and Noelle jumped forward just as a man from the next table also stepped in and yanked Jordan off. I ducked out from under Jordan's arm and darted left, my chest heaving.

"Mila?"

My gaze slammed into Murphy's. His blue-gray eyes widened, his mouth dropping open in shock. I couldn't move. Murphy was so close. Anger seeped into his eyes. His lashes lowered, and then the arse the world saw was back, his face and shoulders stiff.

"You're not getting away again," Jordan growled, into my ear.

I'd forgotten him. So focused on Murphy, his disgust turning palpable, I'd forgotten to run. Defeat weighted on my back. But then Jordan's fingers were at my throat, arching my neck back. My eyes pleaded Murphy to understand. *This was why I left, but I still love you. I'll always love you.*

Someone pulled on Jordan, and I screamed as his fingernails raked across my skin. Murphy's eyes widened, taking in my struggle, the man behind me—the man who broke us. Somehow I read his lips, heard his voice even over the tumult around us.

"Mila." Just my name, but it was more than I could handle.

I ran.

My arm was up, and I flung open the door of the closest cab. "Pike Place Market," I panted. No choice but to get back to my house, get out the suitcase. Tears blurred my vision.

I pulled up my Uber app and set a pickup in the Pike Place Market. Crowded, lots of black cars coming and going. Best chance of losing Jordan was there.

I scuttled from the cab to the new ride, glancing over my shoulder each time. My text app chimed as I slammed the door shut. Noelle.

Are you okay?

I'm in an Uber car. Going back to my place.

No!

I can't be near Jordan. You saw—he won't stop. He wouldn't. Not until I submitted or he killed me. Maybe both. The hurt in Murphy's eyes. No. I wouldn't think about that. He could hate me all he wanted, but he wouldn't break me. Jordan already tried. Almost succeeded.

Noelle responded. *Head over to my place. I'll meet you there.*

No, don't worry about me. I'll go home. Lock all my doors.

My phone rang. "Hello?"

Loud voices slammed against my eardrums and I winced. "You will *not* go home by yourself," Noelle yelled into the phone. She mustn't realize how loud she was. The volume behind her was insane. "Go back to my condo. I have security at the door. I've already called Arnold. He's expecting you. I'll be there shortly. One more thing I have to do."

"Noelle—I can't. I can't let Jordan near me again. I can't get Murphy more involved in this."

"Considering he kept calling your name, even after security mobbed Jordan, I'd say he's already involved."

CHAPTER FOUR
Murphy

Shock still reverberated through me, even all these hours later. Mila. At the venue. The fear in her eyes. Her soul-wrenching scream as that man—the man who'd slipped from six fucking security members—touched her.

That last fleeting peep she'd thrown at me. So much sadness, the pleading with me to understand…what? *What* in bloody hell was I supposed to understand?

I didn't know, which was why I was edgy, angry, and way too keyed up to sleep.

I wasn't surprised when Jake knocked on my door not much past dawn and not long after I returned from staking out Mila's house. "Here to tell me how bad I blew my cues?" I grumbled.

"Considering how much seeing Mila again, seeing her mauled by that arsewipe bothered you, I'd say you did a pretty damn good job."

"Ben tell you anything? He hadn't found her when I spoke with him earlier."

Jake shook his head. "Just what you know—she lives here. In Federal Way, according to her mortgage."

"She wasn't there." I sighed as I collapsed into one of the suite's chairs. My fingers tunneled through my hair and I pressed the heels of my hands to my gritty eyes. "I waited for hours but she never showed up. What the hell do we pay Ben so much money for?"

"To protect your sorry arse," Jake said, settling into the chair across from me. "How are you? Really."

I met his worried gaze. "Knackered. She was so scared, Jake. I can't…what if that bloke hurt her? He's out there still."

Jake folded his hands over his stomach. "I talked to one of Mila's friends, Noelle Markham, while you were trying to find Mila. Noelle said the bloke—Jordan Jones—is Mila's step-uncle. And that he's been stalking her for years."

The weight on my chest pressed down even harder. "You think that's true?" I gasped.

"No reason for her to lie."

"But that means…"

"Before you broke up. *Why* you broke up. That's what Noelle said."

He raised his brow. Of course he thought of the lyrics *That sweet smile hid an ice-cold heart. You tried to pull me down, to destroy me from the start. After I promised you forever, you cut our time short to be with him—the man of your past. I ain't never gonna forget you, sweetheart, nor your tears of glass. From our affair, I got a great story to sell, and it's the only thing from you I'll ever tell.*

"You read the news?" He dropped his iPad into my hand and headed into the suite's dining area where a coffee pot was set up in the corner. The pot rumbled to life.

"What news?"

"You don't have some sheila here, do you?" He waited for my negation before continuing. "Okay, good. Read it."

I bit back the angry retort and did as he asked. "States Mila was attacked last night at the Tractor Tavern. Nothing we didn't already know."

"Confirms the arsewipe is, indeed, Jordan Jones, stepbrother to one Rosemary Jones. Mila's mum."

Pouring a steaming cuppa, I slammed it back, shuddering

as the liquid burned the roof of my mouth and all down my throat. "The hell, Jake?" I set the iPad down on the table and met his gaze. "Let's go."

"Where?"

"To find this lady. Noelle."

"Why should we do that?"

"Because…" Hell if I knew why.

"You can't break down the woman's door, demanding answers. Anyway, you and I have a plane home to Sydney to catch."

"Then why bother me with this?" I asked.

"You said Mila left her mum's house before you first started dating, right? She didn't ever want to go there, even when she was between places to stay."

I nodded. I refilled my coffee cup and sipped more cautiously. My mouth hurt, but I needed the caffeine. The awareness of why Jake was bringing this up was slow to dawn, but when it did, all the breath left my lungs and nausea rooted deep in my stomach. "Bloody hell. Mila left the house because this stalker, her step-uncle, used to live with her."

Jake pulled up the article again. He pointed at the artist's rendering of the man next to an old snapshot, which was next to a grainy photo taken last night. Mila's back bowed away from Jordan, her fingernails gouged into his hand where it was clamped around her neck. She was in profile, but even the small amount of her face showed soul-deep fear.

"Seems like this might be the man who threatened our mum—what was it, the message he'd left? He keeps what's his?"

I paused, thinking back to that night. A large man, masked, armed with a bush knife, strode up to my mum on the street out front of her house during her evening walk with her dog, Shimzie. He'd told her next time he came back, it wouldn't be to leave a message. Shimzie barked his head off enough for neighbors to step outside, concerned about the racket. When the bloke stepped forward to stuff a paper in Mum's hand, good ole Shimzie bit his ankle with those tiny Pekinese teeth. The message was direct but odd. *I keep what's mine.*

Jake, the police, and I had puzzled over those words. If he planned to steal from my mum, how could he claim the items were his? He didn't take anything, and Mum was firm in her stance not to make a bigger fuss out of the situation. But now... what if the bloke meant Mila? Chewing my lip, I considered the news story.

"I can't go home," I said. The need to protect Mila shocked me even as it overpowered my good sense and the reasons I shouldn't care—mainly that she'd dumped me. "I have to go see this Noelle woman. Find Mila. Talk to her."

A deep furrow built between Jake's eyebrows. "You think seeing her is a good idea?"

No. Seeing Mila again was a terrible idea. I wasn't ready for it—would never be ready.

She broke my bloody heart. Then, when I found out she was preggo with some other man's baby, she shredded it so small, I still didn't have all the pieces. I shrugged.

"You planning to be your typical charming self? How much further do you plan to blacken your image and that of the band, Ets?"

"She'll deserve anything I say. And I don't have to explain myself to you," I said, shoving him out of the way as I headed

37

toward the bedroom. A quick shower and then I was off to find answers.

———◆———

Fifteen minutes later, I was dressed. I shoved my wallet into my back pocket and headed back to the living room. Stopping short, I gaped at the sight of my mum.

"What the hell are you doing here?"

She rose from the couch, her gray curls bouncing around her face. Her cheeks were the same soft pink as usual, but her eyes were red-rimmed, and her mouth pinched tight.

"Nice to see you, too, son. Lovely greeting."

I wrapped my arm around her shoulders, pulling her into a tight hug. "I'm chuffed to see you. Course I am. But… you hate to fly."

She'd never come to any of our concerts because of it. The fear was deep, instilled in her as a teen when she'd hit turbulence over the Pacific Ocean coming back from her one trip abroad to Japan. No matter how much Jake and I coaxed her, we never got her near an airport again.

She swallowed hard against my shoulder, clutching me with her fingertips. "It was awful. Worse than I imagined. But I had to tell you in person what I know."

I settled her onto the cushion next to me on the couch and took her shaking hand in mine. "You're scaring me, Mum."

She brushed her hair back off her forehead, her pale blue eyes settling on my face. "I'm sorry, Murphy. What I did at the time, I did as Mila asked me."

I stiffened, yanking my hand from her grip. My stomach spun, dipped, all the while aching with the knowledge I wouldn't like what came next. "What…" No other words came.

"I knew there was more to Mila's leaving than you told me!" Jake crowed.

"Doesn't matter if there is," I snapped. I narrowed my eyes and willed the words to be true. "I'm totally over her."

Jake raised his brow again, calling me on my shit. He'd known, more than Hayden, how much Mila meant to me, and he'd been the one to suggest I go talk to her in Perth—for my sanity. I hadn't, and Jake dealt with the fallout from my misery this past year.

"So no worries that I've set up to have drinks with her later tonight then. Ben found her and we talked. Be good to catch up."

Both my hands were in his shirt as I shoved him against the wall. "You don't touch her. Ever."

Jake shoved me back, his boot catching on the edge of the fancy carpet, causing him to stumble.

I stalked away, trying to ignore the growl building in my throat. Jake couldn't put his hands on her curves. Her soft white breasts with those luscious pink nipples. The slight curve of her belly. The firm give of her bum.

"Stay away from her," I snarled.

"You can't have it both ways, mate. You walk around like an angry, wounded bear and, all the while, collect more women than a sheik has in a harem." I saw Mum flinch at those words. Can't say I've been winning any son-of-the-year awards with my shoddy behavior.

"One of the perks of being famous," I gritted out, my jaw locked down solid. I was seconds away from swinging at my

39

brother. Bad as the shit got with the band these last few months, I'd never come to blows with Jake. He meant too much to me. But now, my ears filled with a loud, vicious ring. The same sound I'd fought off when Hayden came back from his jaunt to Seattle a few months ago so bummed out and lovesick over a piece of arse—who turned out to be the love of his life. Yeah, no wonder Briar was wary of me, and Hayden considered me the excrement on his shoe. I'd tried hard to destroy their relationship from the get-go.

Stupid of me to foist my issues with Mila onto Hayden's relationship with Briar. Stupid and wrong.

Jake shook his head, eyes filled with disgust but also sorrow. "This is your chance to fix it. Forgive Mila for her mistake and let the past go. Especially if she left because of a *stalker*. That's serious. And mental."

"Mila didn't make a mistake," I bellowed, so many of my emotions spilling over. "She told me she couldn't see me anymore. Left me that note." I still had it. It was in my wallet. I pulled it out sometimes to remind myself why I was so fucking angry with her. *I love you, Murphy, I always will, but there's a man from my past. I need to sort things with him if I can ever truly be with you properly.* "She said if I came round, she'd leave. Which she did anyway. Ran away, got pregnant with some other man's bub. She wasn't supposed to ever. Come. Back."

"So are you angry she showed up here or are you angry you still love her?" Jake snapped back.

I tugged at the piercing in my eyebrow. The one I got when Mila chickened out and wouldn't do her second hole at the top of her other ear. We'd had matching loops put in and for some stupid shit reason, I'd never been willing to take mine out.

"You've cracked a fruity, Murphy." Mum's face paled to chalk-white, her mouth pulled into a tight pucker. "This should never have gone so far."

Bloody *hell*. Why couldn't Mila have stayed buried in my past, nothing more than the genesis for the song that bought me my fame?

"There are things you need to know," she said, a tremble building in her voice. "That you should have known then. That I wanted to tell you but I was asked not to share."

"Then why's it fine to tell me now?" I asked, the sick feeling of dread creeping up my throat.

"Because I keep an eye on Rosemary, but it's mainly to keep an eye on that—that… Jordan. Once Mila told me who he was, what he'd threatened, what he did to her, seemed prudent. When Rosemary said Jordan was flying to Seattle—where you and Mila both were—" Mum swallowed hard. "I caught the next flight."

"Why?" I asked.

"Because… you really need to talk to Mila." Mum sighed, her eyes and the tip of her nose reddening. "That car accident. It wasn't one."

Shit. From the moment my mother appeared, I'd worried she might tell me I'd been wrong about Mila. "She was hit by a car. I read that," I said. I rubbed my chest, trying to ease the bloody tightness there. Oh. Bloody hell. Mila'd written *there's a man from my past. I need to sort things with him if I can ever truly be with you properly.* I'd thought she meant a lover. But I'd seen the bloke last night, felt her fear, but… Oh, bloody hell. She'd been hit by a car and miscarried. My baby. Gone. And I'd sung that song and made a point to make it in all the papers with as many women as possible.

Oh. Fuck. No.

I stood, needing to do something. If I didn't get out, didn't move, I was going to explode with the awfulness of the truths slamming into me. Jake stepped in front of me, his movements jerky. Unsure what to do.

"No, Jakey. Let him go. Murphy has to deal with this," I heard Mum say.

But I wasn't sure I could deal. She'd carried *my* bub. Left me, knowing that. Left me *because* of it, sounded like. My bub, dead. An innocent life snuffed out, much too soon, because of violence.

I walked out the door, wracked with pain, sadness, and yes, guilt. I *let* Mila leave.

Probably a good thing I didn't have keys to a vehicle at the moment, as I couldn't focus on anything other than the next step, next breath. Trying to out-walk the hurt ripping through my heart. I walked and walked and walked. My phone rang, and I fumbled to silence it. Eventually, I made it to the beach.

By sheer luck, I'd headed north, toward Alki Beach, the closest I could come to our place. I glanced around, half expecting her, the Mila of my past, but she didn't come out to haunt me.

I shoved my hands in my pockets and tipped my head up toward the storm cloud–studded sky. Anything to try to calm my raging thoughts.

Didn't work.

She'd left to protect me and my family. The very reason I'd wanted her close—to keep her safe and happy. Why didn't she tell me the truth?

My head drooped and I tunneled my fingers through my hair, wishing—needing—to take back everything that happened since that moment when she walked out of that venue in Sydney nearly fourteen months ago.

I wrote that song about her. Opened up our private life to the world so they could hate her, too.

Not sure what else to do, I walked along the surf's edge. Frigid water soaked my boots and jeans, but I kept walking. How else to move beyond the feelings swamping me?

My phone rang, but I ignored it again.

My heart broke for the child I never knew. The one I *should* have had with Mila. She'd been fragile beneath her tough exterior; it's part of what drew me to her that first night. She'd refused to go out with me for months. Finally holding her in my arms, my lips touching hers, was the highlight of my life.

What if the bub was a girl with Mila's eyes? I'd never get to see them widen with surprise like Mila's did when I brought her with flowers or that simple ring. I'd never hold my daughter, cuddle her. Tell her I love her.

Because I did. Bollocks. Jake, the sneaky little shit, was right.

I was angry, but if I'd asked Mila why, begged her to stay, maybe… maybe I'd be sitting with her and our child right now.

My phone rang again.

"What, Jake?"

"Where are you? Mum's worried."

I dropped my head to my knees. "Right. I'm on the beach. Send Ben to pick me up?"

"Give a street name and we'll be there in a few."

I headed back up the beach, straining to catch a glimpse of a street sign.

Jake and Ben pulled up within minutes of me exiting the beach access and about a half minute before a younger, hungrier crowd mobbed me. My personal guard, Kevin, appeared—he'd probably been with me the whole time but I'd been too distracted to notice.

"Bloody hell," I said, slamming the car door shut. "Ferals everywhere these days." One of the blokes slammed his hand against my window, causing me to jump. "The attention is even worse. I didn't think that was possible."

"Harry was right to increase the security detail after Hayden and Briar's big makeup in Amsterdam."

"Thanks, Kevin," I said, reaching forward to clap him on the shoulder.

"So what are you going to do?" Jake asked.

"About what?" I asked. I wanted to close my eyes. I wanted to shut him out.

"About Mila, dickhead."

"I'll go see her. Hear what she has to say for herself." I clenched my jaw, anger and hurt building into a noxious mass that sickened my gut. I had to hear her say it. I needed to look in her eyes when she told me *why* she left that day.

"Not like that you won't," Jake said with a disgusted glance.

"Like what?"

"You're covered in sand and your eyes have more red than any other color. You look hungover. And mean."

"Well, I'm not," I snapped. "Didn't touch a drop. And I've never raised my hand to a woman, Jake."

"First time for everything, I reckon," Jake responded.

"You think I'd do that?" Hurt seeped into my words. "After

the way Dad treated Mum, you really think I could ever abuse a woman?"

Jake repositioned his hands, his jaw clamped just as tight as mine.

"No, I don't. But, bloody hell, Murphy. This is serious. Dead serious. And Mila… She's all alone."

"What do you want me to say?" I sighed, raking my hand through my disheveled hair. "I don't know what to do about Mila. Not yet."

"I don't want you to say anything, you idiot. I want you to *be* the brother you used to be. The one who walked me to school so I wouldn't have to face Perry Evans and his gang of wankers by myself. The one who cares about a woman's feelings and doesn't discard her faster than a sweat towel."

"Thanks for the words of encouragement, mate."

"Why were you so shocked to hear the kid was yours?"

"She told me she was with another bloke, that he'd been hanging around a while. He was older, knew her secrets. He was waiting for her outside and she had to go." I turned my head to stare at my brother. "Do you think she tried to tell me something. Like in code?"

My hands clenched into fists. Mila was so bloody smart. I'd bet my left nut she'd been trying to give me information. To tell me why, and I didn't understand.

"Sounds like," Jake said.

"From what Mum said, turns out she ran away to protect me. And if I'm right, she tried to tell me why that night but I was too stupid to understand."

"So now you're angry with her about that, too?"

"Hell, yes, I'm angry. She didn't trust me to take care of her." I rolled my head, but the tension in my neck and shoulders increased.

"Do you think… was Mum's attack related to her leaving?" Jake asked.

My throat burned from the acid building in my stomach. "Timing's about right."

Jake nodded as Ben pulled into the hotel's parking garage. I shot out from the car, heading toward the elevator. I opened my hotel room and toed off my boots at the door, planning to toss the sand-crusted and water-logged mess in the bin later.

I padded through the suite in my bare feet, thankful my mum stayed out of sight for the time being. Turning on the bath water, I turned toward the mirror and gasped, jumping back in horror. A half dead bag of roadkill was more attractive than me. My eyes were redder than the crimson tides. Peeling off my sand-caked jeans and shirt, I stepped into the shower, clenched my teeth, and pressed my face into the hot stream of cleansing, pounding spray.

I left the shower cleaner but more drained than ever. I wasn't going anywhere just yet. Pulling on some boxers, I slumped against the sink's edge. I was tired. No, worse. I was sick at heart. I pulled on some clothes and went in search of more caffeine.

Mum puttered about the dining space, pulling some muffins out of a paper sack. So she'd been downstairs to purchase muffins. Great woman, my mum.

"Coffee's in the mug there, Murphy. I'll get you a muffin before we talk more."

Mum fretted and clucked her way around the suite while I sipped the coffee she'd made me. Little kindnesses like this, these were the details that made life richer and—dare I say it?—happier. No one on the road cared to do more than shove a water or beer bottle in my hand. But Mum here, she'd doctored my coffee with cream and sugar, and she'd found my favorite muffins.

I'm sure she'd gotten Jake's, too. I liked blueberry and Jake always preferred banana nut. Even when money was so tight we weren't sure we'd keep the house, Mum managed to make us muffins every Sunday.

I pulled her into my side for a cuddle and kissed the top of her head. She glanced up at me, somewhere between exasperated and loving. Pretty much her standard expression for me these days.

"Thanks, Mum. For the effort."

She patted my chest. "Now, none of that. Just drink up so you're not angrier than a Tasmanian devil when I tell you the rest of what I know. Well, more show you."

With a groan I tipped the mug to my mouth and gulped down the rest of the coffee. Not that it would help so much.

She pulled out her smartphone and pressed a few buttons. She flattened the case to her chest so I couldn't see the screen. "I went to visit Rosemary Jones. I told you that. What I didn't tell you was I videoed our conversation. In case you needed proof." She raised her eyebrows.

Everything in me stilled. I met her eyes, calm even as anger and hurt bubbled up into my chest.

"Bloody hell."

"Murphy!"

"You knew she was leaving!" I stood so fast, the chair shot out behind me, falling over.

"Oi!" Jake said from the door. "Why are you yelling at Mum?"

I pointed a shaking finger at my mother, the traitor. "She helped Mila leave." Of course. Mum's job at the passport office would make her the perfect person for Mila to visit.

Mum had the decency to drop her eyes to the table. "It was only supposed to be for a short time. How was I supposed to know you'd give up on her like that?"

With those words, I deflated. I *had* given up on Mila. I never called her, never went to see her, never tried to find out from her—the woman I'd told I'd love forever—what happened. Why she'd left.

All this time… For more than a year, I'd operated under the sense I was the injured party. I stood, paced. I wanted to crack a tinnie or all twelve in the case. Nah. Beer wasn't strong enough. I need a bottle of whiskey to drown out the pain ripping through my black bastard heart.

"Are you finally ready to listen to what Mila has to say?" Mum asked, giving me back the glare. "That girl's been through a lot, and I won't have you hurting her more."

"I get that," I gritted out. My jaw hurt from clamping it so tight. "I'm mad as a cut snake because where's the loyalty, woman? I'm your bloody son!"

Mum's cheeks were ruddier than usual and those gray curls bristled out over her head. "My son, who disappointed me, and more importantly, the woman he loves and who loved him back. I taught you better than that!"

"You should have told me," I growled.

Mum drew herself up, quivering with indignation. "How was I supposed to know you'd be such a tosser?"

I opened my mouth but Jake's quiet words stopped the spew

of anger that might well have destroyed my relationship with my mum forever. I started, having forgotten he was in the room.

"Could you talk to the police? Here but also in Sydney and Perth, too. Get them to coordinate the information. The Sydney police brought Jordan in because he was out front of Mum's house. The Perth police have Mila's car accident on record even if she didn't file charges, they have to write a report, right? And the police here have the assault last night on file. Kevin and Ben might be able to help you navigate the system."

"Good call," I said. I turned on my heel and stalked from the room.

———◆———

Jake knocked as I shoved the last of my clothes back into my suitcase. Unpacking was a ridiculous exercise.

"You heading out then?"

"Yeah. We were supposed to check out an hour ago. I'll book some place for tonight once I talk to Mila. Hear the whole story from her."

"Good."

I zipped the bag and turned to him. "Did you know Mum helped her leave the country?"

Jake shook his head. "No, mate. I knew what you did—that Mila left. I saw how much you were hurting. I would've told you. She was important to me, too."

Mila had been a part of our family. Until she wasn't. I'd never considered he'd lost a sister as much as I'd lost my lover. I set the bag on the floor, satisfied.

Jake and I grew up just thirteen months apart, which made us closer than most, I reckoned. The loss of Logan, the baby brother we'd both wanted, unified us further.

"Aren't you going to talk to Mum about her part?" Jake asked. I flicked my eyes up, and Jake stepped back. "I take that as a no."

"Nothing she says will help right now." I slid my hands into my hair and dug my fingers into my scalp, my palms pressed to my eyes. "What if the bub had Mila's eyes? Her smile? She'd be crawling, possibly walking. Talking, I think."

That ate at me. What could have been. Of course I would've taken care of Mila and our baby. I would've quit the band and worked ten jobs to provide for her. This life of luxury, of constant high-profile dates, security guards and paparazzi, would be a pipedream I wouldn't know to wish away. Much as I disliked some aspects of the fame, the financial perks outweighed the downside of being noticed wherever I went. But the price of wealth—losing Mila, our baby—*that* was too high.

"Would it help if I came with you to the police department? To see Mila?"

I dropped my hands and looked at my brother. Even after all the problems I stirred up this year, Jake wanted to help.

"I'm 'right, mate. You have your holidays."

He swallowed hard. I waited. Jake handed me a paper with an American number in my mum's sharp handwriting.

"This Mila's number?"

"Probably," Jake said. "Mum told me what Jordan said to Mila after he mowed her down with the car in Perth. He said he'd kill Mila before she got back with you."

"Well, isn't that fantastic?"

"Reckoned you should tell the police here," Jake said with a shrug.

"Will do."

"Do police departments work together and share information?"

I scratched my chin. "From what the detective here said when I called in, the case is international. But he didn't tell me if they have to go through a national agency here."

"Like Interpol?" Jake asked.

"Don't think the Yanks use Interpol. The FBI, CIA. At least, those are the names of the agencies in those crime dramas Mum likes to watch." I smirked. "We never did get to know the inner workings of police departments."

Jake grinned back. "Right-o. Mum would've killed us dead."

I snorted. "I've called in a favor to fly you and Mum home. Private," I said, patting my pockets to reconfirm my phone, wallet, and passport were where they should be. "Best pilot I could find. Decades of experience and heaps of credentials. Should help ease Mum's worries. Flight leaves in a couple of hours. Ben's going back with you. No arguments. Not now that we know Jordan is the one who threatened Mum and why." I let him see the worry building in my eyes. "Kevin will stick with you until you're on the flight. I want to know Mum's safe. You'll do that—keep Mum safe?—while I sort this mess here?"

"Course, Murphy. I'll help any way I can."

"Flip make it on to his flight?"

"Yep. Should be home tonight."

"Let him know what's happening, will you?"

Jake nodded. "Mum's not going to handle the flight home well. She's already tetchy."

"She might not want to go, but I don't want her in the same city as this Jordan bloke. He's already threatened her. You, too." I tugged at my eyebrow ring. "His hands on Mila last night… she's tiny. He hurt her, Jake. That's why she was so scared."

Jake cleared his throat. "There's something else you should know. That Mum told me." Jake met my eyes, his uncertain. "Mum said Jordan found her from that picture of you in the paper."

There'd only been one of Mila and me. We were in front of a jewelry store in Darling Harbor and I'd kissed the ring I slid onto her finger. My lowest moment, that, showing the world my feelings only to have them slapped back in my face.

I let the dig slide and stepped in so I could hug him. "Thanks, mate. Take care of Mum."

Jake pounded my back, both of us teary-eyed.

"Kinda funny. I need to fix shit with two people, and they're both here."

"Fate is alive and well," Jake said, a ghost of a smile sliding across his lips. "Good luck."

"Who with?"

"You're going to need it with both. Hayden's royal angry, but I have a feeling Mila's going to be harder to win over. Especially once Hayden hears the full story about Mila and you. That bloke has a heart softer than a fresh marshmallow."

I picked up my bag and squared my shoulders. "If I hadn't been such a wanker about her dumping me, Jordan wouldn't have hurt her. She has every reason to hate me."

"You reckon she does?"

I sucked in a breath, trying to calm my racing heart. "Gonna find out."

Jake put his hands on my shoulders. "Be careful. He's danger-ous, mate."

I nodded, unable to speak around the lump growing in my throat. I grabbed the back of his head and pulled him in for one last older-brother bear hug before I stepped back. "Right. I'll be in touch."

"Should I let Hayden know you're sticking around?" Jake asked, his brows pulling down in a scowl. Because he didn't like the situation with Hayden or because he didn't want to be emo-tional? Hard to say.

I needed to apologize for being such a dickhead to my band-mate and to his girlfriend, who'd reminded me a bit too much of Mila. Not physically, but in her hold over Hayden. I didn't want to see him go through the same hell I lived through, but instead of expressing any of those concerns, I hid behind a false bravado and torched every relationship that mattered to me. I ran my fin-ger across the piercings in my eyebrow, considering my situation.

"No. I'll handle that when I'm ready. Mila comes first."

CHAPTER FIVE
Mila

Noelle was gone before I woke the next morning. I'd huddled in my bed, too strung out to sleep. Or so I'd thought. Somehow I missed Noelle coming home last night. I'd awakened around 2:00 a.m. and tossed for hours, the images of Murphy's disdain and Jordan's lust-filled eyes chasing away my ability to relax.

I must have fallen back to sleep again because now it was after 8:00 a.m. I bounded to the shower and rushed through getting dressed. Even though traffic would be horrendous, I needed to drive home and feed Alpie. She was sure to be out of fresh fruit. That bird ate mango by the pound, but she wasn't as keen on her kale and other leafy greens. Smart bird.

I'd finished drying my hair when someone knocked on the door. I grabbed my phone and my pepper spray. I edged to the door and glanced through the peephole. My moment of elation turned to dread. Not Jordan, but a uniformed officer stood there, rocking back on forth on his heels.

I opened the door, pepper spray positioned at my waist in case I needed it.

"Yes?"

"Mila Trask?"

"Yes?" I asked again, my heart thudding a frantic rhythm. Who knew I was here? Noelle, of course. And Maura. But a man? No way Noelle would tell, and I didn't know many people in the city besides my two friends and the handful of people I worked with.

"I'm Officer Reims." He held up his badge. My suspicion melted away. I remembered a similar experience, blurred by blood loss and pain. "Your friend, Noelle Markham, was accosted outside the building earlier this morning. She's been taken to the emergency room. She asked us to escort you there after we go over some details of the assault."

"Details of the assault? How can I help with that?"

"She said you knew the perpetrator."

"Oh, God, no," I whispered, the pepper spray falling to the ground as I clutched the door frame. "No."

"Please, ma'am. Come with me."

I breathed deeply and nodded. "I just need to get my purse. Where is she?"

"University. It was closest and she said she worked there. Should take an hour, maybe two, for our interview."

I left the door open but still chained and found my purse. I checked my phone. Noelle had texted. *At University. Please come with the officer. His name is Reims.*

Relief swamped me, and I settled on the edge of the bed. Noelle mustn't be too hurt. She also knew me well. I wanted to shut the door on the officer and hunker down in the safety of the condo; my suspicion ran deep.

After collecting my items, I met the officer, who still stood at the door, albeit with lessening patience. "Can we talk here?" I asked.

"We could if you want to invite me in. But if we do that, it'll take longer for me to write up my report and get it to a detective who'll investigate the case."

"Why does the case have to go to a detective?"

"Because my job is to stop crimes as they're happening. The detective's job is to ensure the perpetrator of a previous crime is apprehended after the fact."

"But you said you know who attacked Noelle. So what good am I?"

"You know Jordan Jones. The man who also assaulted you last night at the Tractor Tavern. I need you to give that statement, press formal charges. If you'd come with me to the station now, I'll get one of the detectives to sit in while I get your statement."

"But I'm not in trouble? I thought people were only brought to the police station when they'd done something illegal."

Officer Reims crossed his arms over his chest. "Have you, Ms. Trask? Done something illegal."

I shook my head.

"Then you have nothing to worry about and everything to gain by helping us find the man responsible." He stepped back so I could lock the deadbolt and then he led me to his police car. I stared at it, nervous, but he opened the passenger door. He grabbed a black bag and what looked like a traffic ticket book. There was one of those traffic guns as well. Arms full, he tipped his head toward the now-clean seat.

"Didn't figure you'd want to sit in the cage."

"C-cage?" I asked.

"Back seat. Where we put suspects. But you're not one, and I don't think you're going to shoot me." He narrowed his eyes, his lips set in a stern line. "Don't."

Unsure how to handle this man, I settled in, ignoring my clammy palms.

After dropping his equipment into the trunk, Officer Reims settled into his seat, radioed his dispatcher, and started the vehicle. The ride to the police station took longer because of the building traffic, but we made it in relative quiet, Officer Reims asking if I was comfortable once before lapsing into silence.

"Do you know what happened to Noelle?" I asked.

"She was attacked."

Not the loquacious type. I wrapped my hands around my phone, willing it to tell me more. It, too, remained silent.

"Oh! I need to let my boss now what's going on. Do you mind if I make a call?"

Officer Reims frowned, his eyes darting toward me like I was insane. I took that as an affirmative. I told both Dr. Cahill and the staff coordinator Noelle was at the hospital and the police wanted me there, too.

I tucked my phone back into my purse as we pulled up in front of the building. I started to open the door, but Officer Reims, said, "Hold tight. I'll escort you."

I dropped my hand back to my lap and waited for him to lead me to the entrance. Together we walked into the modern glass-and-brick main campus building. My knees shook but I made it into the building and through a series of doors before Officer Reims settled me into a conference room that was more sterile than the one at my hospital. The long table gleamed in the fluorescent light, the weak sunshine a nonexistent light source.

"I called ahead for the detective, but I want to let him know we're here. Help yourself to some water." He motioned toward the bottles on the table. Then he was gone. Unsure what to do, I grabbed a bottle and took a long sip. I wandered over to the windows and stared out.

The clouds were low, gray. People streamed into the building, some in blue uniforms, others in dress clothes. I turned to face the door as it opened.

"Thanks for coming, Ms. Trask. I'm Detective Jim Davenport." He held out his hand and I shook it, my gaze staying steady on his light brown eyes, a shade or two lighter than his skin. Letting go, he gestured toward the table. I settled into the chair he held out, taking in his neat, mint-green dress shirt and pinstripe blue-and-green tie. He settled into the head chair next to mine and we were still the same height.

Officer Reims sat into the chair across from me, reaching down the table to snag a couple more waters. He passed the first to Detective Davenport before uncapping his own.

"Why don't you start at the beginning, Ms. Trask." Detective Davenport suggested. "The first time you met Jordan Jones."

I dropped my purse next to me onto the floor, folded my hands on the table, and launched into the story no one had ever believed.

———— ◆ ————

More than three hours later, Officer Reims once again opened the passenger door to his vehicle. Another thought occurred. "Is this normal? I mean, you escorting me to the police station and now the hospital like this?"

Officer Reims's neck reddened but he'd already put on his aviator glasses so I couldn't see his eyes. "Not normal. To the police station, yes, but normally we'd let you head over to the hospital on your own. While we were meeting, your boyfriend called the department, alerting our chief to your history with Jordan Jones. Since we were sifting through the details of yours and your friend's attack, both with matching descriptions, Chief Bennett sent orders through my sergeant for me to escort you around today."

My boyfriend? I let that slide for a moment, more interested in reassuring myself Noelle wasn't injured. Officer Reims took my elbow and led me through the hospital and up the elevator. At the door to one of the rooms, he ushered me in.

My heart rate escalated and my mouth dried up faster than an Outback stream. I was three feet from a man's broad back. Jordan? Here? I stumbled back. But no, that hair. The tall, lithe back tapering into narrow jean-clad hips...

"Murphy?" I asked, my voice cracking.

He turned quickly, his eyes snapping quick images of me before he wrapped me in his arms and pulled me tight against his chest. "You worried me." Murphy's voice hit my ear but so did the rumble in his chest, and déjà vu slammed through me.

"Why are you here?" I asked, confused.

His lashes were long and dark. They were straight with no curl, giving him a sleepy look. I used to smooth those dark brows before I kissed him in the morning. His nose was a tad too long. Still the most handsome man I'd ever seen.

"I phoned the police department to talk to one of the detectives. He told me your friend was here."

"But—"

"Hey, Mila. Sending Murphy Etsam to check in on me kind of makes up for your scary-mean stalker."

Much as I didn't want to, I extricated myself from Murphy's embrace and went to Noelle's side. "I'm so sorry. Are you okay? What happened? Where are you hurt? How bad is it?"

"First, I'm pretty much fine. He scared me pretty bad, and

I sprained my wrist, but otherwise, no problem. Second, that creepy asshole waited outside my building. He must have followed you after all. Well, probably me since I came in after he'd been detained and I wasn't particularly stealthy about it. Still, I'm so glad you went to my place since I have door security."

"Outside? Waiting for you?"

Noelle threw me a pitying look. Her blue scrubs were wrinkled and her left wrist was bandaged. A bruise bloomed, red and angry, under her eye.

"No, sweetie. He was waiting for you."

I turned to Officer Reims, who hovered at the door. "So you know, we consider him armed and dangerous now that he's attacked Ms. Markham," he said.

"You'll find him? Put him in jail?" I asked. "And you'll tell me when that happens?" The mere idea of Jordan in jail weakened my knees. God, I needed to believe the police would finally take care of him, keep my friends safe. Relief swept through me, making me lightheaded. I wouldn't have to keep running.

"You'll be contacted as soon as he's apprehended," Officer Reims affirmed. "But in the meantime, it's probably not smart for you to go out alone."

Constant company appealed much more than disappearing, trying to start over again.

But a word Office Reims had said lingered in my mind, causing the panic to build in my stomach again. "Armed?" I asked Noelle.

She shuddered. "He came at me with this big knife."

I squeezed Noelle into another hug, my heart racing at what could have happened.

"I'll make sure she's not alone," Murphy volunteered. My

shock was echoed in his rapid blinking and the tightening around his mouth.

I stiffened. "No way." The words tore from my throat. I couldn't handle being near Murphy for five more minutes, let alone *days*. Seeing him, here and now, made my heart clench. Much as I wanted to be over him, I wasn't.

Noelle gripped my wrist and pressed her lips to my ear. "You're going along with him hanging out with you," she whispered. "If for no other reason than your stalker-uncle attacked me, and I'm asking you to. But there are other reasons, not least of which is talking to Murphy like you'd planned."

She released my wrist. I never planned to *talk* to him. I wanted to watch him sing that awful song, flinging my words back at me with cavalier disdain so I could decimate my heart and never love anyone but Alpie and Noelle again.

Murphy was mucking up my plan—with Noelle's blessing. My eyes darted back and forth as I touched the middle of my top lip with my tongue. I didn't want to be alone with Murphy. Not while I was so raw and rung out from worrying about Noelle not to mention my own scare with Jordan. The cuts on my neck itched, reminding me how much worse the situation could have been.

I inched away, preparing to dart from the room. Murphy must have sensed my desire to get away because he touched me. Just three fingers on my shoulder. Noelle's eyes widened as I melted. I always did when it came to Murphy, the cheating rat-bastard. Except... except we weren't together when he decided to bed all those bloody women. We weren't together because I *broke up* with him. *There's a man from my past. I need to sort things with him if I can ever truly be with you properly.* Bloody damn Murphy for taking me at my word.

"Let me do this for you, Mila. I have the resources to speed up the process so the police can find him. I have a few days until I need to leave. And… and we need to talk."

My spine snapped to attention when his voice cracked. Sure, now that he'd seen Jordan attack me, he wanted to talk. Anger sizzled along my nerve endings and I stepped away from him. Better the anger than the deep despair.

"I'm not sure I have anything to say to you," I said. "And I definitely do not want *your* help."

"Well, I sure as hell have questions for you," he snapped back.

"Because of the report in the paper this morning? Too little interest way too late, Etsam."

He breathed out through his nose, his nostrils flaring. "My mum flew here to see me," he said, his voice quiet. He swallowed hard as his eyes shadowed with pain. "I-I didn't know."

My anger faded, replaced by the same soul-deep sadness emanating from Murphy. After all this time, he finally knew why I left. And he was here, asking me to talk to him.

Noelle slipped her arm around my shoulder, pulling me closer to her side as I sagged under the weight of his words and the emotions they evoked. I hugged her back with my right arm, desperate for some support. Noelle, my rock, the one person who didn't ask a million questions about my motivation and integrity. Well, her and Alpie. They were the only ones I needed.

"You better take care of her," Noelle said in her best nursing voice. I dropped my arm and gaped at her. "She's been through a lot since your breakup and she deserves to be happy and safe."

"Noted," Murphy said.

He shifted in so I felt his body heat against my side. He smelled like my happiness. Home. That was stupid. And ridiculous. Murphy couldn't be what I'd imagined any more than I was the same girl he'd loved. I was different. Broken. And Murphy played his part in destroying me.

"Would that work, Officer?" Noelle asked. She slid off the bed, cringing slightly as she landed. "Shit, that hurts," she hissed.

"You're sure it isn't broken?" I asked.

"I have the x-ray to prove it," Noelle quipped. She smiled and her eyes glinted. "I punched him in the nuts. It's worth the sprain to know he's running around with bruised balls."

"Good on ya," Murphy said, his voice low. "I'd like to get in a few myself."

"We don't advocate assault, Mr. Etsam," Officer Reims said, but his voice didn't hold much censure.

"He said he'd like to, not that he would." I glanced up at Murphy. A mistake. That tiny smile lifted the corner of his mouth while his gunmetal eyes glinted with humor. They'd always reminded me of the ocean just before a storm. All the pictures of him over the last year showed his icy gaze. But here, now, his eyes were filled with warmth.

"Mila will keep me in line. Always has."

Murphy winked and Noelle moaned softly. I understood her distress. Hell, he affected me the same way.

"Turn off the charm, Etsam," I said. "It isn't going to work."

"Oh, it's working," Noelle simpered.

"Well, I gotta go," Noelle said.

"Whoa!" I said. "Where do you think you're going?"

Her widening eyes expressed concerns for my stupidity. Maybe

I *was* stupid. "I'm going to finish my shift."

"But your wrist," I said, my voice as feeble as my will whenever Murphy was involved. Noelle couldn't leave me. I turned on my most pleading expression.

"I'll get some pain meds and some help," she said, waving her good hand in a dismissive gesture. "Don't worry about it. I'll call you later."

"I want you to stay with me. That way I can be sure you're safe. And you can help me." I finished the last words a breath above a whisper.

She gripped my shoulders. "Until your uncle's caught, I think I'm going to keep a real low profile. He can't be happy I tried to emasculate him."

"Wish you managed," I whispered. Murphy stiffened behind me. Dammit. Not his business.

Noelle cupped my cheek as her eyes found mine, steadying me. "Would've been too late, sweetie."

Too late—for my baby and for my happiness. I wiped away the tears clinging to my lashes. No point in letting them fall. They didn't change the past.

Nothing could.

CHAPTER SIX
Murphy

Mila walking into the hospital room a few minutes ago about brought me to my knees. Her voice, usually so confident, dripped with hesitation. And her eyes... bloody hell. Those brown eyes were muddied with fear and shock. Because of me or her uncle, I wasn't sure.

Had I changed so much that she couldn't lean on me for help? Reckon so.

At first, it'd been self-preservation, but somewhere along the line, when the songs wouldn't come and Hayden stepped up, I became a walled-off hoon. Sure, I couldn't create new songs, but I could still perform. I was the band's greatest asset at live shows.

None of it helped me in this situation. Thrown back to the night Mila left, my chest ripped open, and I was just as empty as I'd been then but I had a year's bitterness sloshing through my midsection.

Mila's gaze pleaded with her friend, who pretended to ignore her. Nice sheila, Noelle. Anything she wanted, Noelle could have as far as I was concerned. Noelle narrowed her eyes, darting them back to Mila. No idea what Noelle was trying to tell me but, as I'd told Jake, Mila came first. Protecting her from her uncle and... well, finding a way to put the past to rest.

My teeth clacked shut as a growl built in my throat. Mila forced me into debt I didn't want to owe but had no choice but to repay.

"You sure you're up to your rounds?" I asked. "I could get you home and settled. Rather, my security team can. I'm sticking close to Mila till the wanker's caught." Once again, I ignored Mila's stink eye she sent me.

"That's okay. I'll probably stay with a friend." She took a shuddering breath. Jordan had said more to her than Noelle shared with Mila. Much as I appreciated her discretion, Mila needed to understand the peril. "Rather not meet him again. Especially now that he has a reason to hate me, too."

Mila flinched. Her pale skin faded to an intense white. I shuffled in a bit closer, ready to wrap my arms around her in case she fainted.

"Well, then, how about you call Mila after your shift? Voice, not text. I want to make sure you're okay, too. And Mila will feel better knowing."

Mila glanced up, surprise and gratitude swirling through those brown depths. Yeah, yeah, I still remembered how to take care of others.

Noelle grinned, her eyes lighting with impish excitement. "Sure will. So you're staying with Mila? That's good. I won't have to worry."

"Noelle—"

"Yes," I said, cutting Mila off. I reached out and squeezed her shoulder. Her breathing paused before she exhaled hard.

"I can't worry about you and also focus here," Noelle said, her attention back on Mila, her face falling into stern lines. "I need you to do this for me. Please."

After an interminable moment, Mila dipped her dark head in agreement. I rubbed my thumb up and down the side of her neck, trying to say thank you. I paused on her hammering pulse. From nerves or excitement? Both at the moment, I reckoned, and

I didn't like it.

I'd moved years beyond sweating over what a girl thought of me. The last time was before I asked Mila on a date. Some things never changed.

"We've got to find a place to stay," I said.

"I have to go home," Mila said, her voice filled with tension.

"No you don't. We should go somewhere Jordan won't look for you."

"I have to check on Alpie. My pet," Mila said.

Bollocks. Of course the woman had a pet. She'd always been too softhearted—didn't matter if the hurt being was an animal or a person, Mila wanted to take away the hurt.

"We'll go by your place then," I said.

"I don't think that's a good idea, Murphy," she replied.

"Let me help," I ground out. Being noble was bloody hard. Or maybe I wanted to punch something and that was why I struggled to get my desire under control.

In response to my tone, Mila's spine shot straight and her chin tipped up to a defiant angle. She pulled back, but I settled my hands along her spine and held her hips. "I don't need your pity."

"This isn't pity," I coaxed. I sucked in a gulp of air, released it along with some of the tension building in my neck. "I—I need to hear your story. From your mouth. Please, Mila."

Her cheeks flamed with color. My words dropped liked stones onto both of us. I didn't want to rehash our pain in such a public place, and Mila's stiffening body didn't bode well for us to move our very important convo private.

"Will you do one thing for me?" I waited but she didn't raise her head. "We've always been truthful. At least I thought we

ALEXA PADGETT

were. I promise, no matter how hard it is to say, I'll tell you the truth. Just as I always have." She tried to push me, gain some space but I just outwaited her. Our dynamic snapped back into place that fast. And it was so fucking perfect. I'd missed this. No. I'd missed Mila.

Except under that missing was a sea of anger. She'd lied to me, broke up with me.

"Fine. I'll tell you everything." Her shoulders slumped in defeat.

"Not what I want, love. I want you to promise you'll tell me what you're thinking and feeling. Even when it's hard."

The silence stretched between us as she studied my eyes and I studied hers. I would never understand how people overlooked brown hair and brown eyes. Jake once called such women mono-chromatic, but Mila wasn't. In her eyes, green swirled deeper and richer against the brown. Her hair spanned an amazing array of colors from the palest blonde to a rich auburn.

"I'll start," I said. "I've been very, very angry with you for a long time. It's fucked with my head. I don't want to be that bloke anymore. Hell, I haven't wanted to be him ever."

She pulled back, out of my arms, but I followed. "You can't blame me for that, too," she said, struggling against my grip.

"I'm not blaming you for anything. I'm explaining to you that I made mistakes."

"You are blaming me! I can't take on your emotions. I won't."

I sighed as I wrapped her tighter in my arms. "I handled losing you poorly. Now, I'd like to take you home so that we can talk. Because we have a lot to speak about."

She stilled, a gazelle having scented a lion, waiting, preparing to run. I caressed her careening pulse, as much in comfort as to point out my effect on her. Finally, she gave a little nod. I maneuvered her out the door, and we met Officer Reims in the waiting room. He held a Styrofoam cup filled with a foul-smelling substance—no way to confuse that with coffee—while chatting up a nurse. Must be a mutual love of uniform because the woman never bothered to glance at me. Usually, women loved to gawp at me. Ten minutes in her company, and Mila destroyed my mojo. Not that I cared, really, but still…

Chalking it up to a surreal experience, I reached out my arm and tucked it over her shoulder. As we walked to the lift, I adjusted my stride to hers, just as I used to. I'd missed her, the rightness of her scent and the warmth of her hip against my thigh. She pressed herself tighter into my side as we walked, just like she used to. Like she wanted to get closer, be nearer me.

For the first time, I wondered if she was trying to hide from her uncle. Anger settled low in my gut, burning in sharp bursts. Mila wouldn't have run from me if her mum helped her go to the police the first time Jordan tried something—she'd been young, just twenty-one, when she left her first uni and fallen into the anonymity of Sydney's less savory side. A side she dressed to fit into—all tight tops and ripped jeans, too much makeup, and a don't-mess-with-me vibe. Over time, as more of the real woman appeared from that hard shell, I learned she'd lived fearful, alone, long before we met.

Why hadn't I read the signs then?

In part because I was too dazzled by the woman. The vulnerability and intelligence just under the layer of hard-rock girl. The desire to protect her was *still* strong, and if she turned to me, I wanted her to burrow into me, trust me to take care of her.

We'd just… ended. We'd just never quite gotten to the closure part everyone made such a big deal about.

We stepped out of the elevator as Hayden and Briar turned the corner toward the lift. For a long moment, we stood there, mouths gaping.

"Officer?" I called. He'd continued toward the door. "Would you mind staying with Mila? I need to speak with them." I pointed at Hayden, whose mouth tightened.

Officer Reims nodded, his hand dropping to his holster as he glanced around. Mila tilted her head back so she met my gaze.

"I thought you and Hayden weren't getting along," she murmured. A frown formed as her cheeks reddened. So Mila kept an eye on me via gossip sites. While flattering and scary as hell—spectacularly stupid and I became best mates this past year or so—I needed to set things to rights with Hayden and Briar if I could. And this was a chance I couldn't let pass.

"You'll give me a mo'?"

Her brows pinched tighter. "Mind if I say hi?"

Right-o. She knew Hayden. Not as well as Jake, but I should've known her feelings would be hurt—she'd assumed I wanted to cast her off. Which I did because… didn't. I just… well, sometimes karma's a bitch. Grovel in front of her it was.

I sucked on my lip ring, fiddling with it as I headed toward Hayden and Briar. He wrapped his arm around her shoulders, pulling her closer to his body much as I'd done moments before with Mila.

"Hayden," I said, dipping my head. "Briar. I didn't fancy seeing you here. Thought to call you once I got Mila settled."

Hayden's eyes darted down to Mila's face, his widening before a slow smile crept over his lips, lighting him up. Briar studied Hayden, then Mila, and finally me. I held my breath as she met my gaze, wishing I could take back the worst of my mistakes. No, all of them.

"Mila! If you aren't a sight," Hayden said. He didn't let go of Briar, but he did grab Mila's hand. She stiffened, her body much more rigid than seemed normal. I pulled my gaze from Briar's intense scrutiny to gauge Mila's mood.

"G'day, Hayden," she said. She exhaled softly, her body loosening, then a smile built across her lips as well. "It's nice to see you again."

"Crikey. It's been ages! Where have you been?"

Mila dropped his hand and licked her lips, eyes darting around the lobby. People had stopped, many were openly staring. Not every day two of the biggest names in indie rock stood in a hospital lobby.

I leaned in closer, kept my voice low, even as Hayden stiffened, his jaw tightening. "Mila's got a stalker, mate. You saw him accost her at our show last night. Well, he attacked her friend this morning."

Briar leaned in to hear my comment and Hayden jerked her back, away from me. I understood his reaction—instinct most likely—but his lack of trust still cut deep. I pressed my lips together and stepped back out of their space. This was one more emotional minefield. One I misplayed.

"That's terrible," Briar murmured. "Do you need anything?"

She directed the question toward Mila, but Hayden clutched Briar closer to his side, almost expecting me to physically harm her. Shock detonated through my gut. I was Hayden's version of Mila's stalker. Bloody perfect. He turned her toward the open elevator without answering me.

"Briar's late for a meeting," Hayden said, his voice cooler than his eyes. "Are you in town for a while?"

I glanced down at Mila, who watched the byplay, her eyes darting between the three of us. "I hope so." I ran my tongue over my lip ring. "I'd like to talk to you." I forced my gaze back to Briar's. She deserved to hear the words more than Hayden. "And I need to apologize for the way I treated both of you."

Briar opened her mouth but Hayden jerked his head in a curt nod and turned away. I sighed, regret making it harsh. Mila turned toward the doors so I followed suit. Officer Reims stood nearby, hand hovering near his gun.

"Didn't seem like a friendly conversation," he said. "I wasn't sure if I should intervene."

"Hayden's right angry with me," I said.

"Don't you normally have a security team?" Officer Reims asked.

"Yes. But I asked Kevin—he's my guard—to get my mum and brother to the airport. He'll be back around four thirty. Wherever we are, he'll meet us."

"Good." Officer Reims set his arm in front of me and stepped through the sliding doors. I instinctively moved closer to Mila, doing my part to block her from any potential harm.

"I'm in this lot. There." I pulled the key fob from my pocket and pressed the button. Officer Reims motioned us on, standing near his patrol car parked a few rows in front of my rental.

"You're driving a Chevy?" Mila asked.

"What they had at the rental place."

"But you've always been a car snob."

"Have not. I just appreciate a beautiful machine."

"Not as much as you do a beautiful woman, though." Mila clapped her hand over her mouth and turned a funny shade of yellow. Shock reverberated through me just before satisfaction slicked over the top. She was jealous. Of the other women. Unexpected but not unwelcome because I hated the idea of another man touching her.

"So who's your current chap? There has to be one. You're too gorgeous for the blokes to ignore."

"You know very well I don't have a boyfriend," she snapped. "Officer Reims thinks we're together. You should correct him."

Didn't plan to. Not now. "Well, then in the past year. I had to fend off more than a few interested parties whilst we were together."

"Unlike you, *I* haven't been interested in screwing my way through life. I spent more than a week in ICU and then several more in physical therapy."

My guts hollowed out, all teasing and even the jealousy overcome with remorse. "You shouldn't have gone through all that."

"I did. And then I moved to Seattle because Noelle bought me a ticket and set me up with a great residency here so I can continue to practice medicine. The first few months were hectic, studying for my certification, and they were also scary. America isn't that much like Australia, no matter how much telly you've watched. Took me months to feel settled here."

"Sounds like a lot to handle. But even with all that, no one would expect you to be celibate, Mila." Yes, I was fishing. No, I didn't feel bad about it.

"Seeing as how Noelle loved to lecture me on my lack of love, I'm sure she also told you and anyone else who'd listen all about it." She stopped walking, shading her eyes. "Is this part of that honesty thing you were pushing, Murphy? Want to hear the words straight from my mouth? Here you go: I haven't dated anyone else."

She opened her car door while I gawked at her. No bloody way. She slammed her door shut.

I stepped back. Between Jordan's attack and the loss of the baby… was something wrong with her physically? Mila was too beautiful, too smart and too fun-loving to sit at home, wasting away in solitude.

But she was also the victim of sexual assault.

CHAPTER SEVEN
Mila

Even as the words tumbled out, my skin flamed with mortification. I never spoke first and thought later. That was my mum's philosophy in life, and I'd vowed, at the age of nine, *not* to be like my mum.

I squeezed my eyelids shut. Hard. My phone beeped. Probably the hospital needing me to read some lab results. I was too mortified to open my eyes and focus on someone else's life let alone pretend mine was normal.

Why did Murphy have to come back into my life? Sure, I bought a ticket to his show last night on the off chance I might see him, but my life had taken a turn straight back into a scary, unpredictable mess. All because Jordan's obsessive need to control me kept growing. Initially, I liked having a father figure in my life, and I assumed he wanted my mum, who boasted a handful of years on him.

Over about ten months his desires built, but once I realized what he wanted, what he'd tried to take from me that night midway through my third year at uni, I ran away.

As fast as I could. I changed schools from the University of New South Wales, and I took fewer classes and worked two jobs to complete my undergraduate and then my medical degree at the University of Sydney. Not far, but I used only my initials on my application and transcripts. I didn't list my name on a lease, and I applied for a job in the school clinic and also as a waitress in a ratty bar instead of the doctor's office I'd originally lined up, hoping Jordan wouldn't find me.

But I hadn't been smart enough to keep my picture out of the paper, inciting Jordan's wrath by having a boyfriend. Jordan told me not to get serious about anyone else that night he pinned me to my bed. That my body belonged to him and only him.

I hadn't listened.

Mum coming home when she did, her shocked expression, her babbling questions, was the reason Jordan never actually assaulted my body. He'd wanted to, and that's why I ran.

I shoved the heels of my hands into my eye sockets, trying to force my mind back to blankness. My phone beeped again.

Murphy opened his door and settled into the small sedan. Once upon a time, I would've kept teasing him about the inexpensive car. Instead, I sat, frozen by my words and memories.

"So do you want me to ignore that or should I forge ahead and get all the hard bits out of the way now?" His voice dropped, deeper than usual. I couldn't pinpoint why.

I dropped my hands and cleared my throat. How to answer that? Finally, I said, "What do you want to know?" I kept my head toward my window, unable to look at him while I answered his questions.

"Could we—" Murphy cleared his throat. "I'd like to know about the baby," he said, his words rushed together. "I read about your miscarriage in the paper," he said.

I'd expected it, sure. He'd read about it but never bothered to call. The weight of those words smashed at my crumbling control. He hadn't wanted *me* enough to find out if the child was his.

"I was almost five months pregnant with him when I miscarried. Everything had been going great. The trauma from the accident…" I trailed off. I hated talking about that day. I'd flipped over the handlebars and landed on my side, trying even then to protect my baby. I broke my three lowest ribs and even my leg trying to stop my fall. As soon as I hit the ground, as the sting of scraped skin seared through my awareness, I'd known I wasn't going to last long without support. I didn't go straight into shock, but my body shut down from my injuries within minutes. I didn't get to the hospital fast enough for the initial blood transfusion to stabilize the baby's supply as well as my own.

"The bloke came after you. To Perth. That's where you went after you broke up with me."

I nodded. I didn't want to do this. While I thought I wanted to have this conversation, wanted to share the loss with Murphy, I didn't. I wanted to crawl into my bed and never climb out.

"You said 'him.' A boy," Murphy whispered. "Was he… He was mine?"

"Yes," I said, still refusing to look at him, angry he'd had to confirm that. The ache in my throat built, as did the one in my chest.

The silence between us stretched and built, becoming untenable. My neck tensed with the need to turn my head. But I couldn't. Though I desperately wanted to know what he was thinking, the expression on his face might just devastate me.

"I had a son," he said, his voice thick.

I dug my fingernails into my thighs and opened my eyes wider, unaware of my surroundings. I focused on the small pain, the little grooves in my thighs so I wouldn't cry. Tears wouldn't change anything. A horn honked and we both jumped.

Murphy started the car. "Right. Officer Reims is waiting for us to move. What's your address?"

I gave it to him and Murphy put the car in gear once the route popped up on the screen, reflected in my window.

Such a short time for so many changes in something as basic as a car. Five years ago, few boasted GPS-enabled maps. Now the large LED screen, like cell phones, seemed status quo. The minimum necessity to have a reasonable life in this country.

Moments like this, I missed the more laidback Australian culture. Not because gadgets weren't important. They were. Just not American keeping-up-with-the-Smiths important.

Being nearly dead, losing the only people who mattered in my life, changed me, made me less dependent on other people's opinions. Perhaps because I simply didn't care about their pity or scorn because I generated enough of both for myself.

I refused to bring up the topic of our baby though I did glance at Murphy from the corner of my eye. He fiddled with his lip ring, tonguing the small silver circle. He wasn't just thinking, he was processing the information, and I'd once known him well enough to know now he struggled with the loss of a child he hadn't known existed.

"Did you," he cleared his throat when his voice cracked. "Did you name him? Did our baby have a name? Does he have a grave marker?"

"Yes to both," I said.

"Give me more than that, Mila," he said, voice so full of pleading. I sighed hard enough to fog my window.

"I named him Kyle Murphy Etsam. Your mum had once mentioned Kyle was your grandfather's name. I wanted him to be named after people who would've loved him."

Murphy made a choked sound. I still refused to turn his way. If I did, I wouldn't be able to get through the rest of this conversation without bursting into tears. The pressure built, hard and fast, in my chest and behind my eyes. I hated feeling this way.

I couldn't change the past. I'd tried every night in my dreams for months afterward, waking to a soaked pillow. Nothing would give me the opportunity to hold Kyle, to watch him grow.

"I planned to call you, tell you about the bub, but I ended up in ICU. My leg wasn't a clean break."

"If you'd called me, I would have come," he sighed out. "I still loved you. So much."

I bowed my head, trying to get a handle on my emotions. *Loved*. Past tense. Part of my heart, the little bit still intact, I guessed, broke apart. "I tried. I—I needed someone then. When they told me Kyle died. I called your phone, and some woman answered." The acid still burned the back of my throat when I thought of that. He'd held a woman, rooted her in his bed, while I was in the hospital, mourning our baby. Alone.

"Why didn't you call me back? Or leave a message?"

"With your fuck buddy?" I made a noise filled with disgust.

"Mila." His voice broke.

"I called your mum. Let her know what had happened. I needed someone to grieve with me." I was quiet for a long moment. "That day was horrible. I've never been so alone."

"She never said. She never told me you called."

I turned toward him. He'd wanted honesty. Well, he could have it. In the form of my anger. "I told her not to."

"I would have come," he insisted again.

"How would I know that? You were wrapped around all those sexy blondes. You were singing the hell out of that song, put our relationship out there for the world to rip apart. You used my words in that song." Oh, that still stung. No, the fact he'd used me to further his career hurt.

"I was angry. You didn't give me any warning. Any reason. You just left."

"So that made what you did okay?" I asked. He winced. Good. He should feel guilty.

Not that his guilt now would change the past. We were over. Our baby was dead. "Within a few days of the song hitting You-Tube, you had over two million watches. I couldn't compete with that. All my news would do was land you, hard on your bum, in Perth with a broken and depressed ex. If you even bothered to come at all."

The heat from his skin enveloped my hand. It shook even though my fingers were clenched in my lap. But no tears fell. I wouldn't let them. I wasn't that weak.

Not anymore. More than the attack, I'd struggled with the loss of my child, my last connection to Murphy. One nurse, Sammi, talked me into meeting with her friend, a psychiatrist at the hospital, to help me work through the worst of my depression and help me find a discreet psychiatrist here in Seattle. Now, I could see the aftermath of the miscarriage, of losing Murphy, was debilitating, probably life-threatening. That's when I started taking Xanax, my life saver.

With the little pills working magic through my system, I quit thinking such negative thoughts over the ensuing days, but I learned talking through my feelings didn't make the loss of my baby any less painful.

I fought the growing urge to shake out another pill into my hand, knowing it would take the edge off my reality. Instead, I took a steadying breath and told Murphy the rest of the story, keeping it as unemotional as possible.

I'd see Alpie soon. She'd nuzzle my neck, cuddle me as I needed.

"That's when you decided to leave Australia," Murphy said.

I shrugged. "I didn't have anything there to stay for."

He winced again like I'd hit him. Please. Like he felt that bad about it. I'd seen the pictures. Still, leaving had been hard. But only because I left my baby there, deep in an earthly embrace.

Susan Etsam was the one to suggest I call Noelle. Within hours of hearing my mostly incoherent story, she flew out, got me discharged from the hospital, helped with the funeral arrangements I insisted on for my baby, and booked me on a flight back here. Susan flew out to visit me and try to talk me out of leaving, but by then "She's So Bad" was the number one song in Australia and New Zealand and had begun to climb up the charts in Europe and the United States. Murphy rocketed to stardom as I buried my dreams. Wrong though it was, I couldn't, just could *not* see the man I'd loved so deeply sing about what a bitch I was to the rest of the world.

While Susan resisted my need to break away from Murphy and the failures of our relationship, she'd respected my decision and helped me get out of the country once she realized how poorly I was handling Kyle's death.

Funny. All I ever wanted was a stable home, a loving relationship—the exact opposite of what my childhood was. Instead, the need to run once again built, consuming me. I couldn't breathe in this space. I pulled my hand away.

For someone who craved stability, I was damn good at going walkabout.

CHAPTER EIGHT
Murphy

Mila pulled back. Way back and slammed multiple steel doors between us. Deserved, of course.

As we sat at a stoplight, I made a decision. Hayden had asked how long I planned to stay here, in Seattle. My meeting with a producer in LA about a new project was in a few weeks.

The secondary reason for the trip just became much more vital. Once Harry realized I wasn't excited about flying home to Sydney, he'd talked me into sticking around for a few days to sing at a charity event for a Seattle-area battered women and children, something he knew I cared about—more so now that I'd heard Mila's story. Always trying to improve my image, Harry was, but I didn't care about my image. I cared about the women and children in situations like Mila's—situations not of their making who needed a safe place to go so they didn't end up near-dead, as Mila had.

Seeing Hayden holding Briar earlier brought forth two issues: I needed to work through my shit with him by explaining my reasons for trying to keep them apart, bloody terrible though they were, and by begging their forgiveness. Something to work on while I played Mila's knight, the second but just as important issue to resolve. I sucked on my lip ring, considering my options.

The light turned green and I pressed on the gas. Driving on this side of the road took a lot of concentration. Why would Yanks want to be to the right? We hit another light, and I was glad for surrounding cars, keeping me in line.

Mila deserved better than she'd gotten. Better than I'd given her. I considered what "She's So Bad" must have been like to hear from her perspective, especially knowing she ended up in the hospital trying to protect *me*. My stomach heaved. Why didn't I stop to think?

But—and this was bloody important—she'd broken up with me. *Left* me. So why did I feel guilty for the song? Why should I? I gripped the steering wheel and tried to ease the ache in my neck and chest.

The officer pulled up behind us as I slid the car into park in Mila's driveway. "Can I give him your keys, Mila? He's going to do a walk-through. Make sure your house is safe."

She handed me her key ring. Three keys: one to her place, one to her friend's, I'd bet since Noelle said Mila stayed there often, and a car key. The black plastic on the last told me she drove an Audi. Nice car. Her place was small—probably a two-bedroom—the exterior neat. Different from her mum's house, which stayed one step above ramshackle.

Lush roses bobbed in the late morning sun, a rainbow of pinks, reds, and yellows. The shaker-wood siding was painted a dark gray with lighter trim around the windows. A deep porch ran the length of the front, featuring a white swing in the far corner. Mila'd always wanted a white porch swing, a perfect location to sit out with her coffee in the morning and her occasional glass of wine in the evening. I'd stake my fortune she sat out here at least once a day.

I rolled down the window of the car and dropped the keys into the patrolman's waiting palm. He'd undone the holster of his gun and his lips tensed. His eyes darted quickly around the space, taking in all the details in one thorough sweep.

"My backup should pull up any second. I'll go in when she shows. She's going to monitor my progress, but I want you to sit tight. Hear anything and drive to the closest police station."

"And that would be where?" I asked, overstating my accent.

His lip curled up slightly, but he didn't look away from the house as he rattled off the address. "Plug it into your GPS now so you know where you're going."

I did, grumbling. Mila pressed her lips together, flattening the plump fullness under the hard line of her will. I reached out, wanting to bring her head to my shoulder. Instead, I brushed my hand over the crown over her head, willing her to understand the comfort I needed to offer even as another part of me shook with the need to rail at her for dumping me.

Officer Reims tapped on the glass. A tall woman stood slightly behind him, dressed in her blue uniform, hand resting on her holster. "We're heading on in. Keep the car running."

I nodded, eyes trained on the front door. Tension built as we waited for the officers to exit or for shots to be fired. Officer Reims stepped back out onto the white-washed porch and my neck muscles eased. I didn't want anything to happen to these police personnel.

Kevin would be back from Sea-Tac in a couple of hours with a few extra security guards he and Harry were in process of vetting. Couldn't be soon enough. Just as us moving on from Mila's cute bungalow couldn't come soon enough.

"Ready?" I asked Mila. She'd turned to me in profile, and my gaze followed the soft line of her cheek up to her brow. The skin under her eyes shaded purple, a sure sign she wasn't sleeping well.

She opened her car door and stood, wobbly as a newborn colt.

She dropped her eyes almost as soon as she glanced at my face, and leaning down, she grabbed her purse. Her phone slid out just as it beeped again. I scooped it up, planning to hand it back until I caught a glance at the words on the screen.

You disobeyed me. I'll start with Susan. Just like I did before.

"That fucking piece of shit," I snarled. "I'd kill him myself if I could get away with it."

Mila's eyes finally met mine; her lids rimmed with red, but her eyes surprisingly dry. If I was her, I'd be crying buckets. But no, Mila remained quiet, almost solemn as she held my gaze.

"You can leave," she said. Her voice stayed soft but firm. "This is my fight with my demon."

I handed the phone over to Officer Reims, my eyes never leaving hers.

"You're wrong," I said. "This was always *our* fight. I just didn't know it."

CHAPTER NINE
Mila

My breathing escalated. Murphy's voice dripped sincerity, just as it had when he'd told me he wanted a life with me. No. I couldn't lean on him. Could not. Because he would leave—his glamorous rock-star lifestyle would dictate he fly off to do some concert or charity event or something. And then I'd be alone. Again.

No, that's why I had Alpie. So I wouldn't be alone.

I bolted up the steps and practically fell into my living room. Not good enough. He was still too close, tempting me. I scrambled toward my bedroom, self-preservation my only focus. A locked door. That's what I needed. Distance. Space. Time to consider how best to deal with him. How best to get over him.

I made it to the hall when his fingers wrapped around my wrist. My momentum stopped and my breathing slowed. I hated that he *still* exuded power over my will. He didn't pull me closer, and I yearned to pull away and close the door. I eyed it even as my body relaxed back into Murphy's warmth.

"Hello!" Alpie called from the corner of the room, fluttering her wings and lifting her crown of feathers.

"Hiya, Alpie. How are you?"

"What the fuck is that?" Murphy asked, clearly appalled.

"That's my pet," I walked toward her and she screeched, high-pitched with happiness. Her beak wrapped around the bars of the cage and she fluffed her pink feathers. Her black eyes locked on me. I opened her cage and let her hop onto my wrist. She side-stepped her way up my arm to my shoulder where she stroked her beak against my cheek.

"You broke up with me and bought a fucking cockatoo?"

"Fu-'atoo," Alpie shouted in her screechy bird voice.

Murphy stumbled back. "Make her stop talking."

"Fu-'atoo!"

"What the hell is it saying anyway?"

"*She's* repeating you."

"Fu-'atoo!"

"I didn't say that."

"She's a cockatoo, not a parrot. She does better with intonation than words."

"Put it back in its cage." Murphy stepped forward until Alpie spread her wings, her head swiveling to glare at him with her black eyes. "Now."

"Why should I? Alpie likes to be out. Don't you, sweetie?"

"Mila. I *need* to talk to you. We have important details to discuss."

Alpie brushed her beak down my cheek, making that shushing sound she repeated whenever she sensed my roiling emotions. She hadn't made that noise in a few weeks—more than a month. Clearly, Murphy was bad for my emotional health. "You need to go, Murphy."

"Not till we finish talking," he said.

I stayed stiff and still. I'd called him, needed him, but some other woman was already in my place. Anger burned away the threat of tears.

"You made it very clear over the past year you no longer want me."

He stepped forward ignoring Alpie's spread wings and her dipping head—clear signs of her own agitation. "Don't you *dare* put words in my mouth. You have no idea how much I missed you, how often I've thought of you. You hurt me when you left."

Thoughts swirled through my head. But only one mattered.

"I used to sing to him. I wanted him to be ready to play music with you one day."

Murphy dipped his head and rested his cheek against my forehead. Was he comforting me or drawing strength from our contact?

"I would have loved that. If I could go back, I would. You have to know that, Mila. I would have been thrilled to be his dad."

Kyle. Yes, of course, he wanted his son. He rubbed his palm up and down my back, soothing me with his warmth and touch. My arms crept around his waist and my shivers stopped. I rested my cheek against his chest and sighed. Murphy pulled me a little closer and our breaths synchronized. We could comfort each other now, but this moment wouldn't mean anything later. He'd go back to his touring and I'd continue to survive.

"Bloody hell!" he yelped.

Alpie flew off my shoulder and landed on the bookshelf across the room. A thin line of red oozed from the cut on Murphy's neck. He touched it, cursing when his fingers came away smeared with blood, but he didn't say anything further. Neither did I.

"When you chucked me over," he said in a voice as raw as I felt, "I figured I didn't meet your expectation somehow. That's what hurt the most—the idea that I wasn't enough for you. It never occurred to me you'd lie to protect me."

I sighed as I stepped back. "Perhaps I could have told you then," I said, my voice filled with doubt, "but my mum hadn't

believed me, the staff at uni, even the police didn't believe me."
Some things seemed destined to be repeated.

He squeezed his eyes shut. "I became someone even Jake
hated. I've fucked up my band near as bad as I fucked up with
you. So. I need to hear the rest, know what I'm dealing with. So
I can sort this."

"You want to *sort* me? Salvage your relationship with the band?
With Hayden? Didn't seem like he's interested in being best
mates anymore, and I'm guessing it's because of something that
happened with Briar."

Murphy pressed his head back against the wall and swallowed.
I watched his Adam's apple bob downward. "Yeah, I tried to keep
them apart."

I wasn't surprised; the feud between Murphy and Hayden hit
the pages of both the music and gossip sites. Word was Hayden
had stepped up when Murphy quit writing songs. Their musical
differences poured over into their personal lives. Most music journalists didn't expect Jackaroo to make another record.

"The hurt's been bigger than my anger since I saw you again
and talked to my mum. Stupid as it sounds, I miss the bub."

"*My* baby's death is separate from your problems with the band,
Murphy. Don't you dare try to use it to your advantage."

He met my gaze and hurt built there, deep in his eyes. "That's
what you think of me? That I'd feed the media or Hayden some
sanitized version of our story so they'd realize how wrong they'd
been about me?"

"Don't tell me it didn't cross your mind," I snapped. I didn't
really know this man, and I wasn't sure I wanted to.

CHAPTER TEN
Murphy

She called me on it. But then, Mila always called me on my shit because it was just that—complete shit. "Is that why you didn't tell me?" I bit my lip ring, fiddled with it, trying to find a calmer place. Nope. Not happening. "You never gave me the chance to know about the bub."

"I protected you!" she cried. Her eyes were wild, her breathing short. "I did what I thought was best. Jordan wanted to *kill* you, and I couldn't get anyone to listen. And, yes, before you ask, of course, I went to the police." She shoved at my chest but I didn't move. Instead, I clamped one of my hands over hers.

"I could have protected myself," I ground out. "You and Kyle, too, if you'd let me."

She narrowed her eyes, her lips a thin line of disapproval. "Oh, please. You'd give up the opportunity to be where you are now in this gilded lifestyle to raise a child in the same neighborhood we grew up in?"

"Yes." The word ripped from my chest. I didn't have to think about it. Mila's eyes widened, her mouth parted.

"Fucking hell, Mila." My hands tunneled through my hair. "I wanted you more than you could ever know. Any child that had come from us, yes—hell, *yes*, I wanted the chance at that. And as for the song… I'm a dickhead. Jake's said it, Hayden's thought it. I'm sure Flip has, too. I'm a complete arse, and that song was a fluke. We got lucky. I held lightning in a bottle. It hasn't been anywhere near what I hoped."

She crossed her arms over her chest. "Just all the sex, all the women fawning over you. You were living high on the lifestyle."

"Because you lied to me!" I yelled. I slammed my fist into the wall. Alpie screeched long and loud, adding to the pounding building behind my eyes. "I didn't know it was because you were trying to protect me, did I? So what did you expect? Me to mope around, waiting for you to come back so I could roll over at your feet."

"Yes," she shot back. Then she closed her eyes and sucked in a breath, but her answer, straight from her heart told me so much more than the rational argument she was going to make now. I knew Mila, and while she tried to look at every aspect of an argument, tried to remain rational and logical, her first gut instinct was led by her moral compass, which meant, no matter what she said now, she'd wanted me to wait around. To give her another chance. Hell, like any woman, she'd probably wanted me to fight for her—something I'd refused to do out of pride and hurt.

"No, that's not fair." Mila sighed, rubbing her temples. "I left to protect you, so how could you know? But… but I wanted you to because I would have if I could have. I would have done anything to protect you."

My chest tightened as I held her gaze, the green swirls flaring through her eyes. "I don't know what to do with that," I murmured. "Mila, I'm so—"

"I can't do this right now. There's so much baggage between us. And, quite frankly, I don't want to hear some half-assed apology. You *knew* me." She pressed the heels of her hands to her eyes and her lower lip trembled. "I need some space."

With that, she stepped into her room and closed the door. The lock clicked into place.

No, she couldn't leave yet! How badly had Jordan hurt her? Bollocks. I'd gotten sidetracked, then angry. The not knowing what the bloke did to her ripped at me. I turned to stare at the bird, which was watching me with its head tilted at an unnatural angle.

"She got a bloody bird," I said. "Just stay over there." Great. Now I was talking to a feathered rat.

Since Mila wouldn't talk to me, I called her friend, Noelle. She'd given me her mobile number earlier, before Mila came to the hospital, so I had someone to contact in case Mila refused to see me—Noelle's words.

"What's wrong?"

"Mila's fine. Just mad at me."

"She has a right to be."

"My mum says I got enough stubborn for six people."

I liked Noelle even more because she didn't respond to my obvious opening.

"Why are you calling me?" she asked.

I sighed. I wandered out to the living room and crossed my arm over my chest. "How bad did her uncle hurt her?"

"Why don't you ask Mila?"

"Reckon I did."

"And she said she doesn't talk about that, I bet. Well, I can't say. She doesn't talk about it."

"Please, Noelle. I want to help her."

"Help her, or assuage your guilt?"

I rubbed my hand up the back of my neck and then fiddled with the piercing in my eyebrow. "I never stopped caring about her. And up until today, I had no idea why she broke up with me."

"Past tense." Noelle would point that out. Alpie dipped her

head up and down over and over like she was agreeing with Noelle's words. "And you have a funny way to show your 'caring'—flaunting all those women. You're known as the wild one in the band."

"Never said I was a saint. Or even much of a decent bloke." I hesitated but the changes in Mila's demeanor were startling. "You knew her before. She's not Mila."

"She's not," Noelle said, her voice low. "You have to understand. She moved here as soon as she could, got a job so she could pay her bills and have health insurance, but she never does more than work, go to therapy, and go home. Alone."

"She has a bird." Nope. Still couldn't wrap my head around that choice. A cat, maybe. A dog would be fine as long as it wasn't some miniature version that existed only to make women coo. A ferret or hamster, even a fish would be better than a screechy feathered heathen.

"She hated coming home to her empty house," Noelle said, voice low. "Mila's not meant to be alone."

That sinking feeling in my guts stormed back through me. No. Mila was meant for a house full of kids and their friends. She thrived in a nurturing, take-charge role.

"But... a bird?"

"You don't get it," Noelle's words were clipped with impatience. "Every time she checked her laptop, she'd be so sad. I didn't understand why because I didn't know her Murphy was you—Murphy Etsam. I know she can't sleep without her pills because I flat-out asked her about them when she stayed here before she bought her house. Hell, some days, she barely functions *with* them. So if Alpie makes her life even a tiny bit easier, lay off."

"What's she on? Why? Are they hard to ween off?"

"That's not the *point*."

"Oh, I think it is. You said she's taking stuff to sleep. Does she take other stuff? Is that why she hasn't dated? Do men make her anxious?"

"She knows every one of your exploits and conquests. Each one cut her a little more and that's on top of the depression from the miscarriage. So why are you pushing this?"

"You think I lived this perfect and glamorous life, but I hated it, and I was angry I hated it. I get you think I'm to blame for her pill problem. So, that's one more reason I owe it to Mila—and to myself—to make it right now."

"Talk about a half-assed apology," Noelle huffed.

"Jordan attacked her after he'd threatened *my* family. He held my mum at knife point. This doesn't get any more personal."

Once again, Noelle pondered her words long enough for me to worry she'd hung up. "You could, you know, talk to her about that. See what Mila wants."

"How bad?" I had to know. "How bad did he hurt her?"

Noelle's exasperation blasted through the phone. "What do you think happened, Murphy? This isn't a freaking Disney movie."

Bloody… I slammed my fist into the side of Mila's bookcase, causing the avian monster to screech loud enough to nearly burst my ear drums… I didn't want anything bad happening to Mila. Didn't want to even think about it.

"She needs a new therapist—she hasn't dealt with whatever Jordan did to her." Noelle let that sink in. Someone called her name and she sighed. "I have to go. I'm working."

"Did he rape her?" My stomach ached and I wanted to hit

something. Hard. Over and over again.

"I don't know. The only detail I know—because I was there when the doctor told her—is she'll never have another child."

CHAPTER ELEVEN
Mila

I sat on the edge of my bed, shivers turning into big body-wracking shudders. Jordan's attack on Noelle shocked me, but seeing Murphy, having him here in my house… Everything was wrong.

If I hadn't met Murphy, then my life wouldn't be so convoluted.

Drifting from one flat to another, I'd spent more time at the uni's computer lab and library than my supposed home. Jordan's demands of my time increased while I was at home, he'd made it clear he expected me to be there and to spend time with him.

I hadn't wanted to do either. Especially after Murphy Etsam had walked through the door. Stopping in the shadow next to the bar, my heart thumped out an *oh yeah, oh yeah* beat.

Tall, his build then tended toward rangy. He'd worn old, soft jeans and a gray tee. The dark metal in his lip ring gleamed dully in the neon lights. He'd turned his head to speak to the person behind him, who'd laughed. When he turned back, he smiled, those grayish eyes gleaming with sardonic humor.

That's when I'd noticed the guitar case in his hand. Right. The musicians. My boss, and the bar's owner, branched out into live music, trying to find something to draw the college-aged students from the nearby University of Sydney.

I'd stepped forward, clearing my throat. "You're the band?"

"That we are, sweetheart," he'd said. And, oh, what that voice did to my insides. It was deep, a little cocky, perfect to croon love words late at night.

I cleared my throat again, wiping my sweaty palms on my jeans.

"Howard's stepped out but I can get you settled. My name's Mila."

His brows pulled low. "The owner left you alone?" He'd sized me up, not in the way I wanted but as if ticking off all my faults: my lack of stature, my small hands and delicate features, tight ripped jeans, red halter top. My long dark hair swished against my bare back. "You're a mite. What if some drunk harassed you?"

"We just opened for the night," I'd said, keeping my voice light even though he'd just stated my greatest fear. No need to tell him about the mace in my back pocket and the other bottles I kept behind the bar. "Normally Minskee's here. That's our bartender, but he's down with the flu."

"Right," he'd said, his brows still pulled low as he took in the place. "Oh. I'm Murphy Etsam and this is my brother Jake." He pointed with his thumb over his shoulder. "Rest of our mates should be here in a mo'. Jakey and I, we wanted to get a feel for the place before we set up."

"You can put your instruments in the break room in the back and I'll pour you a pint." I'd motioned toward the door tucked off to the left.

He hadn't known me. There was no reason for him to show an interest in me, especially when his brother settled into a booth, surrounded by no less than a dozen women. More had peered Murphy's way, and why wouldn't they? He glowed with that sheen of glamour. Not like Hollywood fake, but the natural beauty so few are blessed with. That straight nose, those thick brown slash-mark brows, the masculine perfection of his lips. Even the deep dimples in his cheeks only served to highlight his chiseled cheekbones and flashing gray-blue eyes.

As I'd worked my way deeper into his gaze, catching a glimpse of his disappointments and old hurts, I'd wanted to tell him of my own. I wanted to pour out my whole life story to Murphy Etsam, the sexiest musician I'd ever seen. So I had—to a point. I might not have been willing to date but, like every other female in here, I desired to connect, to feel wanted by a gorgeous male.

He'd stayed for the end of my shift, even helping to stack the chairs with me. I let him drive me back to the flat I shared with three other girls at the time. The nicest one I'd ever stayed in, that flat just a block from Bondi Beach. But I'd planned to move out of the room I shared with Kari in another few weeks. I couldn't ever settle down for too long. Jordan would find me if I did.

Ten more performances and Murphy had worn me down enough to say yes to his date request. We'd held a steady, happy course while Jordan searched for me, one of the more than four million city residents.

I blinked my eyes open, shocked I'd fallen asleep. I rubbed my hands over my eyes, trying to focus my mind. Turning my head, I glanced out the window. Straight into Jordan's eyes. I scrambled, falling off the bed, eliciting a startled yelp from my dry throat.

"Mila?" Murphy's voice sounded close, just on the other side of the door. He'd probably been there the whole time I slept. The sweetness of the gesture collapsed under the burgeoning terror. Murphy brushed his knuckle over the door, a whisper of a sound. "You okay?"

Jordan brought the large bush knife up and made a slashing motion across his throat. When he smiled, I finally found my voice.

The first scream was breathy, the second was full-lunged and hysterical.

My door crashed open in an explosion of sound and splinters. "What is it?" Murphy asked, eyes darting around. "Are you hurt?"

I lifted my finger and pointed at the window where Jordan stood. "He…" Jordan darted down my side yard toward my back garden. I swallowed, my throat too dry for more sound. "Jordan. There."

Murphy charged toward the window and I watched, numb and slow, as he slid up the sash. "No!" I managed. I stood, stumbled over and gripped his wrist. "No! Don't leave me." Panic surged and my nails dug deep into Murphy's skin. "He has a knife." Nausea pressed up into my throat. I hated that knife. Hated how it felt pressed to my cheek, my throat, my breasts.

Murphy leaned further out the window. I yanked harder, trying to get him inside. Safe. When tugging didn't work, I threw myself against him, grappling my way closer to the window. He pulled his head back through the window, his eyes dark, his mouth flat. I slammed the sash closed, my breathing ragged. Murphy locked the double clasps before he turned, his arms sliding around my waist.

"I won't leave. Hush now. Hush, love."

"He had a knife."

"So you said."

"He swiped at his throat with the knife. Like he meant to…" I shuddered, pressing even tighter into his chest. Alpie flew in and landed on my arm, sidestepping upward and shoving at Murphy at the same time. Murphy fell back, his face a mix of shock and fear. I wrapped my arms around my waist as Alpie shushed, rubbing her beak up and down my cheek.

"He's going to hurt me, Murphy," I said. My voice broke. "He told me before, in Perth, if I saw you again. That he'd kill me and you if you touched me."

CHAPTER TWELVE
Murphy

A powerful motivator, fear. I'd used it to my advantage when I feared my mum would lose the house after she kicked my father out. I used it again, pushing myself creatively, playing scales, songs, harder songs, everything I could, to prove to myself no fan would laugh at me when I went up on stage. Fear was what *could* happen, not what was happening. And many times, thanks to preparation, fears never came to fruition.

But this moment of fear wasn't healthy. I drew Mila back to my chest and wrapped my arms tight around her, ignoring the bloody bird. But her heart raced and her fingers clenched too tight against my skin. As her fear escalated, I couldn't force down my own, couldn't focus on her warm body snuggled up tight to mine.

I glanced back at the window where Jordan had stood. He planned to hurt her again. And again. Until he stopped.

Bollocks, I was in so much trouble with this woman. Jake would nod his head if I told him all my acting out had been to try to stem the hurt caused by her betrayal. Only I hadn't been smart enough to see that or to come find her and ask her to explain her reasons.

"Noelle said Jordan lived with you whilst you went to uni."

My fingers found her lower back even as she stiffened; her back felt like steel coated in flesh. "I don't want to talk about him."

"I read the police report. I know I shouldn't have but I charmed the secretary at the station into e-mailing me a copy."

She turned away, stroking the bird's shoulder. "Then you already know what he did to me."

"Yeah, but I think it'd be better if you said. Spilled the poison."

Alpie pressed tighter into her neck, her beak opening enough for me to see her beige tongue. Not normal, that. I suppressed a shudder.

"I said I don't want to talk about that. Not with my therapist. Not with Noelle. Definitely not with you."

Fine then. She didn't trust me. Probably best because I'd lied to her. There was no secretary. No one gave me the documents but I had managed to talk some of the details out of the detective. Bollocks! The police.

I hustled toward the front door when a hard pounding filled the room. I checked the peephole, thankful to see Officer Reim's face instead of Jordan's. The bastard was arrogant enough to stand outside Mila's window; I reckoned he'd be the type of bloke to waltz up to her door and force his way in.

"We didn't get him," Officer Reims said as soon as I opened the door. He strode in and locked the door behind him. "Can't be too cautious. Especially right now. I called in backup." Sirens blared, seeming to come from all sides. "Jessup and I hoofed it as far as we could after the car, called in the description and partial license plate. Hopefully, now we can do more with our APB." He let out a shuddering breath, wiped the sweat from his brow. "Wanted to get back and let you know the deets now that patrol cars are pouring in."

"What do you mean you didn't get him?" I asked.

"He disappeared. We think into a car at the intersection."

"So he has an accomplice?" I asked.

"Or he just freaked the hell out of someone by jumping in

their car."

"He's carrying a knife. A bush knife," Mila said. The bird stopped shushing but continued to sit on her shoulder.

Officer Reims pulled out his notebook, pen poised over the page. "And that would be?"

"A big-bladed knife, mate," I said. "Like your switchblade but it doesn't fold in."

"He carries the Ka-Bar Becker," Mila said. "It's got the longest blade."

"And you know this how?" Officer Reims asked.

"He told me. Probably to scare me."

"When?"

She shrank back smaller into the couch and Alpie hopped up on the cushion next to her head, lifting one talon then the other in a pseudo-dance. I hated how small and unhappy she appeared. "When he parked out front of Susan Etsam's house and threatened her, Murphy, and Jake if I continued to see them."

"You never told me that," I said.

"That's because I broke up with you right after that."

"Erm, folks. I don't need to hear more about your disagreements, but I will say that the media's gotten wind of this. They have video from Jordan's attack last night at the Tractor Tavern—from one of the attendee's phones, no doubt—and they learned you both were at the station today, as well as Jordan's subsequent attack on Ms. Markham. The journalists will be knocking down the door here soon. And since Jordan Jones knows where you are, Ms. Trask, it might not be such a bad thing to consider relocating."

Mila's eyes widened and she clutched her fingers into her silk blouse. "Where?"

He shrugged. "A hotel. Someplace with good security. We don't have the means to do more than offer support and run the investigation."

"I can do that," I said, considering. "My personal security and manager are sending over more bodyguards to be Mila's security team. I hoped they could be stationed here, but if you think it's better to move again, I can make that happen."

"Has he made any demands? Do we know what he wants?" she asked.

I gripped her hand as I sat next to her on the soft couch. Mila liked homey things. Perhaps because she never owned them. While our shabby furniture had embarrassed me, Mila had delighted in the well-wornness of my mum's house. Mila would make an amazing mum, reveling in the dirty footprints on her pristine floors and gooey handprints on the fridge.

She'd already have that if I hadn't screwed up. Noelle said she couldn't have kids, which wasn't right. Instead, she had a bloody bird. Jake told me once parrots could live sixty years or more. The shudder at the base of my spine rippled over me. I didn't like birds much, not since the one dive-bombed my head in elementary school. Mila knew this, which was probably why she ended up with one.

"He wants you, Mila." The words sounded harsh.

"Yeah, that's the demand," Officer Reims said. "Came through your friend this morning."

"He won't go away." She didn't ask. The words were flat, a statement.

"Did he ever hit you?" My voice turned gentle like you'd talk to a scared pup. I figured it was as close as I could get to outright asking about Jordan's actions now that Mila said she wouldn't discuss them.

"He liked to grab me, force me to sit with him. Touch me in ways I wasn't comfortable with." Her cheeks fluctuated between milk-white and rose, but her voice held steady. She didn't turn toward me, kept her focus singularly on the officer. Alpie fluttered down and settled in her lap. "My mum said he'd scared off all my potential boyfriends. She chuckled about my protective uncle. I didn't ask more questions then."

"Men who are physically abusive are more likely to stalk, and the longer they stalk their victims the more likely they are to sexually assault them." Officer Reims directed his comment to me.

Mila sat up straight, hands clamped together in her lap. "He didn't rape me. I mean, he wanted to…" Her cheeks flamed, and she pressed her lips together into a thin line.

Some of the tension faded from my shoulders at her words. I'd worried—no—I'd been *sure* that's what happened when Jordan attacked her.

"He told the Perth PD he couldn't stop the car," Officer Reims said.

She dropped her gaze, her jaw tense. "That's how I lost the baby. Well, sort of. More the shock from all the broken bones. And blood loss."

"You never pressed formal charges, said it was an accident," Officer Reims said.

Mila's jaw tensed. "That's not true. I *never* said it was an accident." She hesitated, her eyes flitting to mine. "But I didn't follow up with the officer. Didn't see much point since Jordan kept getting away with hurting people. I just… I just wanted to get away. From all of it."

I shot off the couch. I didn't know how to deal with that. What was I supposed to say? How could I comfort her? "We're going to a hotel. Should have earlier."

She made a disgusted sound before wrapping her arms tighter around her waist. *Not the way to handle the situ, mate.* Right. What was I supposed to do now? Reaching out wasn't something I was used to, but I didn't like the strain between Mila and me. It was making me yobbo as a stepped-on taipan. Mean bastards, those snakes.

"He almost killed you." I swallowed. Hard. "He did kill our baby." Officer Reims shifted behind us, probably uncomfortable with our little display. The man held a small fortune worth of my dirt, and I'd probably regret being this open. But I *needed* Mila to agree. "Don't get in a guff over this. Let me protect you. The police are looking. Hell, if the media's in on it, Jordan's face has been posted on every news report from here to Darwin and back, not to mention the million social media accounts."

"I'll give you a moment," Officer Reims said, beating a strategic retreat. Smart bloke. I liked him and would be sure to tell his boss so.

She searched my eyes like she used to. I worried the small ring in my lip as I waited, knowing she'd break my heart into dust specks this go-round. Hell, she already was and she wasn't even trying.

"I don't like you spending the money on me."

"That's ridiculous. I made it, in part because of you."

She dropped her gaze. "I hate that song."

Too right she did. Wasn't my fave before today and the lyrics were falling fast into the rubbish bin.

"So we're sorted," I said. "We'll go to the hotel—"

"That I'll pay for," Mila snapped.

No, she bloody well wouldn't, but I'd let her think she could if it would get her out of her house and into a place with better security. A place Jordan couldn't hurt her again.

"Collect your stuff," I said. I eyed the bird, hoping Mila wouldn't insist on her "pet" coming with us.

CHAPTER THIRTEEN
Mila

I hated packing up my belongings. I pulled out a small suitcase I'd tucked away when I moved in here four months ago—and had planned not to use again for a good long while. Like most of my belongings, it was new. Too new, a showcase of everything I'd left behind in Australia.

"We'll take my rental car. I'll get a new one sent over to our hotel."

"Won't the media know where you are? They always know where you are."

He gripped my free hand. My other one wound tightly in Alpie's carrier. "Don't worry. First call I made when I realized Jordan was in Seattle was to my manager, and he's working even now to send over some bodyguards. If we have to change hotels, then we'll change. Seattle has plenty. I'll get your luggage. Why don't you check around? Make sure there's nothing you've forgotten."

I walked through each of the rooms, touching an item here and there, hating that this moment felt like a goodbye. I grabbed the small photo album from the bottom shelf of my coffee table. It held a few snapshots from my years in Australia, including the only picture where you could tell I was pregnant. I dropped it into my purse. Alpie shushed me.

"Ready?" Murphy asked.

No, I wasn't but I didn't have much of a choice. I hitched my purse up my shoulder, gripped Alpie's cage tighter and walked toward the door.

"I know this is hard on you, Mila."

I nodded.

"We'll get through this."

"Do you think it'd be better if we split up? I mean, you're pretty well-known, and if the media find you, Jordan can find me." *And hurt you.* I didn't say the words, and I tried to ignore the anger, which was quickly stifled by hurt, building in his eyes.

"Is that what you want? For me to walk away?"

I should. Murphy didn't understand he'd been my lifeline this past year. Remembering our time together was the only reason I managed to keep going. Now we were changing those memories. They'd be overlaid with the bitterness of lies and the pain of loss. When Murphy left this time, my heart would break deeper because it never healed properly from last time.

He stepped closer, his fingers trailing across my cheek. My lids closed and my breath shivered passed my lips.

"Let me help. Please."

Much as I tried not to, I pressed my face into his hand and he cupped my cheek, his fingers tangling in my hair. It was shorter than I'd worn it when we were together, opting for a professional cut with a few flirty layers around my face.

"Mila, tell me what you're thinking."

"Yes, I'll go with you." Then because we both deserved to hear the words, I said, "I—I've missed you, Murphy."

His lips pressed against my forehead and tears pressed hard against my lids. I sniffled, wanting to pull back but not wanting to lose the comfort of his embrace. Of his warmth. Alpie screeched and fluttered in her cage. In the end, Murphy stepped away.

"Let's get you settled." The gruffness in his voice was a balm over my tortured nerve endings.

I glanced around my living room. Neat, orderly, the kind of space I'd always wanted to live in. My two couches were made of chenille—soft and cozy. I loved to curl up on them to read during the long, dark months of Seattle's winter. I even learned how to knit with Noelle's help, and one of the throws I'd made draped over the back, just begging to be pulled into one's lap.

I wanted to stay here, defend my little house and the world I'd created. I took a deep breath and walked out onto the porch. Whatever happened, Jordan didn't get the satisfaction of beating me down.

———————

"We're at Hotel 1000. Security's better at these high-end places. And they have Zipcars so if we need to go out, it'll be easy to remain anonymous." Murphy sucked on his lip ring, clearly nervous about my reaction. "They okayed your bird, seeing as how the situation is extreme."

I settled Alpie's cage in the back seat as she fluttered and squawked. Travel wasn't her favorite past time. "Okay."

"I talked to Jake," he said. "He's worried about you."

"That's nice of him."

We were silent—even Alpie—until we parked the car. Murphy insisted on carting my luggage himself, and we were whisked through the check in process. No one batted an eye at my bird carrier, much to my relief. Alpie, for her part, stayed quiet.

"Which room do you want?" I asked, sliding the bolt on the door with a grim satisfaction. Murphy's manager booked us a two-room suite that would probably drain my savings in a matter of days, but I'd worry about that later. Fatigue shivered through my limbs, thanks to the emotional drain on top of a mostly sleepless night and the fright of Jordan's reappearance outside my window earlier today.

I set Alpie's carrier on the coffee table and inspected the tall bird cage in the corner. It was three times the size of Alpie's normal cage, but then I usually let her roam the house. In this posh space, she'd need to be enclosed—not something she was going to like. But to my surprise, Alpie waddled into the new cage without any fuss.

"Fu-'atoo," she said, her voice soft, like a coo, as she settled on the sturdy tree branch. "Shh. Love-oo."

"You choose the room you prefer." Murphy slid onto the couch, one eye on me, the other starting to slide closed until it snapped wide open again. "Kevin's walked the suite and settled into his room next door. Oh, hell, they have a piano." He grimaced. "I'm going to need to talk to Hayden again. Soon."

"We're both tuckered. We should call it a night," I suggested. I looked around for the night shading that let Alpie know to be quiet.

"You gotta eat something, Mila. Far as I know, you haven't eaten all day. I bet you aren't eating much at all."

I sighed. "It's fine. I'll wait till tomorrow."

"You will not," Murphy said, his need to protect flaming to the surface. My stubbornness reared forth, delighting in the opportunity to turn my fear into anger. But arguing was a form of passion best removed from my time with Murphy. He used to kiss the arguments from my lips, turning that burning need to win into an inferno of desire. For him.

Not a place I should go. I crossed my arms over my chest, using

111

them as a shield to my heart. "Then order me whatever you're having. I'm off to a bath."

Murphy's eyes flared at the mention, and I could have kicked myself. Wet. Naked. Skin-to-skin. Just what I didn't need to be considering. Especially now that I was essentially Murphy's only companion in an elegant suite.

"Fu-a'too," Alpie growled in an excellent imitation of Murphy's voice.

"You are that," Murphy replied.

I scampered into my room, dragging my suitcase in haphazard patterns behind me, managing to miss the sofa by inches before I was within the solitary confines of my new living space. I shut the door and pulled in a ragged breath.

The large bed invited me to flop across it but I resisted the urge. I trudged passed it and took my toiletries into the bathroom. Turning on the taps, I pulled out my phone.

"I'm in a hotel suite with Murphy, and I'm pretty sure it's all your fault," I said in lieu of a greeting.

"Hey, Mil. How are you feeling?" Noelle asked.

"I should be asking you. Wrist any better? No more stalker sightings, right? Where are you staying tonight?"

"My wrist is fine. Painkillers are keeping the swelling down. I did light duty today, which was awesome because Blanche did the heavy lifting." Noelle chuckled. Blanche, a fifty-six-year-old harridan, used intimidation to get the other nurses to do her bidding. She ruled her hospital ward, but Noelle ignored her jibes and the worst of the assignments, performing so well under pressure she'd managed to knock Blanche off her pedestal and back down into the nursing pool.

"That's good, then."

"It is. She was tired so she couldn't give the rest of us as much hell. I think my wrist is going to be hurting for a few weeks. And, no, no more Jordan sightings. I'm staying at Kent's tonight."

Kent was a surgeon Noelle dated off and on. With their busy schedules, neither of them claimed enough time for a normal relationship, but Noelle mentioned him consistently for months.

"Hang on." I set the phone down and stripped out. I settled into the hot water, a murmur of pleasure building up my throat.

"I'm back. Are you sleeping with him?"

"Of course, sweetie. Where's the fun in a pseudo-relationship without the special sauce? That's all we are—a way to pass time. So Kent better bring his A game."

Her voice quavered just a bit. Turning thirty a few months ago hit Noelle hard. She went from loving her job and her crazy schedule to analyzing how everything she did would work with a child. She'd been bitten so hard with the baby bug, she'd dragged me into those baby boutiques and bought things she didn't need. I put my foot down the last time she insisted I go with her, telling her I couldn't go into another. Not with my history. While Noelle stopped talking about her need to settle down, those types of deep-seated desires didn't simply vanish.

"Is he worth your smexy moves?" I asked, hoping to distract her from her careening thoughts. Boy, did I know all about might-have-been scenarios. *So* not healthy.

"He's great, Mil. In fact, he's just finished making me dinner. Making it! He poured me a glass of wine to bring out on his porch while I talked to you."

"Then why isn't he more than a good tumble?"

"This is about you and the fact you're locked away in a gorgeous hotel suite with Mr. Famous Rock Star. It's avoidance. I can tell."

I toed off the tap and leaned back, staring up at the coved ceiling. "He'll break my heart all over again, Noelle. It's not mended from the last time."

"So give him a reason to stay."

"Why would he want me when he could have—and has had—any other woman in the world?"

"He doesn't do brunettes, Mila. I double-checked on my break earlier this afternoon. He's never been photographed with one." She paused to let those words sink in. I pressed a trembling hand to my chest. Yep, my heart pattered faster than a sprinter's. "He called me, trying to pry out details he didn't want to ask you. He cares about you."

"As he would any woman from his past."

"As he would his first love. I found the stupid photo that started this mess. Great gooey goodness, Murphy can smolder." Noelle sighed. "I mean, the way that man eyed you is hot. So don't throw away this chance before you see where it could go."

"That's the trouble. It can't go anywhere, and I don't want it to."

"You are the worst liar."

Murphy knocked on the bedroom door. "Room service just left."

"Did I just hear him say room service?" Noelle asked. "Let him wine and dine you. I'll do the same here. Who knows? Tonight could be the romance we both deserve."

"Night, Noelle."

"Night. Call you tomorrow. And, shug?" she said, her voice lowering.

"What?"

"Stay safe."

"You, too."

I hung up and tossed my phone onto the counter before ducking my head under the water. I held my breath for fifteen, then popped up.

"Mila?"

Murphy's voice grew more insistent, almost worried.

"Be right there."

I clambered out, pulling the plug. I wrapped my head in a large, fluffy towel and then my body in another. I didn't like hotel robes; I didn't trust them to be clean. A weird affectation of staying so long—and working—in a hospital, I supposed.

I scrambled into some pajamas and combed my hair, straightening the bathroom. All avoidance techniques. With Murphy right there, on the other side of the door, I was afraid I'd forget myself and touch him. Want him to touch me.

Noelle didn't understand. While Jordan wanted to own my body—through brute force that would leave me bloody and broken—Murphy wanted to get back that sweet innocent love we'd shared. But we'd both changed so much. Sure, I still loved him, but could he possibly still love me? Would it be possible to pick up the tattered bits of our former relationship and make a go at it again?

Would he even want to?

CHAPTER FOURTEEN
Murphy

I paced the living area, hoping the motion would keep me awake. The adrenaline of the day's revelations faded and the restless night caught up with me. I was bone tired and not much good for conversation.

But Mila needed to eat. During the years we dated, she tended to skip meals, especially when busy or worried. Now, though, she wasn't much more than a waif. I didn't like her so fragile. My Mila was robust. Full of love and fire.

I might never see that woman again. I rubbed my hands over my tired eyes before staring out the large windows at the twinkling lights. They were hypnotic, soothing.

I pressed my forehead against the glass, wanting nothing more than to give in to my need to hold her close as I slept. I hadn't wanted that for months—more than a year. But the urge, now, was overwhelming. Even stronger than my need to rail at her for destroying our relationship.

Mila's door opened and she padded out of her room. Catching her reflection in the mirror, I gulped. Her hair fell in wet, messy waves around her face, now devoid of makeup. Her small toes peeped out of her flannel pajama bottoms while the cotton tee hugged her ribs and breasts. Mmm, she might be thin, but she was mouthwatering.

"Why didn't you start eating?" she asked.

"I wasn't sure what you'd like." I turned toward her, swallowing a groan. Clean and soft, ready to pull into my arms and cuddle into sleep. I missed how she'd curled up into my side, her head

116

on my shoulder, a hand flattened on my chest. I'd loved pulling her closer, even during slumber.

"Crab cakes!" She exclaimed. "They're my favorite."

I blinked away the fantasy, focusing instead on the food in front of us. She'd always moan and sigh when she ate crab cakes. The biggest turn-on in the world. Probably not the best choice for my continued comfort, but she settled at the table, her face lighting with the simple joy of a good meal. I missed seeing that, too.

I took the seat next to hers, ignoring her stiffening shoulders, and reached for another plate. Some local fish, deep-fried, with coleslaw. Not the Aussie way, but still delicious. Hot and fresh. My stomach gurgled its appreciation. We ate in silence. At least this one was companionable.

"Thank you for ordering," Mila said after she swallowed the last of her bite. "I was hungry." She stood up and carried some dry greens over to the bird's cage, dropping them in as Alpie bobbed her head, saying, "Thank-oo. Thank-oo."

Polite bugger.

"Me, too. Been a long day, though."

"It has."

"Right."

We stared at each other. I should get up and walk to my bedroom. Shut the door and go to sleep.

"I want to know what happened, Mila. The whole story."

Her eyelids slid down over her eyes, and she heaved a breath. She pushed her plate back farther. "There isn't much more to tell."

"Don't." My tone turned sharp. "Don't block me out of this. I deserve to know."

Her mouth settled in that tight, angry line, but her gaze

softened when she met mine. "All right." She sighed, her brow pulling together.

"I was nineteen when I met Jordan. My mum's mum married his father. He's a few years younger than my mum and I guess they talked occasionally, I don't know how it all came about, but he stopped over for dinner one night. He watched me the whole meal." She shuddered, pushing back from the table. "I didn't like him, but he left, and I went on with my life until he transferred to Sydney, or he moved there—I don't know. Mum let him stay with us."

I followed her with my eyes as she moved around the room. "He'd bring presents every day, trinkets really, fixed a leaky spot on the roof. Mum was over the moon to have his attention and help."

She turned toward me. "Over time, he began to open my bedroom door at night and watch me. One time, he'd followed me to school and sat in his car whilst I talked to my friends. Another time, he pulled me out of a bar because the boy I danced with got too close."

"Did you tell your mum?"

Mila gave me that impatient flick of her eyes that said more than words ever could. "I was paranoid, stupid, crazy. That's what she told the counselor when I told her about Jordan opening my bedroom door at night."

Sounded like Mrs. Jones and ran true to what I learned so far today. Right then.

"When he pinned me to my bed and…" she blew out a breath. "Mum came home, freaked out. While she cried and screamed, I ran out the door and stayed the night on a friend's couch. But I needed to move out for good, which I did, and I changed universities in hopes he wouldn't find me. Then I met you." She sank onto the couch, her voice changing. "I told you I shouldn't date you."

My heart pounded. "And I pushed."

Her eyes met mine and even across the distance some of that old passion sparked. I clamped my hands on the edge of the table.

"You persisted. And I wanted you to," she said, her voice soft. Her lips flipped up in an insouciant grin. "Best time of my life."

I dipped my head in response. Our years together were the highlight of mine as well.

"Everything was fine whilst you were toiling away, just another musician with a dream. But your music was so good, and you gained fans. The media took notice. And then that picture of us came out in the paper."

She sighed, her throat convulsing. She wasn't aware of her fingers playing with the ring on her finger, but my gaze stayed there. I'd noticed it on her hand within moments of seeing her today. The ring I gave her. Satisfaction mixed with regret, a strange boil of emotions that didn't set well in my gut. Or my head.

"Jordan found me, at the hospital. The article said where we'd met, mentioned my residency position in labor and delivery. Jordan was so angry. Angry enough to force me into his car and drive to your mum's house and threaten her, too. I sat in the car, too scared to get out. He'd taken my phone. I couldn't call for help."

Mila licked her lips. "He said next time he'd start carving and he'd start with you. Murphy, I…" Tears pooled in her eyes as she met my gaze. "He didn't just want to hurt you, he planned to kill you. I couldn't let that happen. So when he drove me to your gig from your mum's house, I did the only thing I could think to do. I lied to you. And I disappeared."

"Because it worked before," I said, my breathing just as ragged as hers.

"Except it didn't. You wrote that song. It immediately blew up, the band was everywhere online. Some reporter in Perth spotted me, made the connection. I didn't know he'd written about me, but Jordan found the article. He found me. I'd picked up a pushy at a yard sale so I didn't have to walk to work."

The tears shimmered on her lids for a long moment before they spilled over. Great big tears that held worlds of pain. "I went over the handlebars." Her throat convulsed and her eyes blazed. "I might've been able to hang on through the shock. But Jordan dragged me into the alley. I bled. A lot. That's what finally did it. I bled too much and there was nothing left for Kyle."

I didn't want to close my eyes. I'd picture her, broken, bleeding, needing help.

"He was perfect," Mila whispered against my shirt. "I got to see him. One more month and his chances of survival were between fifty and eighty percent. Four weeks. His life ended because I couldn't stay away from Jordan for twenty-eight days."

I gathered her closer, wanting to kiss away the sadness that clung to her lips. I didn't move, aching for all we'd lost. This past year, I'd searched for intimacy, impossible to achieve without baring one's secrets, one's fear and thoughts, with a partner.

"I'm so sorry," I said, meaning the words. "For not being there. For you losing the baby. For everything you were dealing with that you couldn't share with me." But under those words was that anger—a big, thick pit stewing in my gut.

"I was scared that you'd leave me if you found out," she said, her voice nothing more than a whisper.

My chest tightened. Had I done such a poor job of loving her that she'd had to worry I'd quit? Soon as she walked away, I tried my damnedest to hate her. When that didn't work, I'd turned to other women. Many of them. But the solace was empty; their arms were wrong.

"You were there alone? You didn't call your mum?"

Mila shook her head. "I didn't want her there. She never believed me. She didn't back me up when I went to the police after he made threats against your family. In fact, she gave him an alibi for the night. They never would have picked him up at all if he wasn't parked outside your mum's house when the police drove by."

I brushed her hair back from her pallid cheeks, liking the weight and tangled softness as it stuck to my fingers. The first time I saw her, in that dingy bar, she'd seemed small, compact but self-assured in her worth. Hearing her talk about her class-es, about her past, I'd been knocked on my arse. She was smart enough, capable enough to make great changes.

She wasn't the woman standing before me now: this Mila was vulnerable, fragile, fighting to keep her life from tipping her over the edge. But both the Mila of six years ago and this older version ripped at my heart. And yet, there was a piece to the story I couldn't resolve.

"So what changed? Why did you come to the Tractor Tavern last night?"

She glanced up for a moment, her eyes flashing darker, the green swirling like bits of mosaic amidst the deep brown. But her lips pulled down at the corners like they did when she felt guilty about something.

"I wanted to see you," she said, her voice too soft. But I heard her. She dropped her gaze as if she'd just admitted a giant sin. Her words were a punch to the gut. Well, just… fuck. I leaned in, needing to taste her.

She didn't try to stop me, and when my lips touched hers, I wanted more. No, I needed it. We'd always shared amazing chemistry. In this kiss, I poured all my sorrow at what we'd lost. Mila did, too. So deep. Just lips caressing, testing, re-learning each other.

The best kiss. Because this connection *meant* something.

"Because I planned to listen to you sing 'She's So Bad' and finally—*finally*—put you in my past."

A moment ago, I wanted to gather her closer. Lay her back on the couch and make her forget her sorrow. Now… I ran my hand through my hair. Bloody hell. She wanted to get over me? I was the injured party here—she'd broken up with me.

Noelle's voice rang through my head. *She knows every one of your exploits and conquests. Each one cut her a little more. So why are you pushing this?*

Why indeed?

I wasn't sure yet, just knew that for the first time in months, I was whole. Maybe… maybe Mila was exactly what I needed.

Problem was, I had no idea how to convince her to give me another chance. Worse, I wasn't sure I could ever get past my anger—the betrayal of her leaving.

"Fu-'atoo," Alpie growled.

That bloody bird was smart.

CHAPTER FIFTEEN
Mila

Maybe in the months since I knew him, that was his go-to; he'd kiss a girl to get her to shut up. If they ended up in bed, well, so much the better.

I was a cynical, cynical being. I ducked my head, shuffling my feet to put more space between us.

Both our phones rang. Murphy snagged his out of his pocket while I dashed back to my room to grab mine off the night stand. I missed the call; I frowned at the local area code but not a number I knew. I debated calling back.

"Mila? You'd better come see this."

I wandered back into the living room, staring at my screen, waiting for the voice mail message to pop up. I glanced up at the telly, which took up most of the wall near the fireplace. My phone slid from my fingers.

"That's my house," I whispered.

Flames licked with cheerful hunger from the windows and out the doors. The roof heaved and steamed.

Vaguely, Murphy's hands on my shoulders, guiding me to the couch. The back of my knees hitting the cushion forced me to sit, my eyes never leaving the horrible image on the screen.

"I'm so sorry."

"My house," I whispered again. I wrapped my arms around my middle, trying to hold in the ache. Nothing there wasn't replaceable. They were just things. But they were my possessions—the ones I purchased to surround myself with something more than the sad, white walls for Jundaloo or even Noelle's guest room.

Gone.

I still had Alpie. I rose, ran to her cage and let her out. She side-stepped up my arm. "Nuff," she said. "Shush."

"Detective Davenport called me. Jordan's the prime suspect. If they can connect him to the fire, arson is on his growing list of crimes."

I nodded, my eyes still glued to the hypnotic view of my house being consumed by flames. "Did they get him?"

"No."

Again, I nodded. I needed a pill. I made to stand when the scene cut to a newsroom. "Breaking news: Jackaroo's lead guitarist's on-again-off-again girlfriend Mila Trask's house in flames here in a Seattle suburb. The fire department believes they've contained the fire to just Ms. Trask's residence."

I breathed out a deep sigh. Mr. Henley lived next door in the house he'd moved into with his wife a half century earlier. Mrs. Henley passed before I moved here, but Mr. Henley loved to show me all her crocheted blankets and the pictures of their four rowdy boys growing up. Jordan couldn't destroy that man's memories as he did mine. Again.

"Do you think the police will find him?" I asked.

Murphy sat next to me, hauling me closer to his side—the opposite side from Alpie, who screeched and dug her talons into my shoulder at Murphy's manhandling. I let him, in part because I wanted the warmth from his skin, but also because I loved that I still fit him.

Murphy would go back to his big life—soon. But in this minute, I needed his solid presence.

"Hard not to. We're the main story both here and back in Oz."

Heat flamed over my skin as my back bowed straight. "No."

"Nuff, shush." Alpie rubbed against my neck.

"Sorry, love, we're the 'it' couple."

I shouldn't have eaten; my stomach sloshed in an unhappy morass of shame and guilt.

"But we're not together," I blurted.

Murphy turned my chin, forcing me to meet his eyes. I wanted to ignore how good his fingers felt against my skin. I couldn't. "We have a sad history. For some people, it'll be an interest in my life. For others, they'll pay attention once they learn you were ever connected to me. Some will cheer for you because of your stalker. Anyway, the story's interesting enough for some staying power. And we'll use that."

"How?"

"To get more pictures of Jordan out there and find the bastard. It's free PR."

I shuddered, my eyes squeezing tight. I didn't want to be plastered on the news. After a deep breath, I forced my gaze to the television where the reporter still spoke about Murphy and my failed relationship. "Sources tell us Ms. Trask spent a few weeks in Jundaloo, a trauma hospital in Perth, Australia after she was hit by a car biking to work. Her injuries were extensive and she allegedly miscarried Murphy Etsam's child then."

I bolted off the couch. Alpie shrieked again, flying into the dining room. My shame, my heartache laid out there, all over the telly, for the *whole world* to see. I hurried to my temporary bedroom. Home, I guessed. Once again I was alone, homeless.

I glanced over at the pills sitting on my nightstand. One was in my hand, my mouth in the next heartbeat. I curled up on my bed with my photo album clutched to my chest. The one memento from my life in Australia. Well, this one narrow book and my accent I couldn't seem to lose.

"Come on," I whispered. Twenty-nine minutes and the sweet relief would start to trickle through my blood stream.

Noelle and Maura would call. Soon, probably. They'd fuss over me. My phone vibrated with a text. From Susan. Murphy's mum making sure I was holding up okay. I wasn't, but I didn't want to tell her that. My door opened and I sighed, wishing I'd taken the time to lock it.

"I need to be alone."

Murphy moved steadily toward the bed. "That's the worst thing you can do right now. Being left alone with your thoughts will just make it seem bigger. Scarier."

"It is scary. Every time I think I've gotten away, started to build a life, Jordan shows up and destroys it. And each time he takes something huge from me."

"See? You can't be alone." Murphy nudged me with his hip. "Show me the pictures."

I hesitated. Sharing this with him would bring back even more memories. I glanced again at the pill bottle. How long until it kicked in? Twenty-four minutes?

"Why are you clutching it like a teddy bear?"

Heat swamped my face. Oh, this was going to be mortifying. I shook my head. I didn't want to share this, not with him.

"My friends are going to call." The phone rang, and I sighed in relief. Murphy beat me to the phone.

"Hello, Noelle. She's fine, sitting here on her bed. She'll call you back later." He powered down my phone and dropped it on the nightstand, next to the bottle.

Soon. I'd relax soon.

"Why don't you show me what's in there, Mila?"

I loosened my grip, knowing he'd keep after it until I showed him. He snagged the album from my arms and flipped it open.

The picture of us at Bondi beach, both of us holding surfboards, wasn't what he'd expected. His hand trembled as he touched the page, his finger landing on my cheek in the photo. I frowned. I wanted his fingers on my face now, not an image of it.

Wait. No, I didn't. If Murphy touched me with such tender concern, I would fall into his arms and be just another one of his conquests.

I scooted up against the pillows and flipped the page to one of his shows, our cheeks pressed tight together, eyes shining with excitement. We'd hoped this would be his band's big break. Hadn't worked out that way, and in hindsight, I was glad. We were together two more years because the record label's intern didn't show at that gig.

The other picture was of just Murphy, at his twenty-sixth birthday party. He'd worn two party hats, one on each side of his head like horns. He grinned at the camera, a huge cake lit with tons of candles in front of him.

He took the book from me and continued to flip through the pages, studying each one. He wiggled his lip ring as he turned another page. I wanted to snatch the album from his hands. These were my memories, and I didn't want to share them even with him. Especially with him. I prepared to bolt off the bed and hide in the bathroom. My movements felt slower than usual. I tried to remember how many pills I'd taken today. From my reaction time, too many.

But he'd flipped to the last page. I stood out front of our favorite beach, my hands forming a heart over my tiny tummy bump.

His whole hand covered the photo. "I never saw this one," he said. His voice was hoarse.

"No."

"You're pregnant in it. I can see this little curve above your bikini bottoms."

"Yes."

"When was this taken?"

"The day before Jordan found me in Sydney."

Murphy flicked at his lip ring. He dipped his head in acknowledgment. I didn't add that I'd hoped he'd ask me to marry him before I told him about the baby. Silly though it was, I was old-fashioned, perhaps because of the way I was raised, and I wanted the ring and the vows before the baby. My mother married many men, none my actual father. Trask was the name of her third husband, a kind teacher who'd remained hurt and befuddled when my mother cheated on him. He'd been in the process to adopt me, already legally changed my surname to Trask so we could all be a family. My mum didn't have the money or inclination to change my name back to Jones.

Murphy met my gaze, his eyes stormy. "What would you have done with this, Mila? I know you—you had a plan. This is staged. Who took the photo?"

"Your mum took it." Much as I wanted to shut the album, I worried I'd have to wrestle it from his hands. I wasn't about to sully the photo.

"What was your plan?" he asked again.

"I'd planned to give it to you before your show that night. As a surprise. I'd hoped you'd be as happy about the bub as I was."

"Fuck." The word was harsh but his fingers traced the lines of my belly with extreme gentleness. "Fuck. If you'd just told me the truth, Mila."

His sigh was harsh. He closed the album, his hand stroking over the cover. His brows pinched tight over his nose. "I planned that night, too."

His voice was all gravelly with emotion. A thrill raced across my stomach. I loved Murphy's voice like this, private, something he didn't share with many people. He raised his hand to cup my cheek, his thumb drifting in lazy swipes against my temple.

"Do you want to know what it was?"

Did I? I wasn't sure. If he told me, I'd obsess about it. If he didn't tell me, I'd obsess about what it could have been.

He smirked at me, probably knowing my thoughts. Murphy knew how my mind worked. And he'd played me well.

"Yes," I said.

He brought his other hand up and pushed my hair from my cheek, his eyes following the sweep of my bangs back from my forehead. His eyes returned to mine. Held them in a long embrace.

"I'd written this song, see. A ballad. Soft and sweet. Just me and my guitar. I wanted to have you come up on stage whilst I played it. You'd love it, have to hug me, arms twined tightly around my neck."

I shook my head again, my eyes widening. I wouldn't cry. No way. I opened them even wider.

"When the show ended, I planned to take you there, to our spot on the beach."

129

My lips parted and a guttural sound drifted from my throat. Murphy's lips flipped up in a sad smile. He kept his eyes on mine.

"I'd bought you an engagement ring, Mila." His eyes filled with sadness. "Not that big or fancy, but it felt right."

My breath broke. I scrambled back, but Murphy caught me before I fell off the far edge of the mattress. He brought me back toward him, though I shook my head, mouthing no.

"I was going to ask you to marry me that night, Mila."

CHAPTER SIXTEEN
Murphy

She'd managed another pill before I got in here. I could tell by the way her eyes were filming over, glassy instead of sharp. Anger warred with a sad kind of understanding. I didn't want Mila turning to substances for relief; I'd seen too many good musicians ruined by them.

At the same time, she'd been through so much. So much of it alone. At some point, she'd made the decision to survive, no matter what. While I didn't agree with her methods, my chest tightened at the other possibilities: Mila too broken to find her way back to the strong, loving woman she'd been or perhaps worse, Mila apathetic to it all, giving in to Jordan's sick needs.

The longer we toured, the more musicians I met, the more I realized many people had a string of bad luck who felt as though they'd deserved it.

She sniffled. "Why did you tell me that?"

"Because you needed to know how much I cared about you." I waited until she met my gaze. Took ten seconds—longer than it used to. "I still do."

She shook her head. "You don't mean that," her voice was quiet. And I bit the tip of my tongue, unwilling to fight with her.

"I mean, you care about me as a past lover," she said. "But we don't know each other anymore."

I patted the spot next to me. "Lay here."

She eyed the narrow strip of space between us with trepidation. "I don't think this is a good idea."

"Now, Mila."

Her eyes met mine and she sighed, longing softening her features. I hoped her medication wasn't too powerful. The withdrawal effects were going to rip her, but that wasn't a good enough reason to let her keep abusing the medication.

I couldn't let her keep digging herself deeper into the hole she'd managed to fall into. She'd destroy the life she'd clawed together. She paused again, sucking at her lower lip as she eyed my body stretched out on her bed. I gripped her wrist and gently pulled her down, tucking her next to me. She sighed and snuggled closer in increments, a tiny kitten unused to and afraid of anyone's touch.

I tipped my head back against the headboard. Bloody hell, being with her again hurt. Not just because I wanted to touch her—that desire never left—but I wanted to fix her life and make sure she could stand alone.

Then I'd leave—to deal with my record exec's meeting, decide how to handle the solo project. Go home to Sydney or start recording in LA, touring somewhere else. Leaving wasn't an option. My life *demanded* it.

I stroked her hair, letting my thumbs brush the sensitive skin against her nape. I didn't say anything else, just held her until the pill's effect trickled through her system.

Once she was deep into her slumber, I picked up the album and stared at the picture of her on the beach. Her smile shone brighter than the warm Sydney sun. Her eyes laughed into the camera, thrilled with her secret.

Prison wasn't enough for Jordan Jones.

I slid from under her. She mewled in protest, her shoulders stiffening. I sat on the edge of the bed just out of her reach and rubbed my hand over her head.

"Murphy," she breathed.

My name from her lips and I was on the verge of an emotional breakdown. She turned, snuggling deeper into the pillow. I picked up her pill bottle and studied the label. A depression or anxiety pill. A lot of musicians took it. Ironic how many of them didn't like to perform.

I took the bottle and my phone into the living room.

I dialed Noelle's number from my Recents list.

"What do you want?" she said, stifling a yawn.

"Sorry to wake you."

"You didn't wake me, but I am in bed."

I made a sound in the back of my throat as I thought of Mila on her bed, curled around me. Great, now my dick was hard. Again. Almost a permanent affliction in the past few hours. So very mature of me.

"Mila's abusing her Xanax," I blurted out.

"You're crazy," Noelle said, but doubt threaded through her words.

"I'm holding the bottle in my hand. It says she filled it ten days ago and there are only ten left."

"It's an easy med to become dependent on." Noelle sighed.

"Gets into the system in about half an hour but back out in about six to eight hours."

"Right," she said. "So the mind starts to want more of it if the stress doesn't go."

"How do I break her of the habit?"

"You think now's the time to do that?"

I flicked my lip ring, considering her question. "Is there ever a good time to treat an addiction?"

"She's dealing with a lot, Murphy. The stress has to be crushing."

"And it'll only get harder to stop when she becomes more dependent."

"Dammit. I hate that you're right," Noelle sighed. "Can you hold on a minute?"

Noelle muffled the phone. A deep, male voice responded. So it was like that? Just tattoo "dickhead" across my forehead.

"Kent says she needs to ease off. Slowly. If you do cold turkey right now, she might have a very adverse reaction."

"What does that mean? Some of us don't have medical degrees."

"It means wean her off." The bloke spoke again. Ah, Noelle had put me on speaker. "You have the bottle?"

"Yep."

"Keep it," he said. "Look to see if she has any others and confiscate those as well. Then dole out her normal dose for the next few days. When she runs low, she'll need to see a psychiatrist to get another script. Noelle will send you a couple of names for good ones that one of my colleagues recommend his patients to."

"She'll need to be occupied to keep her mind off the stress, especially the waiting to find out about Jordan. And, Murphy, she's going to be cranky," Noelle said.

"Cranky I can handle."

Noelle snorted. "We'll see. Mila's always so even-keeled. This ought to be interesting." She yawned. "Call me tomorrow."

"Yes, ma'am."

Clicking off, I went back into Mila's room. She lay on her side, facing away from me. Her ribs rose and fell in a steady rhythm. I did a methodical search through all her bags, the pockets of her long cardigan, and her purse. I pulled out a printed script for another round of pills from her wallet but didn't find any more pills.

Good. Maybe the problem wasn't that serious.

I clutched the pill bottle in my fist. Mila mewled, shoving her hands between her thighs. I tugged a blanket from the bottom of the bed, dragging it up to her chin.

Time to do a little more research before I could sleep for the night.

I walked out into the living room, stifling a cry when the rustle of feathers and a rush of air brushed my cheek. The bloody bird landed on my shoulder and I cringed back from its beak nuzzling my chin—barely.

"Right. In your cage."

"Mil?" Alpie asked, tilting her head. Her black eyes bored into mine. "Mil?"

Bollocks. Its beak was mere inches from my eye.

"You want to see Mila?" I asked. Anything to get it off me and into its cage.

I opened Mila's door and Alpie fluttered in, landing on the headboard. She bent down, wings spread, to peer at Mila's slumbering face. "Shush. Mil."

"Time for sleep… er… Alpie."

The bird made a soft humming noise for a long moment before flying out of the room, just missing my head. I ducked, cursing. Alpie settled into her cage.

"Night. Mil." She dipped her head, her crest feathers fluffing. "Fu-'atoo," she said in that voice that was so close to my own.

Mila would choose a bloody damn bird.

CHAPTER SEVENTEEN
Mila

I woke, shocked. I'd slept the whole night for the first time in… I couldn't remember. I stood and stretched. After a trip to the bathroom, I snuggled into my cardigan, running my tongue over my clean teeth. I loved that feeling.

I walked out to the living area, unsurprised to see Murphy up and about. He'd always been an early riser. He was talking to a man, big bloke with a no-nonsense buzz cut and sharp hazel eyes. I shied away, planning to head back into the quiet of my room.

"Mila. Good. This is Kevin, my main security detail. He's heading up the rest of the guards here."

"G'day," I said, feeling uncertain.

"Ms. Trask." He dipped his head. "I'll introduce you to your personal close guard for the duration of this assignment in a moment, but if you ever feel uncomfortable or see something odd, don't hesitate to tell me."

"Yes. Right."

I stuck my hand into my pocket, planning to grip my pill bottle. Nothing.

The fear pulled me under immediately. Murphy clamped onto my elbow, steering me into the dining room. He spoke to Kevin, who answered, but I didn't understand the words. I was too busy trying to keep the shaking under control.

Murphy settled me onto his lap and placed a pill in my hand. I shoved it into my mouth and took the glass of orange juice he handed me, my hand shaking with such force, Murphy steadied me so I didn't miss my mouth.

He set the juice down and pulled me tighter to his chest, his hand rubbing up and down my back in slow soothing strokes.

"I've got you, Mila. Breathe it out."

"Alpie," I whispered.

Murphy maneuvered me into the chair and went to open Alpie's cage. The bird shrieked and shot out. "Mil!"

"I didn't know she knew my name," I stuttered.

"She checked on you before she'd settle in last night." Murphy eyed the bird with diffidence. Not the best of mates, these two. Not that I expected them to be. He resettled me in his lap as Alpie shushed from the table.

As my breathing calmed, I tried to scoot off his lap. But Murphy hugged me tighter to his chest.

"Not yet," he murmured. "I quite like you here."

I buried my face into his chest, preferring to breathe in his scent—that woodsy soap and fresh laundered cotton—than fight. So much for my early morning peace.

"I'm sorry," I muttered.

"Is it always so bad? The fear?"

I shook my head.

"When did it get like this?"

"When Jordan showed up here."

He tipped my chin up. I kept my eyes downcast. I didn't want him to see the few secrets I still hid from him.

"How long have you been abusing the pills, Mila?"

My eyes flew to his. I searched his eyes, mouth open to deny. I snapped it shut. My back stiffened and anger built in my sternum, spreading outward to fire my belly. How dare he?

"I want to help you, love. So let's talk it through."

I tried to clamber from his lap again, but Murphy held me tight. The ensuing struggle was brief and certain. I remained in Murphy's lap, but now I seethed. I turned my face away, refusing to let him see how lost I was without my pill bottle.

"You popped one in your mouth last night before I came to your room."

I gritted my teeth.

"I talked to Noelle," he said.

"What?" I cried. After another short attempt to disengage from his lap, I sat there stiffer than the queen of England on her throne. He waited. The bastard knew I hated these kinds of silences. Finally, I broke and raised my eyes.

"Nuff!" Alpie cried, coming to land on my shoulder. Murphy pulled back but still kept his hand on my hip.

Concern lit his eyes. He reached up and brushed my hair back from my forehead. Much as I wanted to lean back and not give him the satisfaction, I froze.

"How long have you been doubling up?"

My shoulders sagged. I couldn't fight him, too. "Since I flew to Perth five weeks ago."

"You did what?"

"I went to Perth. To check on Kyle's grave."

Murphy's mouth opened. Shut. His eyes darkened.

Too much of my limbs draped off him. This position worked so much better when I curled into him. But I couldn't do that. We weren't together. Not even close.

Alpie jumped back onto the table, her attention caught on the small bowl of fresh fruit. "Ooh," she said, waddling toward it. "Ooh. Yum. Shh. Yum."

"Why?"

"To see my baby," I snapped. "To tell him I missed him and wish him a happy one-year. Unfortunately for him, his birth date is also his death date. Made for a rather morbid experience."

Murphy's eyes slid shut and he rested his forehead against my chest. Of their own volition, my arms wrapped around his shoulders. They were so tense. He hurt. I hated that I was the cause. My fingers itched for my pill bottle.

"You had no right to take my pills, Murphy."

"Give me a mo', love. I'm still processing our baby has a grave. You'd said it before but realizing it, knowing it's there, hurts."

I fumbled in my pocket, pulled out my phone. I scrolled down until I found the picture. Handing it over, I studied Murphy's face as he studied the picture.

His lip ring was made of a dark metal and did nothing to detract from the sexiness of his firm lips. Murphy's kisses were soft but his lip ring spoke of his edgier side.

A tear spilled onto his cheek. Another quivered on the tip of his lashes of the other eye. This time I couldn't fight the need to lean in and wipe them away.

"The angel is lovely," he murmured, his voice catching.

"It is," I whispered.

"You're right. Seeing his name... it makes it all more real." He set my phone down on the table and buried his face into my neck. "Bloody fucking hell, Mila. I don't want him to be gone."

The sting in my eyes was too much. My own tears spilled over. We held each other for a long time. I rubbed my hands over Murphy's hair and neck, and he clutched my back, pressing me tighter to his chest.

This is what I'd missed. What I needed when I lay alone in the hospital.

"You wanted to know how long I've been abusing the Xanax?" I sighed. "Probably from the beginning. It helps me function. Keeps the sadness at bay."

Murphy nodded against my neck. "I get that," he said, pulling back. "But you can't keep taking more, Mila. You've got to cut back. Preferably cut it out."

I barked out a laugh. "Because it's that simple. My life's an absolute mess."

He cupped my cheeks, thumbs swiping away the last remnants of my tears. "Doesn't have to be. I'm here to help."

"For how long?" I exhaled a harsh breath and dropped my gaze. The words needed to be said. Murphy's life—a big one—didn't involve me. I couldn't go back to Sydney. Any of Australia. I'd said my final goodbyes to my birth country on that last plane ride.

Murphy blew out a breath. "Too right. I'm… I'm hurt, Mil," he said. "Angry you didn't trust me."

I opened my mouth to respond, but Murphy covered it with his hand. "How about this? Let's start with breakfast." He glanced at the table, lip curling in disgust when Alpie dipped her head and broke off another chunk of melon. "What your bird didn't touch anyway. Then we can strategize with what to do next."

"I have patients I need to see, Murphy."

"Not this week. Hopefully not for a few days." He backpedaled when he saw my face. "You wouldn't want to endanger any of them, and Jordan's listed as both armed and dangerous. I've arranged a leave of absence for you."

After wondering constantly if Jordan followed me if I'd be run down again, I didn't think this would end in a few days. Jordan liked being the hunter—of toying with his prey before he went in for the kill.

I shuddered. The glint in Jordan's eyes as he raised the knife to his neck outside my house… This time, he wouldn't stop.

"We should give an interview," Murphy said. His tongue flicked over his lip ring.

Horror built in my chest. "Why would I want to do that?" I gasped.

"We give people want they want. Our story. And we let them know what Jordan's done to you, why he's here and needs to be in jail."

I shoved harder this time, hard enough to finally break out of Murphy's arms. I stood, shaking, arms akimbo. "You want me to explain to some reporter my history? Why we broke up? Have me confirmed as the woman in 'She's so Bad,' and what? You become more popular and I'm pitied or hated or skewered for being stupid?"

Murphy spread his hands out and leaned back in his chair. "It's an idea. We don't have to do it, but getting the correct information out there would help *your* reputation more than mine."

I glared, my chest heaving, until I stormed out of the room.

———◆———

The day passed in tiny increments. Even though I wanted to ignore him, Murphy refused to let me. His constant supervision grated as did his desire to check my room any time I went in there.

Alpie was snuggled on the couch next to me, preening her feathers.

Murphy glanced at her, then back at me. "Why a bird?"

"She needed a home."

He raised an eyebrow, his way of telling me he was calling bullshit on my answer. I stroked my hand over her head. Alpie turned and nipped my finger, lifting the crown of hot pink feathers.

"Noelle took me to this bird sanctuary and Alpie hopped onto my shoulder. When Noelle wanted to leave, Alpie wouldn't get off my shoulder. She kept saying, 'No. You.'"

"The bird chose you and you accepted? I didn't think you liked birds much. And don't cockatoos live for decades?"

Another one of those moments of raw honesty. None of the last few days had turned out how I'd expected. "You were gone." At the dark look he shot me, I held up my hand. "Arguing over why doesn't change the fact I assumed our relationship was over. I never planned to fall in love again. I can't have children, so Alpie seemed like a smart choice. I'd have her for thirty to forty years, and then when I needed more medical support, she'd be gone."

"You planned to be a spinster with a bird?"

I glared, refusing to answer. I'd wanted Murphy, but I'd tried to move on. Alpie helped heal some of the worst of my emotional scars. On cue, Alpie climbed into my lap and shushed. Murphy waited, but I ignored him. Instead, I picked up the remote and turned on the telly.

By three that afternoon, I was strung out too tight, even my skin ached with desperate need for another pill. The stress of close quarters wore me down. While Murphy spent time at the piano—he wasn't as bad as he'd led me to believe—and bent over his notepad, I moped. Daytime telly was horrendous, even with a million channel options. I watched two movies I couldn't recall by name. Now, out of sheer boredom, I pulled out my laptop, planning to start searching for a new house.

Murphy's phone beeped again, the seventh such text. I'd peeked at one earlier—it was a former lover. Three other women called him, but he brushed them off easier than old lint. My scowl deepened as he sighed, mumbling something about territorial craziness. Oh, so the women were crazy for thinking the sex meant something?

I slammed my laptop shut. Murphy glanced up from his notebook, pulling the sleek black spectacles from his nose. I huffed out a breath, annoyed by how sexy the man was, even in eyewear. Hell, there was nothing he didn't look good in. *Kill me now.*

Everything about him screamed sex and sweaty nights—but since our talk at breakfast, he hadn't gotten any closer to me than absolutely necessary. Ergo, he no longer found me attractive. And I suffered—suffered!—from near-constant desire laced with anxiety.

"I want to go down to the pool," I said.

"All right. I'll go with you."

I gritted my teeth, annoyed by his pleasantness. I was like the stray dog he couldn't shake so he'd finally given in and let me go everywhere with him. Well, I didn't *want* to go anywhere with Murphy Etsam. I didn't want my name linked to his, and I sure as hell didn't want people thinking we were a reconciled, happy celebrity couple. My shoulders tensed. Nothing could be further from the truth when I wasn't even worth a pity petting. Preferably naked with lots of bumping and grinding.

I nearly moaned before the irritation I'd been fighting all day slammed back through me. *Stop thinking about sex.*

"You were engrossed. I wouldn't want to pull you away from something important."

"I keep telling you, Mila. Nothing's as important as keeping you safe."

I curbed the desire to jump up and down and smash things. Barely. The need still shimmered there, just under my skin. I wanted a pill, but Murphy wouldn't give me one. I settled Alpie in her cage.

"I need to be alone," I bit out.

"Well, you can't be. I have to go with you." He said this good-naturedly. I didn't even warrant the annoyance of his former root buddies who were too clingy. No, Mila Trask wasn't import-ant enough to waste real emotions on. Not anymore.

"I'll take one of the guards standing outside. What's his name? Hank. Or Lew. I'm sure either would like a change of scenery." I stalked toward my room, contemplating how many laps I could swim before I passed out. Probably fifty.

Murphy coughed, and I near-panted with want. I was a bloody hot mess.

"They are not seeing you in your swimsuit," Murphy said, his voice curt. "They'll have permanent hard-ons and won't be able to watch anything but your breasts bobbing in the water."

I whirled back toward him, eyebrow raised. "A fantasy that you've played out probably a million times in the last year with a million different women. So if it's a perk of their babysitting job, so be it."

He stood and stretched. "You're in a helluva mood."

I wasn't being fair, I knew, but I couldn't stop. "You could give me back my pills," I said, my voice saccharine.

"No can do, love. You need to break the habit."

"Not going to happen in a day," I gritted out.

"It's a start." When he scratched his abs, I bit back a whimper. I wanted to run my hands, my tongue, over that skin.

My flashes of irritation boiled into a hard knot of need. His phone beeped again. He scowled at the screen. The need deflated back into frustrated anger.

"What? Don't like having your long, long list of fuck buddies thrown back at you? Then you shouldn't have used and tossed so many."

He shoved his hands into pockets. "I shouldn't have."

"Stop trying to placate me," I grouched. "It won't work."

"Already figured that out. Your knickers are twisted so far up your bum, they may never come out."

I laid my palm flat against his chest, planning to shove him away. Murphy's hand closed over mine as his other slid around the curve of my waist. He felt good. I wanted nothing more than to melt into him, watch his eyes darken with lust. Feel the first sweep of his finger across the curve of my cheek before he cupped my jaw, tilting my head just so. But he didn't make any move closer, and I vibrated with suppressed need.

"If you want me, love, you're going to have to tell me."

"I don't want you," I spat, reeling. Even I could hear the lie in my voice.

I'd suppressed the need for another's touch for so long, now I could hardly breathe but for the need. One of the bodyguards would do just as well. At the pool. Without Murphy.

"Whatever you just thought, you're not doing it," Murphy said.

145

"Let me go."

"Mil," Alpie cried. "Mil. Mil."

"Don't want to," he said. "In fact, this is the best idea. You still fit me, Mila, like a glove." He ran the pad of his thumb down my cheek just as I'd dreamed of before, and I quivered.

That caress—casual but sensual—was still my undoing. And he knew it, the smug bastard.

"No, I don't," I said. "You're just saying that because you're bored and it's been more than twenty-four hours since some woman plastered herself against you."

"Much as I like women, you're the only one who's ever fit me."

"I don't want you holding me."

"You used to love me holding you. You used to slide into my arms, all quicksilver and sweet lust." His voice dipped low, into that panty-melting space, and my core melted. He tightened his arm around my waist, snuggling me tighter to him.

Oh, spaghetti on toast, he lowered his head. His lips were inches from mine. I held my breath. He stiffened and stopped, pulled back. "What changed?"

My temper snapped. I needed another pill, had been craving its dulling effects for hours. Being near him, not touching him, knowing what he'd thought of me, what he'd done afterward. Too much. The tidal wave crested, and I was its first—only—victim.

"Everything!" I shrieked. "You walked away from me." Bringing up my other hand, I slapped at his chest. Alpie squawked, fluttering around in her cage. Fury spurred me on, and I kicked him. "You believed I'd cheated on you. I can't believe you thought I'd do that."

"You told me you couldn't be with me anymore." Murphy gritted out, dropping his arms. "What did you expect, Mila? I'm not a fucking mind reader."

"You wrote a song about me that everyone loves to sing! You wrote it to be hurtful and it *is*." My breathing escalated to sharp staccato gasps. "You screwed half the female population."

"We weren't together. I'm sorry about the song. Especially now that I know why you left—"

"You should have loved me enough to come after me." I'd never understood the whole seeing-red-with-rage thing. I did then. Sure, I left him, but he believed I wanted to do so. "You should have *trusted* me."

I wanted him to suffer as I did each time I opened my computer to find Murphy wrapped around another beautiful woman. God, I hated those women. Skinny, model-perfect bodies in tiny bikinis. He'd put his hands on them, his tongue. He'd brought them to peaks of pleasure I hadn't felt since I was last in his arms. I hated them for their knowledge of his body almost as much as I hated him.

"You broke up with me," he said. "You *hurt* me."

I slammed my foot into his shin. When he didn't let go, I pulled at his shirt as I drove my foot forward, just as my self-defense teacher showed me.

Murphy grunted, stumbled back. "That hurt!"

"Good," I panted. "You deserved it."

"You need to settle down. Then we can talk about this like rational people."

"Don't tell me to settle down!" I screeched like a dying dingo, a sound Alpie echoed. "You ruined my life."

He reeled back, his eyes dark with pain. "Mila."

"Call back one of those women. I'm sure they'll be happy to give you a gobby."

"No one here's talking about blow jobs, Mila."

"I'm going to swim laps. By myself."

I stormed from the room, slamming the bedroom door shut behind me.

He didn't follow.

CHAPTER EIGHTEEN
Murphy

She'd snapped. Tension wound tight around her mouth, worsened by the lowered dose of her meds. But the shock of her anger still reverberated through me. Mila was so smart—she always analyzed her problems. She never yelled, never used force.

I scrubbed my hand over my face. My phone beeped again. Why couldn't those women leave me the fuck alone? It's not like I wanted any of them.

And that, right there, was the crux of the problem. The woman I wanted thought I'd ruined her life. I dragged my hand from my face to massage my chest. The pain of that dart continued to spread its poison through my system.

Bloody hell. That accusation hurt because she was right. The picture of us never would've been in the paper if we hadn't been playing an important gig that weekend. Jordan wouldn't have scared her, accosted my mum, if I hadn't cared more about being a public figure than about my relationships with the people I loved.

Just one of those choices—if I could go back, I'd change them all, but just one decision might have given Mila a different life now. I picked up my phone, prepared to delete the text, but stopped short when I saw who it was from.

Let me know if you're free. Probably best to meet at Briar's. The media is slavering to get pics of either of us, especially after my performance yesterday.

Hayden. Much better than another woman I wasn't interested in. I'd left him a text last night after seeing him at the hospital, once again requesting the opportunity to talk. Maybe heading over there would give Mila time to cool off.

I walked over to Mila's door and raised my hand to knock. I paused when I heard her muffled sobs. Hell. I pressed my hand to the door, wishing I could walk in and gather her up. To kiss away her tears. But I'd never have that right, not if she thought I ruined her life. Just because I was thinking about rekindling our relationship didn't mean Mila would want to. Worse, that she could be in a normal relationship again. What did I know about assault victims?

Only what I'd seen from my mum. My dad chose to beat the snot out of my mum for serving him a pot roast dinner—typically one of his favorites—after he'd lost his job at the freight company. Because pounding on my preggo mum was a healthy outlet for his anxiety.

Few people knew Jake and I had a younger brother. Born eight weeks early, Logan spent four weeks in the Neonatal Intensive Care Unit at Westmead in Sydney until the day his tiny body left the hospital in a much-too-small casket. All preventable.

Going to a funeral at the age of six confused me. The casket lowering into the ground still haunted my dreams—nightmares made worse now that I'd lost a son of my own.

Which was why I was performing at the charity concert no matter the risk to my own safety. If my name would help bring in more money and keep child abuse front-and-center in the media for a day or two, then I was willing to stand up on stage with a bloody target on my chest just for Jordan, who'd managed to slink into some slimy hole overnight.

He'd turn up, especially if I made myself available.

So that's what I'd do—I'd go out, be seen over and over again until Jordan came after me this time. Me, not Mila. And I'd make sure the sack of sorry shit never saw the outside of prison walls again.

I hesitated another moment at Mila's door, but she wasn't in the mood to talk. I snagged my key card and headed to the front door. I let the two new guards in, annoyed when they looked anywhere but me. They'd heard Mila. Thank God for Harry's sense to have anyone who worked for Jackaroo to sign nondisclosure agreements. If I read even a hint about our fight, I knew who to sue.

"Mila's struggling under the enforced solitude. She wants to go to the pool. Please take her. I have to meet up with my bandmate."

Lew, the bigger of the two guards, crossed his arms over his massive chest and nodded his bald head. The bloke was intimidating as all hell. "We'll take care of her."

"See that you do," I said.

"You get any new credible threat information?" Hank asked. "Want someone in the water with her?" Former military police, he'd said. Not much older than me. Fit. Probably considered an attractive bloke with his conservative haircut and the straight, even features. I almost dismissed him on the spot until I realized I was jealous. Dammit, I didn't do jealous.

But I always had with Mila. Something I was going to have to relearn. Because Mila and I needed to spend time together, see if we could give our relationship another go. All those emotions, that anger she'd spewed, stemmed from hurt. At least I think it did. And if I was correct in that assumption, if what Noelle had said was true, Mila still cared about me just as I still cared about her.

I stood there for a moment, the need to fix the situation with

Mila warring with the need to talk to Hayden. I'd texted him back, letting him know I'd stop by soon. He'd sent me the address, which wasn't too far from here.

I'd talk to Mila first, make sure she knew I wanted what was best for her, then go meet up with Hayden. The shower turned on in Mila's half of the suite. Bollocks. Missed my chance to talk to her and left the wound festering ever wider. If I was braver, I'd simply tell her I still loved her.

But I wasn't that brave. Not now that I knew she thought I ruined her life.

I slammed out of the suite, irritation at the situation catching up with me. I settled into the new rental car next to Kevin and closed my eyes. Mila needed me to be her rock, which required me to handle my emotions better. To act better, period. I used to without thought. But now, since my every whim was anticipated, my every action justified thanks to my multiplatinum album, my lack of civility—humanity—was appalling and obvious.

No wonder Jake, Hayden, and Flip wanted to get rid of me.

—◆—

Briar's flat was small, but the exterior wall was made of windows and the hardwood doors and floors were only some of the subtle touches that made it feel both homey and roomier than it actually was. The main room consisted of a tiny dining nook, a decent-sized living room and a functional kitchen done up in stainless steel appliances and bright white countertops. A whole three feet of it, upon which sat a brand new espresso maker.

"Briar bought that for me. Said I needed to learn how to

make real coffee like they serve in Melbourne since I made the mistake of saying coffee there's better than here. She's waiting for a brilliant cuppa, she says." Hayden shrugged. "Your shadow coming inside?"

I glanced back at the guard. "Be decent, Hayden. Kevin's just doing his job."

Hayden's brow shot up, shocked, no doubt, to find a decent bone in my body. Or that I'd chastise him. Both, I reckoned.

"Right-o. Sorry, there, Kevin. Come in. I'll grab you a drink—a coffee?" At Kevin's nod, Hayden moved over to the kitchen and pulled out a premade Starbuck's mocha. "I don't know how to use the bloody thing," he sighed. "It's more complicated than that freaking airplane we took up in Cairns last year. Best part: the instructions are in, like, Korean."

Kevin and I chuckled. "I'll step outside, Mr. Etsam. Holler if you need anything. Thanks for the coffee." Kevin raised his glass container and stepped out the door, shutting it firmly behind him.

I walked to the living space. The couch was tattered and I wondered why they'd keep such a nasty old piece of rubbish when a fluffy gray cat with bright green eyes sashayed around the corner.

"You even have a cat?"

Hayden settled into the corner of the couch and the cat leaped with light grace into his lap. "She came as part of the package. Bit moody, this girl, but she's all right. Aren't you, Princess?"

"That cat's name is Princess?" I couldn't stop the snort of laughter.

"Better watch yourself, mate. If Princess doesn't like you, this convo ends."

"You're still angry," I said, holding up my hand. "Mila has a bird. A bloody cockatoo. For emotional support." Hayden shook his head but his lips curved up. I cleared my throat. "Right. I didn't come to talk about animals. I acted like a complete douche canoe."

"That you did. But… seeing you with Mila, knowing how you loved her, how I love Briar, I can understand part of it. The acting out from hurt anyway."

I leaned forward, my hands clasped between my spread knees. "You can't because I just learned how bad it's been."

"Her stalker, you mean? The step-uncle? It's been all over the news."

"That part, yeah. I'd told her I wanted to marry her a few days before everything went to shit because of that bloke."

Hayden hissed out a curse. "Not that I'm surprised. Mila's fabulous. Kept you in line, didn't she?" Hayden reached down to scratch Princess under her chin. She blinked up at him and began to purr.

"So when she broke it off, I wasn't just angry, which I was. Really angry." I met Hayden's light brown eyes. So different from Mila's wild swirls of color. "I didn't handle that well."

"Too right. Jake, Flip, and I, we got that. What we didn't get was the escalation of the behavior."

"I didn't, either," I said, shame washing over me. "It just happened. Jake says I was hurt and I handled it with avoidance."

"The parade of women I can see as avoidance, but what about the desire to make the rest of us as shitty as you?"

"I don't know." Shaking my head, I hoped some profound thought broke through, helping me understand my self-destruction. "I was—am—messed up." I blew out a breath. Somehow, admitting my jumbled emotions helped. "You heard Mila had been pregnant?"

Hayden dipped his head in acknowledgment.

"I didn't know before. She hadn't told me. I found out after she miscarried, and I thought... I thought it was some other bloke's bub." I closed my eyes and swallowed hard. "I would have a son if that bastard left her alone."

"Crikey." Hayden dragged out the word, his eyes filling with sympathy.

"'Bout sums it up." I glanced down at my hands, white-knuckled and fisted. "I left her now at the hotel, angry with me for not trusting her more then."

"Seems like you've fumbled more than one dance."

The cat wandered over, wending its way between my legs. "I'm still in love with her." I laughed, but it was humorless, and I choked it off just before the sound shifted toward a sob. "Not that my feelings do me much good. I've handled her, you, the fame, all of it, like a complete wanker."

"Not a surprise. You couldn't have written 'She's So Bad' if you weren't so heart sore."

I bit my tongue against the snide comeback. That wouldn't help. "I'm not asking you to forgive me for how I treated your relationship with Briar. I was wrong. Dead wrong. I just didn't want you to end up like me, mate."

Hayden ran his finger over his upper lip. I dropped my fingers down into the cat's long, silky fur.

"I'm not sure I forgive you for what could have happened to Briar."

"I understand. I should never have involved myself. And I shouldn't have tried to keep her from seeing you."

"True."

The cat put its paw on my knee. I moved my hands. A moment later, Princess jumped into my lap. Her purrs rumbled across my thighs and stomach.

"You're a loud bugger," I crooned. Princess tipped her head and twitched her ears.

"Princess doesn't like a lot of people," Hayden said.

"Smart cat."

"I told Briar I'd listen. She wants us to work it out. She said you were hurt and she reckons Mila's the reason."

"No, I was an arse because of me."

"Truth."

"But," I sighed, "Mila really fucking hurt me, leaving as she did. I'd only sorted through my response to this a bit before seeing her at the Tractor Tavern." I swallowed hard. "Seeing Jordan's hands on her... Hayden, he *broke* her. Killed my nipper. I don't know how to handle any of that."

Hayden cleared his throat. "Reckon you don't. Not really. Just be there for her. If you want to be. Which I'm assuming you do since you're with her now."

I nodded. I continued to pet the cat. She nuzzled into my chest.

"I'm not sure I'm ready to tour with you again, but I won't slam the door shut on another Jackaroo album," Hayden said. "At some later date."

The tension eased from my chest. "I can't leave Mila now. Not until her stalker's in prison."

"Understood. She's one in a million, that lady. Don't bugger your second chance. I won't stick around to see if you survive it."

"I want to write her a new song. Problem is there's so much I have to say. More important things." I paused, testing a phrase in my head. They sounded terrible. I shook my head, unable to meet Hayden's gaze. "I'm not sure I can. Write another song, I mean. I haven't been able to finish anything halfway decent since I wrote 'She's So Bad.'"

"I've wondered on that. We all have." Hayden's light brown brow pulled low over his nose. "You're stuck in the hotel. Use the time to reflect. Consider what you want. The music might come now that you've admitted to your emotions."

"That's easy. I want Mila in my life." Hayden was my best mate. Or had been. And I needed someone to confide in. "I'm just not sure I'm good for her future."

"Make her see you *are* good." Hayden leaned forward. "You fucked up. I did, too, but I managed to talk Briar into taking me back. I'm still in awe for her capacity to forgive. I was a dickhead all in my own right. Without any help from you."

Hayden stood, walked over to the fridge and pulled out two beers in tall bronze cans. A large dog panted a smile but there weren't words anywhere on the can. Weird. He handed me one and then clinked my can with his.

"This is different from your epic disappearing act on Briar." I sighed. "Mila and I have serious baggage."

"So you work through it. You should, whether you get together again or not. You're calmer and seem to be in a better mental space than you've been for the last year at least. You need her understanding. Forgiveness would be better. For what it's worth, Briar forgave you."

"She's one helluva sheila, your Briar."

"That she is." His eyes met mine, his face set in serious lines that matched the tenor of his voice. "Don't hurt her again or I'll rip you apart."

I patted the cat one more time. "Understood." I sipped my beer. "This is good."

"Mate of Bri's makes it. He has that strange Northwestern thing about pets. Even named his brewery after his first dog."

"This the bugger?" I asked, pointing to the can.

Hayden shrugged. "Don't really care. Just like the beer."

I sipped again, hoping it would keep me from saying something stupid. The silence stretched. I squirmed under the cat. Hayden stretched out his arm no the back of the sofa and considered me over his beer. "When my mum died, I was angry and confused."

I held my can loosely in my hands. Good as it was, I wanted to get back to Mila. Worry didn't come close to my current emotions. Hank, the bastard who wasn't long for his job, wanted her. He was at the pool with her now. If the prick touched her, I would rip him apart. I managed to smooth out my scowl and pay attention. Hayden deserved that.

"Hard not to be, mate," I said.

"You pushed all your feelings out into the world. Onto others. I did the opposite. Held it all in. It's what I'm good at. Because of my dad… you know, him being so old when I came along, taught me to not make a fuss, not to be loud."

"I'm not sure either option's healthy."

"Mine sure wasn't. I've watched you implode same as I did, but that was after you exploded in those first weeks. Don't think you've been any better off."

I waited. When Hayden started talking, it was important to let him finish. The bloke didn't make idle conversation.

"I think what we do, create music, is grounding. But the touring, the cycle of shows and fans and the disruption to any type of normalcy is what turns those coping mechanisms into vices."

"You mean why so many rock stars go too far."

"Something like that. I've been talking to Asher Smith. From the Supernaturals. He's not as interested in touring as he used to be. He's got his boy to consider. And now that Briar and I are together, I want time with her. Time to let her finish her degree and to spend in our pajamas on a Sunday morning. Normal time."

Something Hayden never experienced in his life. His dad sat him at the piano at age three, and he was touring by ten.

"Right. So take your time. A year won't kill us." I hoped not. All of us were set financially until we found our next passion.

"Actually, it's more than that. There's a collective of musicians that have started a community here. It's not the same as traveling around the world but YouTube still lets you connect with them for a lot cheaper than the price of a stadium ticket."

Hayden stood and the cat jumped from my lap to run into the kitchen, tail straight up.

"Expecting your salmon, Princess? Right, girl." Hayden pulled a large platter out of the fridge. I shook my head and he just smirked. "Keeps her happy. Anyway, there's a get together a week from Thursday at the Showbox with some of the collective. You should come and get the vibe of what we're doing, how we plan to change the endless tour cycle without giving up the music we love so much. We can add a few Jackaroo tunes."

I pressed my lips together, trying hard to hold together my emotions. Hayden offered an olive branch I didn't deserve. I stepped forward and pulled him into a brief, hard hug. "Thanks, mate. I'll try. Not sure if Mila will be able to come, and I hate the idea of leaving her alone at the hotel."

Hayden slapped my back once. "I'm glad you ran into Mila again, though I don't like the circumstances around your reunion. You're acting more like my best mate again. I've missed him."

"Yeah. Me, too." I pressed my lips together in a firm line, unwilling to let my chin tremble. I cleared my throat twice. Hard. "Thanks, Hayden. Really."

After he plated up the raw salmon, the cat's purrs hit a new level of loud. Holy Christ. Hayden put the fish back in the fridge and washed his hands. I set my beer on the counter, assuming our meeting was done. Towel in hand, Hayden cocked his head. "You want to see my new Taylor?"

Surprise burst through me. "You got a guitar?"

Hayden grinned. "I had to. I've been jamming a lot with Asher and the piano's too big."

"Love to, mate. I haven't opened mine in a couple of days."

"Let's work on that tune of yours. Got an idea of what you want to say?"

"Matter of fact, I do," I said. "I brought my notebook to scribble notes in the car. It's not much."

"Never is when you start."

———— ◆ ————

We'd invited Kevin in for another premade mocha, which he drank with relish. Poor bloke, he'd told me he'd grown up in a small town in Missouri, and he obviously didn't know good coffee.

Not only had Hayden and I worked through some of our shit,

we'd played music together. I'd missed that time, those sessions. Best part was the backbone of the song was Mila.

The chorus lyrics came together with ease. Just like they used to. We'd found a good rhythm to fit the lyrics I wanted and messed around with chords. This tune was soft but still edgy because that's what Mila and I were together.

After another hour, I decided Hayden was well rid of me.

"I better get back."

"Worried about your girl?"

"Never stop." I sighed.

Hayden picked up his cat, tickling her under her chin. "I get that. Just gets worse the deeper you fall, mate."

I nodded. "Been there. Know it well." Mila had the power to destroy me, and I'd already hiked well down the path of self-destruction. A problem for another day, perhaps. "Thanks for this."

Hayden smiled. "We'll get that song worked out. Be sure to let me know when you'll be at the Showbox."

"Right." I rubbed my hand down the back of my neck, trying to shove down my nerves. But honesty was important—and Hayden deserved the truth from me. "One more thing. The big wigs asked me to do a charity show later this week. To iron out my shit-tastic image, no doubt. I'm not expecting you to come, but it's for battered kids. Means more to me now than it did before, even." Hayden knew of my mum's abuse, how Jake and I lost a brother much too soon. "I'm going to talk to Jake and Flip, see if they want to perform."

Hayden considered me. He ran his forefinger down his nose, never a good sign. "Thanks for the information. Send me more details. I'll see what Briar thinks."

Fair enough. I sprang that news poorly. "Right. Well, I'll talk to Jake. He'd probably like the time to jam. If it's okay to tell him about your Showbox gigs?"

"I'm always happy to play with Jake."

"C'mon, Kevin. Let's get out of here while Hayden's still speaking to me."

They both laughed, but I wasn't kidding. Hayden slapped my back and opened the door. "The charity concert is more like what we're thinking. With the collective, I mean. Be sure to send the information."

I nodded. I turned, shook his hand, and left.

"Go okay?" Kevin asked as we walked down the hall to the elevator.

"Better than I anticipated."

"Good news, then."

"Am I a bastard?" I blurted out once we entered the elevator. Kevin took his time, studying me. Sweat pooled on my upper lip and the base of my spine. For some reason, his response mattered to me.

"No," he said. "You're a man who's made mistakes. Much like all of us, I expect. But you seem to want to fix them."

I blew out my pent-up breath. "True enough."

We were quiet as the elevator car slid down the last few floors. Kevin was thorough, not letting me cross the lot until he'd checked all the corners, under the car and in the boot. A man I could count on.

"Do you plan to stay in this business long term?" I asked.

Kevin shrugged. "If the right job came along, sure. I'd planned to go back to my government work, but one, I'm still healing from my most recent tussle with the bad guys, and two, my wife gave me an ultimatum: either I find a career that doesn't try to kill me every day, or she walks along with my thirteen-year-old daughter."

"Tough break there." We walked through the lot. Kevin pressed the key fob to unlock the doors.

"No, more of a reality check. I considered what was most important, and my family won."

"What does that mean?"

He started the ignition before he turned to appraise me again. Much as I wanted to squirm under his appraisal, I didn't. I met his gaze and waited.

"I'm staying here, in Seattle. So I can be around while my daughter grows up."

I nodded, absorbing the information. Kevin put his family first, the exact opposite of what I'd done when Mila walked away from me. In fact, I'd been acting like a toddler who'd lost his favorite toy since that moment, having an extended tantrum.

Time to man up. Not just to my feelings for her but to my responsibilities—and the ones I wanted. Taking care of my mum, Jake, and Mila were priority one. Telling Mila I still loved her might not get the response I wanted, but she deserved to know I wanted her in my life. She needed to know that's where I'd always wanted us to end up.

Kevin called ahead, letting the guards in the lobby know we were almost back to the hotel. He pulled into the garage still waiting to hear from them. The next second our windshield shattered.

"Stay down." Kevin shoved me farther into the seat as another bullet slammed into the windshield. "We're under fire. Basement level one," he said, voice calm as he spoke into his phone. I didn't know who he was talking to, and I really didn't care. My only concern was getting to Mila.

Cradling it against his shoulder, he slammed on the gas and sped forward. No way he could see. He dropped the phone on the console, pulled out his gun and twisted the wheel hard. With his other hand, he pulled off three or four rounds in rapid succession, the bullets shattering through what was left of the glass in the window. The entire car shook, the concussion from the gun echoed with a teeth-rattling boom.

Kevin slammed on the brakes, peering through a tiny clear space in the glass.

"Shouldn't we get out?" I yelled over the ringing in my ears. Bloody hell, Kevin's shots from inside the car caused my ears to nearly bleed. If Jordan had gotten to Mila... my hand was on the door handle.

"He'll pick you off much faster from outside the car. Gas tank's in back, protected by the cars behind us. We're safer here." Kevin picked up his phone. "He's moved to the northeast corner of the garage. Murphy's safe. Any word on Mila?"

"We have one down in the pool area."

I didn't wait for more than that. I bolted from the car, darting between the vehicles toward the stairwell.

One down. What did that mean? Mila. I wasn't losing her. Not again. Bullets pinged off the cars, glass shattered right in front of me. Kevin bellowed. I kept running.

Chapter Nineteen
Mila

Stepping out of my bedroom fifteen minutes after I'd bolted from Murphy, I stopped short, shocked to see Lew and Hank lounging on the couches, watching something on the large flat screen television.

"Where's Murphy?" I asked.

"Out. We'll take you down to the pool." Hank held out his hand and took my bag.

Okay, then. I rode the elevator down between the two burly men in suits, wishing I hadn't made such a big deal about swimming. I didn't want to go any more. I waited to enter the pool area with Lew, who stood nearby.

Hank motioned us in, and Lew followed me. After arranging my bag and towel, I took out my goggles and slid them on. I stripped out of my cover up, painfully aware of Hank's eyes on my skin outside the sleek black one-piece made for surfing or swimming laps. Since the accident, I exposed as little of myself as possible.

Diving into the pool, I wished the water here was more like the ocean where I could hide in the waves and churning surf. Two more turns and I was in my zone, my arms starting to burn with that delicious tiring of well-used muscles. Another few laps; this time I turned and flipped onto my back.

Something rippled near me in the water. Too big to be a bug. Another ripple on the other side, closer this time. I could feel the heat coming off it.

What in the world…I stopped mid-stroke as a disturbance

caught my eye. I stopped swimming, popping upward to tread water. Lew held his gun out, eyes focused on the closing door to the pool area. Hank sat on one of the loungers, his gun still holstered, his skin chalky even through my goggles. He hunched over, his bum barely on the seat. Lew strode back and forth in front of him, talking on the phone.

I kicked back to the edge of the pool and hauled myself out. Grabbing my towel, I slung it around my body.

"What's wrong?" I asked.

Hank was pale and he swayed on the bench. His once-pristine shirt slicked with something dark. "You're bleeding." I pressed the towel to the center saturation point. "Not arterial," I muttered. "Good."

Hank hissed, pulling his arm tighter to his chest. "It's not bad. Grazed my ribs."

"Stay still," I said. "I don't know if the bullet's still in."

"Passed through," Hank gritted.

I raised my gaze to Lew, but he continued to sweep the area, gun still drawn. "We need to get you out of here. But I don't want to move you until I know the property's secure."

"You didn't hear us calling," Hank muttered. "He shot into the pool, too."

Everything in me stilled. No. Security crawled all over this place along with cameras and extra police. No way Jordan just walked into the hotel, pretty as you please. I collapsed onto the bench next to Hank, my legs shaking too much to hold me up. "Jordan was *here*? In the hotel?"

"He was here," Hank said. He groaned softly. "On the pool deck. Dressed in maintenance attire."

Murphy slammed into the room, only stopping when he gripped my shoulders, hands sliding down my arms as his eyes tracked their movement. "Why is there blood on your hands? Where are you hurt?"

"I-I'm not," I said. "It's Hank's. Wh-what happened?" My teeth chattered. Shock. I was sliding into shock.

"Jordan's gone," Kevin said, stepping forward. "Through the underground garage."

"Where you were?" I asked, gripping Murphy's shirt in response. I gasped, taking in the bits of glass on his hair. "Oh, God. Call another ambulance! We need to get you to the hospital," I said.

"I'm fine, but Jordan did take some shots at me."

I fell into Murphy's arms, clutching him tight even as my mind whirred with scenarios.

"A gun. He's never used a gun before." My teeth chattered harder and I shivered.

"Cold?" Murphy asked, voice soft.

I nodded. "Mostly scared."

"Come on. We'll go upstairs. You can have a shower."

"But Hank—"

"Needs to go to the hospital," Lew said smoothly. "The wound isn't life-threatening. Kevin will accompany you upstairs and stay in the room while I take care of this down here."

I opened my mouth to argue but I was too scared, felt too exposed. I wanted to check Murphy over, see with my own eyes he was in one piece. When Murphy pulled me up, I stumbled, my vision hazing toward black. Murphy wrapped an arm around my waist and without any thought, I burrowed in closer, finding my spot.

He exhaled hard, pulling me even tighter against him so that I felt the fine tremors wreaking havoc with his body. He dropped a kiss to my forehead, an unconscious gesture, sweeter for its thoughtless response. "You have to stop scaring me," he muttered as he walked forward.

"Believe me, I want to."

Kevin, gun in hand, stepped out in front of us. Seeing the weapon caused me to shake even harder. Murphy tightened his grip and we clung to each other, our forward progress hindered by my inability to peel my arms from Murphy's waist.

Two other guards flanked us. My hair dripped water all over the carpet, and I shivered in my wet suit. We took the stairs up, not waiting for the elevator. My lungs were laboring by the time we got to the top.

"We lost him again," Kevin said, scowling at Murphy, his frustration palpable. "If you'd waited another minute before jumping from the car, I might have been able to corner him."

Murphy scowled back at his guard. His fingers tensed at my waist. "I had to know Mila was safe."

Kevin turned toward me. "He didn't wait to hear any more. He just leapt from the car and started running. I covered him up the stairwell."

Tremors ripped through Murphy and his fingers dug into my skin. Murphy had always been impulsive—too much so, clearly. "I shouldn't have left you. I can't… Mila, you have to stay safe."

I let him wrap me in a hug as my eyes met Kevin's exasperated ones. He shook his head, irritation oozing off him. But he smiled at Murphy's arms around me.

I couldn't see Murphy's face because it was buried in my dripping hair. He cared about me. I sucked on my lip as I considered both his words and his raspy tone. To test my theory, I rested my wet head against his chest and brought my hand up to his abdomen. His muscles clenched and he hissed. I set my hand lower, nearer the button on his jean. The fear, the frustration, the anger… Murphy could help me forget all those emotions. Just let me *feel* again.

"You need to stop."

I started to pull back, my cheeks flaming at the thoughts of what must be going through Kevin's mind but the guard wasn't paying attention to Murphy's softly spoken words. He was on his phone and after a few intent moments, he said, "Got it."

"Staff security and Lance from our team walked the suite. Everything's secure," Kevin said. He opened the door to the suite and I clutched tighter at Murphy, practically dragging him into my room. I shut the door behind us, locking it.

"What's wrong, Mil?"

"I shouldn't have gone to the pool," I said. "I'm sorry for what I said earlier, for insisting on going down there."

"It's the lack of pills, too." Murphy stepped back. His eyes drifting up and down my exposed skin. He paused and I tensed. His callused fingers reached forward, touching the large, ragged scar on my shoulder.

"This is from the accident?"

"They grafted skin from my calf up there. I was pretty banged up." I pulled down the strap of my suit so he could see the full extent of its ugliness—the raised, bumpy skin ran from my shoulder to the top of my breast and down part of my side. So he could see how broken Jordan left me. Jumping out of that car proved once again Murphy wasn't taking this situation as seriously as he needed to.

"I can't believe he did that to you. No wonder…" Murphy pulled me close and kissed the scar, a soft brush of his lips. "This is where you landed? After you fell off the pushy."

I nodded. Murphy pulled me closer, resting his head on my chest. "I can't tell you how sorry I am for what you went through."

I slid my fingers through his hair, loving the way he felt pressed against me. He was gentle as he touched each one, learning the new, ugly parts of me now as he accepted these less-perfect additions.

He kissed the scar again and my blood heated. I wanted him. With the way my life was going, I might be shot or stabbed at any moment. Better to take this opportunity. I might not get another.

I sifted my fingers through his hair again before moving my fingers down over his eyebrow. I traced his eyebrow ring.

"I would've thought you'd get rid of that."

"Reminded me of good times." He sighed, his warm breath washing over my sensitive nipples. "I missed you, but thinking about you hurt near as much as the missing. Does that make sense?"

"Yes. I understand. I kept mine, too. I just moved it."

"What do you mean?"

I took a deep breath and stepped out of his arms. He'd seen the worst of my scars, but that didn't mean the rest of me would measure up to the sculpted, perfect bodies of his more recent bed partners. Still, I started this and Murphy's intense gaze told me he wanted me to continue.

I slipped off the other strap and pulled down. My breasts sprang free and Murphy murmured a sound of pleasure. I wiggled the suit lower, loving his low moan, and my breasts jiggled. I left the suit bunched low on my hips, not quite having the courage to strip nude in front of him. I sucked in my stomach and stood tall. My hand just above my belly button.

"I wanted to share you. With Kyle. So I pierced my belly button. That's the ring you bought me."

Murphy swallowed, his throat working as he struggled to contain some emotion. I sucked on my lip. The silence built as he stared. His hands fisted on his thighs, and I shivered as the air conditioning kicked on, blowing its frigid air over my exposed skin.

"Are you mad?"

In one motion, his arms were wrapped tight around me, his mouth pressed against my navel ring. "Thank you for including me."

I stroked his head again, loving the feel of his silky hair in my hand. "I always planned on you being part of his life, Murphy."

"I would have, Mil." He rained kisses on my abdomen, rubbing his scruffy beard against the sensitive skin. I sucked in a breath as my stomach and sex clenched. He placed a kiss at the dip toward my hip, and I whimpered. His eyes lit as he slid his whiskered cheek across my belly to kiss the other side. I gripped his forearms, shifting closer so my thigh straddled his.

He dipped his tongue into my belly button. His hands wrapped around below my bum to grip the back of my thighs. I arched into him, my skin thrumming as he played me. My thighs and bum clenched as he tightened his hold. He remembered. That spot always drove me wild.

But I knew his secrets, too. I leaned back a little further and

171

pressed my palm against his abdomen, just above his jeans. I rubbed my hand back and forth as he pressed into my hand, wanting me to lower it, his breathing turning ragged.

"You always did like to deal with big emotions this way," I murmured. I pulled my hand back.

"That feels amazing, Mila. Don't stop."

"Is this how you dealt with the stress and frustrations? By screwing some woman?"

He ignored me, but I wasn't sure why. Because I was right? Because he was so wild with lust for me? I tensed, needing space. But he slid his cheek up, over my ribs to the underside of my breasts where he pressed hundreds of tiny kisses, moving toward the shadow between them. I couldn't help running my fingers through his hair as I arched closer. My hands trailed down the back of his neck and over his shoulders, still covered in his t-shirt.

"Like that, do you?" he asked. His voice always edged lower with desire, and the gravelly tone of his speech pumped up my need. It had always been like this—as his desire built, it fed mine, and we spiraled upward into a conflagration only mating could satiate. "I might just die if I don't get us both naked and I get to drive into your warm, wet heaven."

His words doused my desire. I didn't want to be another of Murphy's conquests. I hated thinking of myself as one of the hoards. Sure, we'd talked about our former lovers when we'd been together before, and his list was more extensive than mine then. But now it felt like we were comparing a simple script to a full-fledged health workup.

"I can't!" I cried, covering my face with my hands. "I'm so sorry. I don't mean to be a tease, but I can't do it."

The idea of being nothing more than another cheap screw in Murphy's dissertation of sexing up the ladies… that broke me.

"Hush, love." Murphy crooned.

I shook my head, adamant, shoving his shoulders to put more space between us. "I can't be on that list. You don't even care about those women."

He cupped my cheeks, forcing me to stare into his gray eyes. "You're not, Mila. You've never been a fuck buddy."

I choked, the giggles making my crying seem even more hysterical. "You're right. But only because I haven't fucked you yet."

"Stop it," Murphy kept his voice low, his eyes intent, captivating mine as surely as he held my chin in his grip. My giggles stopped and my eyes dried.

"What?" I asked, my consternation coming through loud and clear.

"You're not a passing fancy."

I nodded, my heart constricting. "Because I'm old news."

CHAPTER TWENTY
Murphy

I clenched my jaw, wishing the ache in my dick would die now that my heart hurt. Her eyes were shadowed, so sad. Even with her pulling away from me, I wanted Mila more than I'd ever wanted another woman. Not a shocker. I *always* wanted Mila even as I freaked out about how she could break my heart again.

What was shocking was how quickly her scorching response turned ice cold. My desire didn't quit burning that quickly, and I didn't want to stop. Bloody hell. Trying to think with a raging hard-on wasn't easy.

"What's wrong, Mila?"

She struggled, trying to climb off my lap. I didn't let her.

"I told you. I'm not one of your groupies."

"I know that," I snapped. "You were the love of my life."

The green swirls in her eyes dimmed, her face crumpling like a pavlova left out in the heat. "*Were*. Now I'm nothing more than a dependent. You don't want my death on your conscience. I understand, Murphy. But I can't be one of your dick-wicks." She pulled her small frame up to attention. "If that means you want to leave me to fend for myself, then—"

"Stop right there," I growled. Black tinged the edges of my vision. I forced my fingers to relax, to let her go. "I'm not leaving you alone whilst Jordan is out there. End of discussion."

"He shot at you today. Because of me."

She appeared so lost. Bollocks. Didn't matter which way I turned, I screwed up and hurt her.

"And he shot at you, too. He's going to keep coming until he's caught."

She dropped her head into her trembling palms. "I want to see my patients, Murphy. I built a life here. My days aren't what I expected, but they mean something. And my whole life is crumbling, and I hate that you're here, because you're just going to leave, and then I'll…" She stopped. Moving to the bathroom, she pulled a robe from the hanger and slid it on.

I sighed, wishing I'd kept my mouth shut and just continued to worship her so we'd both be naked in the bed now. Stifling a groan, I aimed for nonchalance I didn't feel. Leaning back against the edge of the headboard, I raised my brows.

"You'll what?"

She didn't want to answer. But this was one area I wasn't willing to even entertain the idea of playing the gentleman. I *had* to have Mila again. She was mine in a way no other woman ever could be.

"Honesty, remember?"

She grimaced. "Fine. I'll be crushed when you break my heart."

Better than I thought. Scarier though, too. My heart pounded and my mouth went dry.

"Why's that, Mila?"

That earned me a full-on glare. She walked toward the bathroom, intent to put another barrier between us.

Not happening. Jordan shot at me today. Wanted me dead. I refused to allow any fake obstacles like pride and fear get in the way—for either of us. I scrambled forward and caught the door with the toe of my boot.

"Come here."

Her mouth compressed and she shook her head.

"Please, Mila. I want to show you something."

She sighed. "Fine. But I want to take off my suit first."

Heat slammed back into my groin. "By all means, go commando."

"That's not what I meant!"

"Mmm, but it does have its merits." I opened her robe, forcing myself to ignore her creamy flesh. Time for that later. Soon, I hoped. I tugged her suit down her hips, managing to dodge her hands and ignoring her squeal of surprise.

The wet Lycra pooled at her feet and I got my first view and Mila's nakedness. Before I knew it, I'd pressed a kiss to that slight curve just below her belly button. The skin gave a little. She smelled of chlorine but also desire.

I clenched my jaw and stepped back, pulling the edges of her robe together. Her eyes widened. I loved that look. Like I was a bloody magician, capable of anything.

Not quite, sweetheart. I wasn't capable of loving you right last time. I brushed a tangle of hair from her forehead but didn't press the kiss there I wanted to. I had reason to be hurt but so did she. The question was how we moved on—together or apart. I cinched and tied her robe's belt and took her hand.

She whimpered a little as our palms connected and caressed, its own sensual dance. I pulled Mila from her room and toward the piano. Kevin stood by the door, talking to someone. Mila tugged at my hand, trying to get free. Probably to scurry back to her room and hide again.

Nope. I was intent on this—a gesture to alleviate some of the hurt I'd caused her. I could've planned the moment better. Ordered up candles, a bottle of wine. But Mila knew me, which was part of the allure here. She knew I was spontaneous. Unable to control my runaway mouth.

And her heart would break when I left.

Some of my hurt melted away as I eased her down onto the bench next to me. Her brows were pulled tightly together.

Alpie stared at me from her cage, her hot-pink crest rising from her head, but she remained quiet. Maybe she, too, understood the importance of this moment.

"You don't like to play the piano."

"Not often. But then, I've always compared myself to Hayden."

I took a breath and settled my fingers on the keys. "Before I do this, I want to tell you something. It's important."

"Okay."

"I haven't written a new song in over a year. Not because I didn't want to. Really, it's the thing I've wanted most. But I just couldn't."

"Okay," she said, confusion marking the word and swirling in her eyes.

"I thought about you this morning. About how I'd planned to play you a different song that night. I've never performed that one, by the way."

Her lips parted, forming a little O.

"I'm not playing that song now either. One day, maybe, and just for you. But now isn't the time."

"What is the time, then?"

"I want to play this instead."

I closed my eyes and started on the melody Hayden and I worked out earlier today. Mila shifted on the bench next to me, giving me space to work the keys. And I did. I sang the lyrics that

177

flowed effortlessly.

"*Pride ain't that mighty, not when yours is the best love*
I cannot lose,
So baby, I'm here, needing you—
If you stay,
Let me hold you close and keep you warm."

I stopped playing. "It's not finished yet, but I wanted you to hear it." I dropped my fingers from the keys and wrapped them around her waist, hauling her closer. "I needed you back in my life to be able to write again." I let my forehead rest against hers. "Know why?"

She shook her head, just a little, her eyes never leaving mine.

I took a deep breath, the fear of losing her, of Jordan hurting her, a bitter taste in my mouth. I focused on her deep brown eyes, those rich swirls of color. I might be out of practice, but I knew how to say this.

My hand moved to the back of her neck, cupping her head in my hand. Cradling it. "I thought about it before, but when you asked me if that's how I dealt with everything, I realized I hadn't. I mean, I've known for a while I should see you, try to understand why you broke my heart."

"I didn't mean—"

I placed my fingertips on her soft lips, and she inhaled sharply, eyes on mine.

"It never healed. I did stupid shit, then more stupid shit because I didn't know how to fix it and I didn't want to hurt anymore."

I removed my fingertips, scooting closer to her on the bench. Her breathing escalated. My heart tried to thump out of my chest.

178

"Murphy," Kevin said. "The police want to talk to you."

"Later."

"They're here now, and—"

"Blood fucking hell." I stared hard into her eyes. "We're finishing this."

CHAPTER TWENTY-ONE
Mila

I nodded, shoving my tousled hair back from my cheeks. "Yes, please."

He stood as he removed his hand out from behind my knees and my body slid down the length of his. We both hissed out a breath.

"Ms. Trask, Mr. Etsam," Detective Davenport said with a nod. Murphy shook his hand, so I did the same. Once we were all settled again, this time with water I grabbed for us, Detective Davenport leaned forward. "I wanted to let you know where we are with the investigation." He raised his eyebrows. "Especially since you seem busy."

I stiffened and Murphy wrapped his arm around me, squeezing my shoulder. "You're here pretty late," I said.

Davenport sat back and cleared his throat. "Full day. First free minutes I've had to stop by."

"Have you eaten?" I asked. "We can order you something."

Davenport smiled, a full one of appreciation, but shook his head. "So… we have warrants out on Jordan Jones, both for assault with a deadly weapon against Noelle Markham, and for attempted battery and aggravated stalking of you, Ms. Trask."

"Does that mean you're going to arrest him?"

Davenport's lips puckered for a moment. "We want to. But we have to find him first."

"The hell?" Murphy growled. "Do your jobs and get the bloke!"

Kevin cleared his throat and Murphy turned to glare at him, too. "Not that easy," he said, his voice calm. "Seattle proper has over six hundred thousand people in it. Then there're the surrounding areas. It's like finding a needle in a haystack. Especially since he hasn't used any of his credit cards, and he's finding ways to get past security. He wore a disguise to get in through the delivery entrance of the hotel."

"What about burning down Mila's house? You going to charge him for that, too?"

"As soon as I can prove it was him," the detective said, his voice more clipped. Because Murphy was questioning him or because the situation angered him as well?

"What do you need to prove he torched my house?" I asked.

Davenport rubbed his fingers over his eyes. "Arson's tricky. The house flamed really hot, so we know lots of accelerant was used. Gasoline," he clarified. "But Jordan's been smart. Once he was in the country, he hasn't flashed his passport and has paid for everything in cash. And now the disguises. He's sliding under the radar."

"Can you track his mobile? You know, with that find a friend feature." Murphy waved his hand.

Davenport's lip kicked up in sardonic approval. "If I knew his number, sure. Do you happen to have the phone number of the device he's using here? Because the cell phone in his name is sitting in Rosemary Jones' house, back in Sydney."

I tensed again, not liking the mention of my mother *still* spending time with Jordan.

"Right. So. To clarify…" Murphy said. "You have lots of warrants and probable cause. You're actively searching for the wanker but just haven't found him. When you do, you plan to put him in jail for the rest of his ruddy life."

"As soon as we catch him," Davenport averred.

"When will that be?" I asked. I twisted my left fist around my right pointer finger, in an effort to relieve my building anxiety and my burgeoning need for another dose of Xanax. Alpie cooed from her cage, and I considered letting her out to comfort me because Murphy wouldn't give me the pill until tomorrow, and I needed to come up with new coping skills to deal with all this tension.

I licked my lips thinking of the best relaxation method. What was it my psychiatrist said? Skills before pills. Well, Murphy had mad skills in the bedroom, and I'd bet they'd improved this past year. Not that I wanted to think about why that was… and I was back to being concerned about why Murphy wanted to have sex with me.

Davenport took a long drink of water. After setting the glass back on the table, he held first Murphy's gaze then my own. "I want this guy. I want him behind bars. Now. Not because the Seattle PD appears incompetent—that's the chief's PR problem. Jordan Jones is a bad man doing bad things. I don't want another fire or another person harmed. I don't want to have to come back here and tell you we've failed again."

I cleared my throat, thankful for the ability to focus on something besides the rabbit trail of Murphy's sexcapades. I leaned forward, away from Murphy's drugging scent and warmth. "I don't think you've failed. And you're the first police personnel to believe me. Thank you for that."

"We just want him in custody," Murphy added. "Unable to terrorize Mila any further."

"We all do," Kevin said. "Would make my life a lot easier if I didn't have to worry not only about a gunman but also about your reaction to him." He raised his eyebrows, still irritated about

Murphy's stunt in the garage. Murphy shrugged, clearly not willing to apologize for his concern over my safety. Oh, how I wished I really was Murphy's top priority.

"What happens now?" I asked.

"We keep searching and hope we get a good lead," Davenport said. "Something to break the case."

Murphy ended the interviews with a speed that bordered on terseness. If I didn't know him well, I'd think he was being a rock star diva dickhead. But he kept tugging at his eyebrow ring, flicking his lip piercing, fidgeting with his hands. Murphy was nervous about our conversation, and the fear of being shot at still coursed through us. As soon as Detective Davenport shuffled his papers, Murphy stood and practically hauled me from the room.

I would have been embarrassed if I hadn't been so preoccupied with what Murphy had begun to tell me earlier. I'd broken his heart and it hadn't healed. Did that mean he still loved me? Could I believe him if he told me that now?

The situation we'd been thrust in was dangerous. It escalated emotions and physical reactions. I knew that—I was a doctor. Yet, here I stood, my body practically begging for Murphy to touch me, make me forget my fears and anxieties.

He fumbled with the door. "It's locked," he muttered. "Mila, I—" Instead of finishing that thought, he leaned down and kissed me. This meeting of lips, teeth, tongue was slow, soft, banked with more hunger than I'd ever felt from him before. I kissed him back, trying to make up for lost time.

He ripped his lips from mine, his eyes dark with lust. "I want to make love to you, Mila."

I cupped his cheeks. Ignoring my pounding heart, I said, "Because of the adrenaline? To feel more alive?"

He blew out an exasperated breath. "No. Because nearly losing you today, worrying you were hurt or dead, made my heart pound and my hands sweaty and my soul ache."

I blinked up at him. Not the declaration of love I wanted, but the words, their starkness, melted my heart. And… to be honest, I wanted Murphy, too. Just as much—maybe more—than he wanted me.

"I can't have sex with you," I said, sighing. Stepping back was hard.

"Why?" he asked.

"Because I'll want to be in a relationship. An exclusive one."

His frown cleared. "But we are."

"Since when?" I asked.

"Since I saw you again."

"You were so angry at the Tractor Tavern."

He shook his head. "I was *hurt*. Part of me still is. I'm also angry you didn't trust me with the situation with Jordan then."

And here we were. Back to the lack of trust, to the bitterness we'd both created over the last year. If I asked him how we got past this, I might never have another chance to feel Murphy's arms around me, his skin sliding over mine. Was I ready to throw away our chemistry—whatever this second chance was?—because our relationship hadn't aligned perfectly? I was still in love with him, would be for the rest of my life. So if this was all I could get, these few stolen days punctuated by the fear of Jordan's stalking, I'd be a fool to not live them to the fullest.

I stepped back, my limbs shaking. I opened my robe and let it fall from my shoulders. "Make love to me, Murphy."

Meeting his gaze and the emotion there caused me to step back in. Closer. I wanted to be closer to him. I wanted to pleasure and be pleasured.

"You're the most beautiful woman I've ever seen."

I snorted. He placed his hands on my hips, cupping my bum. "I mean it. No one compares to you, Mila."

"Enough sweet talking. Kiss me already."

He did. And it was hot, wet, glorious. His tongue stroked mine, relearning the textures of my mouth. I moaned, pressing my body fully against his, my hands in his hair.

"I've got to feel you against my skin."

He disentangled our arms, and I whimpered. His smirk disappeared behind his T-shirt. And then his chest was bare. I touched his collar bones, slid my hands down his pecs and traced his puckered nipples. His breath hissed out and he moaned when my fingers drifted lower, over his abs to the button of his jeans.

He cupped my shoulder blade with one hand, the other covering my breast. I leaned into his palm, needing the friction. Right… there. I gasped as my nipples hardened.

"Please."

"What do you want, Mila?"

"You. I need you."

I undid the fastening on his jeans. Reaching inside, I cupped his erection. He was so hard, so warm in my hand through his underwear.

"Don't stop," he groaned.

"Don't plan to."

With my free hand, I managed to shove his jeans over his hips. They puddled over his boots. He dipped his head and I tilted

185

mine, knowing he wanted to kiss my jawline. I jumped when his lips, then his tongue, touched the upper swell of my breast. Not what I expected but good. So good.

He quivered as I cupped him harder, pressing him into my palm.

His hand at my shoulder drifted down my spine. His arm tightened around my waist, low, just above my hips. He tipped back and we fell onto the bed.

I sprawled over him, my hair cascading around our faces. His hand cupped my bum, weighing it, caressing it, while his thumb and forefinger plucked at my nipple. This time, he kissed my jaw, near my ear.

I whimpered as I ran my free hand down his side. I needed more of him. I would always need him.

He pulled me up so that my breasts were even with his mouth. When we collapsed on the bed, I lost my grip on his erection, and now my hands were splayed across his chest. I loved the soft, springy hair there, and I tangled my fingers in it, tugging just enough for him to growl.

He toyed with one nipple, his tongue swirling around it until it hardened into a tight bud. He went to the other side, massaging my flesh. I wiggled against him, managing to straddle one of his thighs and I pressed my heated core onto his leg. We both moaned at the contact.

"You're so wet."

"I want you," I gasped.

He chuckled, burying his face between my breasts. "You're going to have me, love."

I pushed up, off him and knelt at his feet. I pulled off his boots, his socks and then his jeans. He'd leaned up on his elbows, and I took my time scrutinizing this delicious man as I crawled back up his big, muscular body.

"Been working out, I see." I touched his broadened shoulders, following my hand with my lips. He shuddered as my hand, then my mouth, drifting down to the more defined muscles at his core.

"Surfing, actually. I spend most of my free time doing that and kayaking."

"It's working for you," I purred.

He flipped me over so I lay beneath him.

"God. You have no idea how much I've wanted you like this."

He ran his fingertips between my breasts and over my stomach. He pressed his palm against my heat and I moaned.

"I like this. How wet you are for me." He kissed me, his teeth tugging on my lower lip. I bucked against his hand, wanting, needing more.

He slid his fingers over my clitoris, and I raised my hips, splaying my legs wider. He licked his way over my lips before delving into my mouth. I kissed him back, fingers tangled in his hair.

He pressed a finger into me and my head fell back, mouth open, as my back bowed.

"Christ, Mila, you're tight."

"Feels good. Don't stop."

He found a rhythm with his finger, sliding in and out of my body, pressing forward into that spot I loved. His thumb circled the bundle of nerves.

"Murphy," I whimpered.

"Here with you. Let go. I've got you."

"No, I want you with me."

"We have all night, Mil." He pressed more insistently against my clit, adding a second finger to pump in and out of my body. My hips bucked wildly. The pleasure built too fast, too big. I kissed him with all that passion inside me as I pushed down his boxer briefs. Soon, I'd admire his bum in them. But right now, I wanted him inside me.

I tugged his cock forward, but he wouldn't stop caressing me with his fingers.

"Murphy, I need you inside me. Please."

His fingers were gone and then he pressed against my entrance. He both moaned and gasped.

"Condom," he muttered.

The crinkle of a foil packet, the weight of his knee next to my hip, his body covering mine. He slid inside me before I really considered the need for protection. I threw my head back and gripped his shoulders, my hips rising to press tighter to his groin. I'd missed him, missed this. He pulled out. I leaned up as he pushed into me and bit into his shoulder. He reared back but I wrapped my legs around his hips and pulled him closer.

I teetered on the edge.

"Christ. I've missed you." He caught my lips in another kiss and I tilted my hips to accept his next thrust. Murphy was back in my body, pulsing inside me. He held himself there, pinning me to the bed with his hips. He stared down into my eyes. His face flushed, his features sharpened with lust. He pulled out once more, his eyes on the place where we joined. He pressed back into me just as slowly. He hissed and I whimpered at the sensations pulsing through me.

One more thrust sent me over the edge. I convulsed around him, my vision going black at the edges as he continued to pump into me, milking my orgasm that seemed to go on and on and on.

I eased back from the pleasure just in time to feel him stiffen over me. He came on a low groan, his forehead against mine. I pressed a kiss to his lips and pulled him tighter to me as he finished falling over the edge.

CHAPTER TWENTY-TWO
Murphy

Intense. The best orgasm ever, and this woman was the reason for it.

Much as I'd wanted to draw our coupling out, bring her to the pinnacle of pleasure multiple times before I entered her body, Mila had her own agenda. Turned out, she knew what she was doing.

Catching my breath, I wrapped my arms around her and shifted us so we both lay on our sides. She reached up and touched my cheek, smoothing back my hair.

The gentleness of the caress combined with the love shining from her eyes loosened something in my chest. Tears filled my eyes. I blinked, shocked. I didn't do much in the way of emotions outside of angry, hungry, lustful, and relaxed. But this was some type of cleansing.

I pulled her tighter to me and dropped my head to the crook of her shoulder. She smoothed her hand over my head, down my back as the tears flowed. When I pulled back, Mila wiped away the wetness from my cheeks and I returned the favor.

Her eyes were bloodshot, the tip of her nose red. I couldn't look any better.

With a sigh, I slid from the bed and padded to the bathroom. After disposing of the condom, I washed my face and wet a cloth for her.

Mila propped herself up on the pillows, the covers pulled up to her chest. Her hair, tangled and wild, spilled across her shoulders. I slipped under the sheets next to her and handed her the cloth.

After she'd cleaned up, she snuggled against my side, her head against my shoulder. My arm wrapped tight around her waist and I breathed in the scent of her hair.

"I always have firsts with you," I said.

"Hmmm?"

"Getting weepy is new."

Mila laid her hand on my chest. "Getting shot at, the constant worry… our feelings over losing Kyle. It's been a lot."

"For the first time in much too long, I'm happy and I think I have a shot at sleeping all night." I ran my thumb across her shoulder and she stiffened, pulling away. Right. The scars. She didn't say a word about it, but I knew she was comparing herself to the women I'd been photographed with—every air-brushed bit of perfection. She stiffened further until she was straighter than a board. Not easy to hold.

"I want my pills," she mumbled.

Yep. She'd decided she came up lacking and wanted to ease the turbulent emotions pinging through her mind. Having seen how dependent other musicians came to the false calm of these types of pills, there was no way I was letting Mila have one now. "Not a good idea."

"I didn't ask you if you thought I should have one. I said I wanted the bottle. I need one."

"You're recovering from an addiction," I said. We'd gone post-coital bliss into a full-blown argument in less than five minutes. If I didn't feel so alive, I'd be angry at how quickly I'd messed up.

"That's your opinion," Mila gritted.

Anxiety drove her now, told her to pull away from me. Not

happening. I rolled over, caging her in my arms. I pressed a kiss to her shoulder, the one with the scars. She tried to push me away, her cheeks flushing enough for me to know she was sensitive about the area. I kissed her again, working my way down to her breast. She hissed a breath. I lapped the space between those beautiful globes.

She clutched me tighter, her body heating as I laved her nipple. I moved to the other side. She made those sweet sounds in the back of her throat. I rested my body between her legs and molded my hands to her hips, thumbs brushing over the sensitive skin on her ribs.

I kissed a path down to her navel, delving my tongue into the small indentation there before tugging at her piercing. She moaned, her head falling back to expose the length of her smooth throat. I levered up, pressing kisses to her jawline, to her throat, running my lips over her collarbone. I savored the valley between her breasts again before heading lower.

Mila vibrated under me, her body so primed for my loving she couldn't remain still. Her nails scored my shoulders and she palmed my back. Her hips tilted up to meet mine, restless, needy.

I planned to give her everything she needed. I drifted down to kiss her hip bones, the tops of her thighs, her pretty knees. I trailed my lips up the inside of her soft, smooth legs. She gasped as I hit an erogenous zone.

I pressed a kiss to her lower lips and she stiffened, then immediately melted against me. Her legs splayed open as I continued to kiss her, pressing in deeper to taste more of her.

God, she tasted sweet. I wanted to do this all night.

———◆———

Sleeping with Mila meant waking with her. Which meant hot morning sex, something I hadn't partaken of in way too long. Much positive to be said for hot morning sex with Mila.

Now we were in the shower, soaping each other's bodies, lingering on our favorite places, peaking together.

I cupped her breast, loving how it filled my hand, as I slid from her body.

Bloody damn hell. No condom.

"Are you on the pill?" I asked.

Mila froze and shook her head. "No." I watched her teeth come out to sink into her lip. She leaned back and rinsed the conditioner from her hair. When she met my gaze again, hers darkened. "It's okay. The likelihood of me getting pregnant again is very low."

I pulled her close to me, needing to share in this moment. I ached for her. For us.

"Can you tell me why?"

"The way I miscarried. The doctor performed a D-and-C afterward, to clean out all the leftover tissue from the placenta, but the trauma… There's scar tissue in my uterus."

I held her as she shuddered against me. "Should I be worried about catching something? Too late now that we've gone bare, I know."

"You're the only woman I've slept since I was last tested." I hoped she didn't ask when that was—she really wouldn't like the answer. "We do it on the reg."

Her shoulders stiffened and she eased from my grasp. Once again, she wasn't ready to hear about my list of previous partners. Not that I could blame her. The idea of Mila sharing her body, let alone her passion, with someone else made me want to break things.

She opened the shower door and grabbed a towel, wiping the water from her face before wrapping it around her head.

I couldn't tell her I'd never been so affected by a woman before—never reached such levels of pleasure—without Mila feeling like I compared her to them. Complete mood killer. I sighed as I reached for the knobs to turn off the spray. I weighed my choices.

"I'd be thrilled to have a child with you. You know that, right?"

"The baby wouldn't replace Kyle."

Anger started a slow burn in my gut. "Never said a new bub would. Or could. What I meant was I'd like to be a father."

"Then you'll need to find another woman."

My olive branch turned into a new battleground where Mila didn't feel as though she lived up to some standard of womanhood because the choice was ripped from her body. I wrapped my towel around my waist and followed her into her bedroom. "Fine. Then we won't have kids."

"You can. I can't."

"There are other ways to have children."

"Not *my* children."

"Don't get your back up."

"I'm just pointing out my shortcomings now. That way you don't have to hear them first through the media. Might as well know you're getting someone so damaged."

She'd pulled on her panties and bra. I watched her slither into leggings and a long top. I couldn't wait to pull it off again and run my hands over her soft curves.

"What do you want me to say?" I asked.

"Nothing. There's *nothing* you can say."

She walked back into the bathroom and hung up her towel. She ran her brush through her hair while I tried to figure out how to control the damage from this conversation. Being with Mila was like walking through a minefield. The other side—us, together forever—was worth the risk, but I wasn't sure we'd both survive to get there intact.

She managed to avoid my arms and open her bedroom door. I strode out behind her, my eyes glued to the back of her head.

"Why can't we talk about this?" I asked.

Mila'd stopped and I tripped over her. I managed to catch her with one arm around her waist, the other going to my loosened towel. Noelle, Jake, and even Briar and Hayden sat in the large living room, a coffee service and multiple plates with crumbs resting around the space.

"Too bad about the towel," Noelle said, a twinkle in her eye. "That would have made my morning."

"Mil!" Alpie cried from her cage. "Hi! Love-oo."

"G'day," I said, not quite catching anyone's eye. I turned and sped into my room, closing the door just shy of a slam.

Bloody fabulous. Mila would be even more upset that others heard our argument. I leaned back against the wood, my fingers gripped tight into the metal of the handle, and fought down the urge to destroy things. I'd just gotten her back, and I sure as shit didn't plan to let her go again.

———◆———

"You didn't answer any of your messages yesterday after the news reported you and Mila were shot at. We were worried," Jake said.

Kevin walked by and dropped my phone into my hand. I winced at the number of texts and messages from my mum.

"Mum upset?"

"Beside herself, mate. It's sorted now, though. I let her know you were alive once I showed up here."

"And that would be?"

Jake rubbed a hand over his tired eyes but glanced down at his watch. "'Bout a half hour ago. I called Hayden to let him know I was in Seattle. He and Briar said they'd meet me here. Noelle was arguing with one of the guards in the lobby, but I remembered her from the show, so I brought her up with me."

I typed out a message to let Mum know I was sorry for worrying her and to let her know I'd been with Mila.

"Who's with Mum?"

"Ben."

I nodded.

Her response: *Good. Please call me soon.*

I inhaled Mila's scent as I pulled her into my lap. She relaxed against me, giving over her trust. A sight better than good, this.

"Glad as I am to have you here, Jake, I'm surprised. Both by you and Hayden." I dipped my head, "Briar," I said.

She smiled back, those blue eyes dancing as she watched me squirm. "Hayden's here on official record label business. They want you out in the spotlight as soon as possible so they can coat-tail off your new level of fame. You're even hotter than Hayden was when he left me in Seattle in June."

"Are you bloody kidding me? I'm not putting any of you at risk so the label can make some more bucks."

Hayden leaned back, a smug expression on his face. "I knew you were still in there, Ets. Glad to see the real human emerging. Wasn't a fan of the troll."

"Piss off," I said. "You are not doing anything with me. No crowds, no performances, nada."

"That's a bit of a struggle, mate. The label's put it out that we'll be at the charity event," Jake said. "The label hired some private firm to watch us and also to prowl through the crowd. I guess even with the huge price tag they're still expecting to make some serious coin. Harry said something about broadcasting it on pay-per-view. They moved the venue to something bigger and it's going to live stream for a fee."

Jake leaned forward. "People are going to pay to hear you sing, and if the telly's good, maybe get shot."

"Shut it, Jake," Hayden said. "No one's getting shot. This isn't a game."

"Just trying to lighten the mood," Jake said, scowling.

"Jordan's still out there, still trying to hurt Mila," I said.

"And you," she replied.

"The label pulled out its lawyers. They're making this happen," Hayden said. "We didn't get a say."

I growled. I wanted to stand and pace. Instead, I pulled Mila even tighter to me. When she didn't take another breath, I loosened my grip.

"How about we have a cuppa?" she said, turning to lay her

palm against my cheek. "Some brekkie. Then we can discuss this more."

"Right. Fine," I grumbled. I caught Jake's smirk from the corner of my eye. The little bastard knew I liked Mila taking charge, handling me. I always had.

"I'll get it for you," Noelle said. She'd been strangely quiet this whole time but Mila appeared happier for her presence.

Noelle came back in a few minutes later with another coffee set and a pile of pastries. Reluctantly, I let go of Mila, who slid onto the cushion in the same chair, making me inordinately pleased she didn't try to go to another chair. She leaned forward and prepared us each a coffee, handing me the first mug, with just one sugar. I didn't know why, but the fact she remembered how I liked my coffee brought a lump to my throat that I worked to swallow down before I could take a sip.

Mila stood and embraced Noelle. "I'm glad to see you," she said.

"And I'm glad to see you took my advice," Noelle's laughing eyes darted to me. Ah, so she'd wanted us back together. Interesting.

"Murphy and I are—"

"Together," I snapped.

"Always the romantic," Jake sighed.

"Rack off."

"And there's the Ets we all know and love," Hayden said. "Seriously, mate, we need to do some planning. The logistics of putting this together without Flip are staggering."

"He stayed in Sydney with Cynthia and the baby," Jake said.

"Good. I don't want him to get hurt. I'm supposed to play the venue *solo*. That's the deal I cut with Harry," I said, crossing my arms over my chest. I'd talked to him last night on the way back from Hayden and Briar's, telling him I wanted to be on the stage alone—mainly so I didn't have to save face with Hayden, who I didn't think would show.

Mila turned to glare at me. Oh, right, I hadn't mentioned my hope Jordan wouldn't be able to resist the free shot—literally—at my head or arse to her. I'd forgotten how to do this sharing-of-lives business.

"But you invited me yesterday," Hayden said, "And I've invited Jake."

"We'll have to borrow a drummer," Jake said. "I've talked to Harry about it and he's got a few options for us to talk over."

"No," I said. "I don't want you there." That sounded the worst kind of harsh. I tugged at my eyebrow ring. "I mean, I do, but I don't want you to get hurt. Bloody hell. I can't let you put yourselves in harm's way. Jake, you can stay here with Mila. So I know she's safe."

"I'm coming with you," Jake said, his chin thrust out with determination. "No way you get all the limelight."

"I can't protect all of you," I gritted.

"Nor should you have to, big brother," Jake said, his face falling into serious lines. "We're all in this because we *choose* to be."

"Right," Hayden said. "We left our band image, hell our relationship with you, a mess for the world to see. It's time everyone realizes we're a group. You're my mate, and I'm there with you—especially through this point in your life."

Hayden kept his eyes trained on me, and that damn lump in my throat swelled up again. I gulped the rest of my coffee so I could get the words out. "But you could get hurt. Any of you."

"Staying here at the hotel almost got me killed yesterday," Mila said. "I don't see how it's more dangerous for us to be on the move."

"You are *not* coming."

She blinked up at me, her eyes filled with hurt. "You don't want me there?"

I shoved my hand through my hair. "That's not what I said, and it's not what I meant. Mila, you almost *died*. He's tried to kill you twice now. One of these times he just might."

"But he hasn't. And if I'm with you, at least I can see what I'd be getting into with the touring and concerts and such. I never did much of that with you before because of my coursework, then my residency."

"You have patients now that you're supposed to be seeing," I said, grasping for something.

She raised her brows. "Someone told my boss I wouldn't be in this week. Apparently, I have loads of free time. Now, if you don't want me there, just say it. I'll figure something out."

"That's not it, Mila! Of course I want you." I huffed out a breath, annoyed to be fighting, baring my soul in front of such a big crowd.

"I'll come, too," Briar said.

Hayden jerked beside her, his eyes narrowed.

"I'll keep Mila company backstage. It'll be good, as Mila pointed out, for me see more of this touring business."

"Well, I don't want to miss the party," Noelle said. "I mean, I'm not involved with one of the members of the band, but it sounds like fun."

I wanted to rip out my hair, break something. "Don't you get that there's a mad man out there with a gun, shooting at us?" I gritted out.

All the eyes in the room blinked up at me. Hayden stood, walked around the coffee table and laid his hand on my tensed shoulder.

"Of course we do. But we're your family, and you're not doing this alone."

CHAPTER TWENTY-THREE
Mila

Murphy stood in a single lunge and pulled Hayden into a bear hug. He turned and did the same to Jake. "You're not allowed to get hurt. No matter what. You're not allowed."

"Can I talk to you, Mila?" Noelle asked.

I nodded and started to leave the room. "No," Murphy said. "Stay where I can see you." Realizing how harsh that command sounded, he added a soft, "please."

I nodded, smiling, and moved to the other side of the room. I reached through the bars of the cage and petted Alpie, who cooed in response.

"What's up."

"Are you okay?" Noelle asked. "I mean, with all the coverage about your miscarriage and hospitalization? Murphy said you're dependent on your pills."

I blinked, surprised to realize I hadn't thought about my next hit since… well, since Murphy made me forget last night, and again this morning.

"It's early days yet," I said, feeling out the words, "but I think I'm going to be fine."

She blew out a slow breath. "Well, if there's anything worth getting addicted to in this world, it's that man. Good Lord, he's hot, Mil. Especially when he goes all alpha male around you, snarling and snapping at anyone who gets too close."

I nodded. He was. But being with Murphy meant sharing him with his adoring fans. The ones who stripped naked at shows and no doubt did all kinds of naughty things I'd never considered. I'd only been with three men in my life, and Murphy was my longest relationship by far. In my last lonely year, I'd read a lot of possibilities for sexual play in the erotic romances Noelle kept leaving at my house or sending me via her Kindle. How could I compete with women who not only knew about those kinky options but put them to good use?

"One of your patients came into my ER last night."

I pulled my mind from its rabbit trail. "Who?"

"Tanya. I happened to be leaving when they admitted her. I helped her get settled in. She said to let you know she's thinking of you."

I closed my eyes. Twenty-seven and alone, Tanya struggled with her pregnancy, first with an inability to hold anything in her stomach and now with bleeding. She'd reminded me of me from that initial appointment—her hope warring with fear and boiled down to an essence of determination to do anything she could for her unborn child. For me, that wasn't enough. I didn't want Tanya to go through the same hell I'd lived.

"What for?" I asked.

"Is there anything I can do to help?" Briar asked. She laid her hand on each of our shoulders, squeezing just enough to let us know she meant her words. I liked her. A lot.

"We're discussing one of my patients. She's in the ER."

"No, they moved her to Labor and Delivery," Noelle said. "They're monitoring her."

"Oh, I'm going to the hospital in a little while. Want me to check on her?"

"Would you mind?" I asked.

Briar smiled. "Not at all. In fact, it's one of my favorite parts of my new position. I like cheering people up. What's wrong with her?"

"Placenta previa," Noelle said. Tanya's situation kept getting worse. She was young, single and about to be put on bed rest. There was no way she'd be able to keep up with the bills, especially without an income.

"Crap," I said. "She's still got eleven weeks left. Bed rest is going to be a real problem."

"The admitting wants to keep her another day or two," Noelle added.

"And then?"

Noelle shrugged, an attempt to wrest away from the pain of getting too involved in a patient's life.

"Why don't I go see her later this morning?" Briar said. "We leave Friday for the concert."

"It's this Friday?" I asked, startled. Definitely some details Murphy and I would have to work out. Number one among them was communicating our schedules.

"From what Hayden's said, they'll do press today and practice with their fill-in drummer," Briar said. "That's the schedule until the concert."

I shook my head, trying to wrap my mind around the fact I planned to tour with one of the hottest bands in the world. "This is so different from when they were playing pubs in Sydney."

"You have no idea," Briar sighed. "It's the part I like least." Her eyes softened as they drifted over to Hayden. Jake, Hayden, and Murphy were huddled together, their sun-kissed locks nearly as beautiful as their faces, all set in concentration. "But I can't imagine being happy without him. So I deal."

"Smart words," Noelle, said.

She fell back into her thought, which made me ask, "This about Kent?"

"Hmmm? I don't know," Noelle responded, a frown pinching her brows.

"He wants more?" I asked.

Noelle shook her head, her lips pressed together. "He wants to keep doing what he's doing. But he'd be perfectly fine if I worked around his schedule, his life."

Briar made a grumbly noise in her throat. "Doctor?" she asked. Noelle nodded.

"Figured," she said with a sigh. "There are some really great ones. Like you, Mila."

"Kent's one of the good ones," Noelle responded. "But his schedule is insane."

"So you're going to coast along with him until something better comes along?" I asked.

Noelle's gaze slid over Murphy before landing back on me. "You're one to talk."

"It's... we're complicated," I sighed as I hugged my arms tighter to my chest.

Briar's smile turned rueful. "Any relationship worth having is. Once emotions get involved, all that cool logic goes right out the window." She shook her head. "I sound like my sister. She's so freaking smart."

Murphy's tears last night haunted me. "I'm worried he's only with me because of the baby. Well, now because he'd feel horrible if Jordan hurt me."

"I don't know him well," Briar said. "In fact, I've made a point to avoid him after he tried to keep me away from Hayden, but I can tell you he never looked at any of the women on tour like he looks at you. He wants to bundle you up and hide you from the world."

"He has," I said, my voice sour.

"Because he cares about you. And that hug when you came out? Even though you two had just been arguing, he couldn't bear to be apart. That's sweet."

"Not the word I would have chosen for Murphy Etsam, but yeah, it was," Noelle said.

"How'd you know?" I asked. "That Hayden was worth the risk? The headaches of the travel schedule?"

Briar's dreamy expression stayed in place, building into a large cat-with-cream smile. "Easy. He ripped my heart out and took it with him when he left. The only way I'd be whole was with him. Thankfully, that goes both ways."

I glanced over at Murphy, who stared at me. His interest created a powerful reaction in my body.

Oh, how I wanted this man. I hoped when he took my heart on his next trip, I held his.

———◆———

After Briar, Hayden, and Noelle left—now each with their own security detail since they'd decided to attach themselves more closely to us—Murphy moved his things from the second bedroom. Jake wanted a lie-in and Murphy said he wanted to spoon me. That wasn't what he wanted, but he did win points for saying so.

"What are you thinking?" he asked when I settled on the side of the bed, too restless to actually lie down.

"One of my patients was admitted to the hospital last night. Briar offered to visit her today, but I'd like to see her. Soon."

"That's not a good idea. Not with Jordan still running around, armed and crazed."

"Murphy, this young woman reminds me so much of me. She's single. Her boyfriend jumped ship when she found out she was pregnant."

Based on Murphy's thin-lipped response, he didn't like that comparison.

"I'm sorry, that started out badly," I sighed. "What I mean is, she's struggling through this pregnancy, fighting and clawing every step of the way to bring this baby into the world. She's been thrown so many curves, Murphy. The baby," I swallowed, "the baby likely has Down Syndrome, and she's never changed her course, never been anything other than a loving mum."

He sighed. "Do you want to go there now?"

I gripped my shirt. "Do you think it's safe?"

"I can ask Kevin if you'd like."

"You don't think it's safe," I whispered.

His arms tightened around me, squeezing too tight. "Christ, Mila. I can't deal with all this heavy shit. The last time I left, you were shot at."

"So were you."

He pressed a kiss to my lips and I melted into him. "For your safety—your sanity—I shouldn't let you go. But I'm a selfish bastard, and I just can't control you. So if you want to go to the hospital today, even though it scares the shit out of me, we'll go visit your patient."

"Where are you going?" I asked.

"To tell Kevin we're going to the hospital."

———◆———

"Your vitals are good," I said. No, I purred. It was late afternoon, almost five, by the time we arrived. I'd had to show Murphy how much I appreciated his willingness to compromise even though he didn't want to. I didn't complain when, an hour and a half later, just as I finally climbed from our bed, he wanted to reassure himself that I was his.

He'd called Nordstrom when he went to talk to Kevin about my desire to visit the hospital, and one of the personal shoppers created and brought over a new wardrobe for me. Thanks to the fire, my clothing choices were sadly depleted.

Still, I protested, not liking the grandness of the gesture. Murphy whispered how much he wanted to see me in the short white shorts and the red checked top, the 1950s-style day dress and especially the corset and garters. I gave in without too much grumbling once Murphy understood I was serious about paying for all of it. Sure, it would put a dent in my savings, but if Murphy and I were going to be seen together in public, I must appear good enough to date him—one of Briar's tenets for reducing publicity. While the idea of expensive clothing was weird and the reasons for such expenditures shallow, I understood her point. I'd read the scathing attacks Briar endured and didn't wish to follow in her footsteps.

I sighed, confused. Much as I wanted to rise above the silliness of gossip sites and Internet memes, the part that bothered me most were the comparisons to Murphy's previous lovers.

Sure, he said he wanted to be with me. But I wasn't sure he'd still feel that way once he saw the gorgeous, cover-model perfect bodies he could have instead. The man was a connoisseur of beautiful women—with even better taste than he had in cars and clothes. With the scars on my shoulder and average stature, I couldn't compete with those women, no matter how beautiful Murphy told me I was. Because while he thought me beautiful, that didn't mean the rest of the world didn't see my flaws in my too-large, boring brown eyes and hair.

So much for my momentary sexual bliss. I blinked at Tanya, trying to restabilize my world. The pills. This depressive crash I was experiencing must be due to my lack of serotonin. Upping my protein levels immediately should show an improvement in a few days.

"Yep, your BP is perfect," I said, patting her shoulder.

"I'm doing great, Dr. Mila."

I smiled, as I always did whenever Tanya called me that.

"But how about you? I was shocked when you were on the news."

I frowned down at my clipboard. What to say? This woman was my patient, but she'd also become my friend. "I'm okay. It's not pleasant having my past exposed to the world at large, but Murphy's been great."

"To think you once dated a rock star," she sighed.

"She is again, but I still think I got the better end of this deal," Murphy said as he entered the doorway, moving in to embrace my middle as he nuzzled into my neck. I melted back into him, unable to stop myself.

Tanya's mouth opened—her tonsils were pink, healthy. She

snapped her jaw closed to grin with more megawatts than I'd ever seen from her before.

"Dr. Mila is amazing. I always thought she was too pretty to be a doctor."

"She's smart enough for the career," Murphy said.

"You'll take good care of her? Not just while the stalker's out there?"

"Oh, I fully intend to," Murphy said.

I couldn't help but smile. He sounded satisfied, a perfectly happy cat with its canary.

"How are you faring?" Murphy asked.

Tanya dropped her gaze to the hospital bed and flushed. "I'm okay. It's the baby, though."

"Yeah, Mila said he's given you some trouble. She also said your background is in PR." Murphy raised his eyebrows.

Tanya nodded, hesitant. Where was Murphy going with this?

"Right. Well, once you get that nipper sorted, give us a call," Murphy said. "I've been known to get in a spot or three. A good PR team is worth its weight."

Tanya smiled again, this time her eyes sparkling with excitement. "Really? You'd do that?"

"Well, I don't hire. My manager does. But seeing as how I'll be spending more time in Seattle so Mila can finish her residency, I'm going to need some staff in this time zone. Here's his information. Tell him I said to talk to you."

"Oh," she whispered. When she lifted her head, her eyes were filled with tears and something close to hero worship. "Thank you."

"Take care," Murphy said. He kissed the top of my head. "I'll be in Briar's office with Hayden. Who knew we'd spend so much time together in a hospital when neither of us was sick or broken?"

I smiled at him, my own heart melting at the sweetness of his gesture to Tanya. I sucked in a deep breath and turned in his arms. Professionalism be damned for the moment. This man was amazing when he wanted to be. I stood on my tiptoes and pulled his head down for a real kiss.

While short, the kiss promised all kinds of hotness later. I trailed my lips along his jaw and whispered in his ear. "Thank you."

He squeezed my hips as he stepped back. "Oh, you can do that. Soon." Glancing back at Tanya, he winked. "See ya."

I pressed my fingers to my lips as he walked from the room, wanting to hold the tingling warmth for another moment.

Tanya sighed. "He might just be the most potent hit of testosterone I've ever met."

"I didn't stand a chance," I sighed.

"He wasn't kidding when he said he's all kinds of into you. Oh, Dr. Mila! Do you think he'll get me a job?"

I smiled, patted her hand. "If Murphy says he'll do it, he will." I needed to believe my words. If it wasn't… well, I'd find out tomorrow if his eye wandered. I cleared my throat. "Now tell me more about the baby's movements."

CHAPTER TWENTY-FOUR
Murphy

Kevin stuck his head back into the living area a couple of hours later. "There's a slew of reporters in the lobby. Just wanted you to know they're refusing to leave until they get a statement from one of you."

I glanced over at Mila, who was curled up with Alpie in the corner of the sofa. She sighed, a long drawn-out sound. Much as she must be struggling with her need for more medication, she never asked for more. Just fallen slowly into a funk that worried me. Was this the start of something more serious? Should I get a counselor in here to monitor her for depression?

I wasn't sure, and the lack of a plan caused my stomach to clench. I couldn't lose Mila again—not now that I'd found my way back into her good graces and her bed. I was settled, happy even. I needed to make sure she stayed in that same emotional place.

I rose from the piano stool and settled onto the couch cushion next to Mila, wrapping my arm around my shoulder. A burst of pleasure filled my chest when she moved Alpie over so she could settle in closer. Trust wasn't something Mila threw around, and now that I understood more about her past, my actions—and how they'd hurt her—caused me pain, too. So, this, this willingness to snuggle against me, even if it was subconscious, warmed me more than I cared to admit.

My phone chirped. Jake strolled out of the second bedroom—formerly my bedroom—rubbing the side of his face. "You get the message from Harry? He set up a press conference for you in ten since all the media outlets are camping in the hotel lobby."

I growled in frustration. Mila rubbed my arm in a soothing pattern.

Kevin glanced around, eyes narrowed. "Might want to bring the media up here. I'll have the security team vet each person on the way in. Easier to manage the crowd and who's in it when they're on your turf."

I tipped my head. "Whatever you think's best," I said. "But let them know this'll be short and sweet since we have no real information to share."

"Do I have to be here for the press conference?" Mila asked. Dark shadows flitted through her beautiful eyes and hazed the skin below them.

"Are you tired?" I asked.

She nodded. "I don't have the mental energy for media."

I was media savvy enough to understand we needed to show a united, happy front. I played with my lip ring, wondering how I could ask it of her.

"Be best if you were here, Mil," Jake said with a yawn. "Otherwise there'll be speculation. Murph and I can answer all the questions. You just need to sit next to him, hold his hand, and look gorgeous."

She nodded, a small frown knitting her brows. "I'll go put on some of my nicer clothes then." Not that I didn't think she rocked her yoga pants and hoodie, but changing was probably smart.

Her shoulders pulled down and in as she trudged toward our shared room, Alpie resting her beak against Mila's neck.

"I'm worried about her," I said, my voice pitched low. She shut the bedroom door with a soft click.

"Noelle said you confiscated her pills. Whilst she's dealing with a stalker and an international media shit storm. None of that's easy on a body. But Mila can handle it."

"I want to handle this for her." Frustration bubbled back up, simmering along with my fear. "Bloody hell! I'm happy for the first time in ages. I want the same for her."

"Give her time, mate. She's been through heaps, sure, but I see how she looks at you. If I'm ever lucky enough to have a woman look at me like that, I'm never leaving her. Ever."

"I was a dipshit," I said with a sigh.

"True words."

"I have to make this right, Jakey."

He pulled at his bottom lip. "Seems to me she wants to be with you. Start there."

"You're a smart one. Sometimes, anyway."

He patted the back of my head. "Might want to comb your hair. I'm going to do mine now."

———◆———

Kevin ushered in the group of twenty or so reporters. They stood in the living area while Mila and I sat on the same sofa she'd commandeered earlier. Much as I tried to stay on top of the questions, the reporters kept asking Mila questions about her miscarriage and our current live-together relationship. While she covered the strain well, her hand shook even in my tight clasp, and she pet Alpie's head in a soothing rhythm.

"What is your comment on 'She's So Bad?' Is it about you?"

Jake took that one. "We never talk about the genesis of our songs. Not all art reflects our lives, just as our lives don't all reflect our art." Good brother, Jake.

"Why didn't you tell Murphy you were pregnant? Are you sure the baby was his?"

"Yes, I'm sure," I said, my voice hard. I dismissed the first part of the question, unwilling to divulge more of our secrets than need-be.

"Jordan's your step-uncle? How does your mother feel about this situation?"

"So Jordan was the reason you broke up with Murphy?"

If the police would just capture Jordan, we'd be able to move on! While I understood their need to follow due process, I wasn't above thinking vigilante justice was more appropriate in this case. After yet another rude, intrusive question about how Mila felt about my sexual exploits, I cleared my throat. I waited until all the cameras and faces turned to me.

My smile was slow, calculated for maximum charm. "As you know, Mila has been threatened by her step-uncle. He's threatened not only her life, but the lives of anyone she cares about. Mila will do *anything* to protect someone she loves. I know this firsthand. I lost her because of it before." I raised our clasped hands up and pressed a kiss to her knuckles before turning back to the rapt crowd. "What I need you to do is make sure the police find that piece of shit before he touches either Mila or another innocent person. Like my mum or Mila's friends. Report that. Find him. The world will be safer."

I stood, pulling Mila up with me, ignoring the chorus of questions and Alpie's shrieking protest.

"Was that smart?" Jake asked as he followed us into the bedroom Mila and I were sharing.

"I don't know." I tried to gauge Mila's reaction. Her face was pinched. Was it fatigue or the pain forced on her by bringing up both Kyle and my playboy days? "Felt like the right thing to do."

"It's going to be a manhunt," Jake said. "Crazies will be out there, trying to find him. Grab some of the glory."

"Good." I gritted my teeth. Was it? Hell if I had the answer. "It'll slow him down, then." I pushed Mila's hair off her forehead. "You all right?"

She closed her eyes and pressed her cheek into my chest. "Honestly? I don't know."

CHAPTER TWENTY-FIVE
Mila

I refused to leave the hotel suite the next day, too strung out by the media's obsession with my dead baby. I refused both Noelle's and Briar's requests to stop by, not wanting either of them in any more danger because of me. By Friday morning, I'd refused to leave the bedroom for more than a quick meal that Murphy practically forced down my throat. My appetite was even more minuscule than it already had been, thanks to Murphy forcing me to ween off Xanax.

The withdrawal symptoms had kicked in and my mind was as listless as my aching body. The only time I felt alive was when Murphy touched me, but thanks to the need for multiple rounds of press and practice—that they did at some studio downtown—I didn't see much of Murphy, which deepened my depressive thoughts.

"You ready?" Murphy asked. Since the meeting with everyone here on Monday, Murphy had done a complete turnabout, now willing to do just about anything to get me to leave the hotel suite and the dark cloud that had been clinging to me for days. He even went so far as to rummage through my new clothes, picking out the outfit he wanted me to wear—tight jeans with multiple rips starting mid-thigh and a form-hugging Jackaroo short-sleeve tee. He'd headed back into the closet for the pair of Chuck Taylors he'd insisted I get, remembering our conversation years ago about how much I'd always wanted to own a pair.

He kissed my forehead and started toward the bedroom door.

"Murphy?" I asked. My body aches and the rebound anxiety

weren't as bad this morning. The symptoms were supposed to fade within a week, and I was within a couple of days of that time frame. I stood and stretched, surprised by the energy once again flowing through my limbs.

"Whatcha need, love?"

I turned back to him, biting the tip of my finger. Lust flared deep in his gunmetal eyes, but he stayed where he was. This carefulness with me was what I disliked most about Murphy this go-round. I wanted—no, I needed—him to need me as much as I needed him.

Subtlety wasn't going to work. I whipped off my sleep shirt and dropped in onto the edge of the bed. "I need you to shower with me."

Murphy's smile was bright. "That'd be my pleasure."

Ended up being mine. Twice.

———◆———

The venue appeared huge—and really open. Originally slated for the Moore Theater, which held an intimate eighteen hundred people, the label had moved the performance to the White River Amphitheater, about an hour south of Seattle. Ten thousand bright-red seats snuggled up close to the stage. Each of the original ticket buyers received an actual seat for the inconvenience of the move and additional drive out of Seattle. An expansive green lawn behind the covered chairs would soon be dotted with blankets, chairs and lots of screaming fans. Large metal towers with banners of each of the band member's faces lined the concrete walkway to the center, sentinels of doom if one of them housed

Jordan and his firearms. I shivered as I walked in.

"Feels like a fishbowl with a really big stage," Noelle muttered, and I tried to stifle my nervous giggle.

Four more security guards met us at the band entrance while another four stood just inside, arms crossed over their chests. The hallways were cavernous and smelled of old sweat mixed with industrial cleaning products. Gross.

Harry, Jackaroo's band manager, met us there, talking into a headset and glaring down at a clipboard. I'd seen him a couple of times this week but hadn't made the effort to say more than hello.

He glanced up and his smile was brilliant. I edged closer to Noelle, wondering if he planned to take a bite out of me. I'd never liked Harry, hating the way he treated his wife and two daughters.

"You've done it, Ets! Packed out the house. Nice job staying top of the media. Press conference went swimmingly."

"Rack off, Harry. This whole situation is because Mila has a stalker. As in someone trying to hurt her."

Harry clucked, concern washing over his features in a water-fall of fakeness. "Right, of course. Absolutely. The record label is thrilled with the attention, just thrilled with your impromptu sales numbers. When you boys get back in the studio, we'll be able to hammer in a nice new deal." Harry's eyes burned brighter as he considered his upcoming windfall.

"I don't like him," Noelle muttered.

"Because he's a reptile dressed in a suit?" I whispered back.

Noelle squeezed my hand. I turned and flashed my own fake smile at Harry, who'd moved over to shake my hand. His gaze calculated my worth to him, his smile never sliding an inch. But I could tell from the look in his eyes that he'd heard me, and he didn't like my thoughts.

"Pleasure to see you again," he said, his voice about as warm as a Tasmanian dawn. "Though I'm surprised you came back after Murphy's success with 'She's So Bad.'"

"Been a while," I responded. "How are your lovely wife and children?"

"Glad for the income I provide them with. Sally's got the shopping bug. Wouldn't do to disappoint her." Why did the words sound menacing? I held my ground, chin up so as not to show my fear.

Harry shook Noelle's hand, and she waited until he'd turned away to rub her palm against her skirt.

Briar stopped next to me and shuddered. "Hayden isn't fond of him," she said.

"I think he heard me refer to him as a reptile," I said, eyeing the back of Harry's expensive and highly style head.

"That's part of what I like about you, Mila," Briar laughed. "You call it as you see it."

"Not sure I made an ally."

Briar shrugged. "He'd never be one. Let's go to the waiting area. I want to see what type of snacks they've stockpiled."

Noelle and I trailed behind her, but soon we were surrounded by bodyguards. Being here, at this venue, with one of the hottest bands in the world was so surreal. Not my life at all. Did Murphy have to put up with this throughout his tour? No wonder he'd been ready for some normalcy.

"Hayden hated the tour. The constancy of being on for the fans grated. Fabulous! Guacamole." Briar dove at the huge bowl of chips and dip. She piled a plate and snagged a water. "I was nervous this morning, so I ran about ten miles. Hayden grumbled through the last four, but I needed to burn off that energy. Now I'm starving." She eyed a plate of cookies and snatched one of those as well.

I snagged a water, too nervous to eat, and wandered over to sit next to Briar. Once settled with her plate balanced on her knees, she devoured her cookie before she began to make headway through her massive pile of chips and guac.

"You run every morning?" Up until this week, I'd always been active. I hadn't run, but this morning I had enjoyed my shower.

Briar chuckled before she popped another chip. "I try to. Before and after Hayden and I spend some quality time together." She raised her brows, and I giggled.

"No wonder you're hungry."

"She's always hungry for me," Hayden said as he walked into the room. Briar tipped her face up for a kiss. Hayden obliged with alacrity and Briar's hands came up to cup his cheeks. Noelle stood near the snack table, holding a baby carrot and talking to Jake. Their budding friendship surprised me because Noelle was interested in pushing forward a permanent relationship with Kent. Or, she had been. She and I needed to talk.

Murphy pulled me into his arms. I loved that he could—and would—sweep me off my feet. I smiled as I pressed my lips to his, savoring the feel of his warm, soft mouth against mine. His days-old stubble chafed at my chin as he tilted my face, bringing me closer and tighter to his body.

Our tongues met, tangled. I moaned against him, thrilling at his rising passion. This time in our relationship was intense as we relearned each other. I couldn't get enough. Murphy pulled back with a groan, placing a soft, chaste kiss to my lips.

We spent the next couple of hours talking, laughing, simply enjoying each other's company.

"Five till show time, boys," Harry called.

Murphy immediately leaned down and kissed me, an even more heated dual of tongue and teeth than earlier.

"Not my best idea just before we have to go on."

"Why's that?" I clasped my hands around his neck as he lowered me to the floor.

"Because now I want to do more with you, and I can't."

"Later," I whispered, pressing my lips back to his.

"Lots of later," he said, his voice dipping low into that sexy rasp I loved so much. "I mean that, Mila. You're wearing my ring." He tipped his head to the platinum band on my finger. I'd removed it to swim, but he'd settled it back on my finger before our press conference, and I hadn't taken it off since. "That means something, just like it did when I slid it on your finger then. Something we'll work out soon."

My eyes felt round, huge. I couldn't breathe. Did he mean… No, I shouldn't get my hopes up. We were different people, learning each other again. While he might be impetuous, that didn't mean he planned to marry me. He pressed his forehead against mine, breathing deep against my neck. "I'm glad you're here, Mila."

He kissed me again, so of course, I responded. "Me, too," I whispered as he pulled back. "I-I hated taking it off."

"Because you weren't meant to."

"Let's go, gents," Harry called.

"You watch from the wings. Don't leave Kevin's sight." Murphy's eyes were filled with concern.

I smiled. "Promise."

He hugged me tight, pulling me off the ground once more. "I'm scared to go on stage, and it has very little to do with the mob out there. I need to see you during the show."

"Okay."

"I need to know you're safe."

"I am."

"I want to forget about this and carry you back to our suite so I can love you all night."

"You can, as soon as you finish working."

"I'm holding you to that."

I giggled and kissed him again. "I hope so."

CHAPTER TWENTY-SIX
Murphy

The lights were too bright, thanks to the setting sun. Hayden and Jake were struggling to look out into the crowd, too. We were three songs in and while we sounded great, this show wouldn't go down in our personal top ten.

I glanced over at the spot I'd told Mila to stay in, and smiled at her, my eyes lighting when she smiled back. I stepped in and sang my part, focusing on the frets as I worked my way through the bridge. We finished hard, and the crowd went wild. I walked to the stage hand.

"Can you fix the bloody lights? They're blinding us."

He nodded, started talking into his headset. I winked at Mila and drifted back onto the stage in time to rev into a faster melody Hayden had written the year before. Good stuff, this was. He had an ear for it. I lost myself in the music, letting the feelings build and crash over me. Jake grinned. Damn, my job was fun.

I didn't even glance at the girls flashing me in the front row. As Hayden and Flip had said most of the tour, not interested. I'd love on Mila later.

We finished the set hard. Now came the screaming-crowd-multiple-encores part of the show that I found the most exhausting. We exited. None of the ladies joined us and dread pooled in my gut.

"Back out, gents."

Hayden scowled, and I'm sure I mirrored the expression. "Where are Mila and Briar?"

"Your fans are waiting," Harry said. He shoved me back on stage. I bowed again and smiled but anger bubbled thick in my chest. No bloody way Harry ever shoved me again.

Hayden and Jake came out but we'd lost our momentum. None of us worried about the final, final encore.

"Thanks everyone for supporting such an important cause! You've been great," I called into the microphone. I'd prepared an entire speech telling the fans about my youngest brother, before our final song. Not happening. Not now. I whipped my guitar strap off, signaling the end of the show. The crowd's calls still rang in my ears as I hustled off the stage. Mila wasn't there, where I asked her to stand. Neither were Briar or Noelle, but the security was still thick. I handed my guitar to one of the roadies and ran across the chords and wires littering the stage floor. I burst into the lounge room where we'd left our personal items, and Briar whipped around, eyelids rimmed in red, tears still shining on her cheeks.

"Where's Mila?" I asked. She's with Noelle, I thought. But when I didn't see her crazy ringlets either, my lungs started to ache. Where was my phone? I'd call her.

Harry cleared his throat. "She called a cab about half way through your set."

I grabbed his shirt, pulling him up until we were nose to nose. "The hell you say?" I growled. Jake yanked on my arm but I didn't let go. I was going to hurt the little wanker. Bad.

"She got a call or a text," Harry said with a shrug. "She said she had to leave. She didn't want her friend to go with her, but the girl insisted."

Kevin was still here, in the lounge. Trying to pull me off Harry. "Wait! She left without a bodyguard? Kevin, how could you do that? You know what Jordan's capable of!"

"I didn't let her go anywhere," Kevin said. His voice was sharp with anger. I dropped Harry and turned, prepared to run from the room. This couldn't be happening. Not again. I wasn't losing Mila again. If Jordan got to her first…

Kevin and Jake stood in front of me, barring the exit.

"Move!"

Hayden joined them. "I've got a car coming round, mate. You can leave in a few minutes. But you have to calm down. You're not rational."

"He's going to try to hurt her again. What could he have threatened her with?"

Briar stepped forward, her right arm folded across her body. "Tanya. The woman at the hospital. He said he'd kill her if Mila didn't come immediately. She called the cab and bolted from the room just as Harry was coming to check on us."

I groaned, slowly becoming aware that Jake had grasped me under my arms and was holding me up. Of course Mila went. She'd do anything for the people she cared about, and she cared deeply for Tanya, for her baby.

"Why didn't you come get me?" I asked, my eyes meeting Briar's, which filled with tears again. I wasn't trying to be accusatory, but my words were sharp, studded with worry.

Hayden went to hug her, but his face settled in a firm line. "We'd have stopped the show, Bri. Mila is more important."

"I know, but Harry locked Kevin and me in this room and you don't have your phones on you." She gestured to where all our mobiles lay on the catering table.

We turned as one to gape at Harry. Before I could open my mouth, Jake said, "You're fired."

"Wait, Murphy, there's more to this," Briar said, her voice shaking. "Jordan also threatened your mom."

"He's in the US. What can he do to my mum?"

"I don't know," Briar said, her eyes stormy. "Mila didn't say, but she was really upset."

"Call Mum," I said. "Tell her what's going on. Stay on the line with her until she gets somewhere safe."

Jake pressed the phone to his ear.

I turned to Kevin. "We need a plan." I yanked at my hair. "Hospital. Fastest route—you get that for me?"

"On it." He typed something into his phone.

"I wanted to call the Seattle PD," Briar said. "But Mila showed me the text. He said he'd kill Tanya if the police came to the hospital before her. Kevin called in some of his friends who do this type of thing. They're going to meet Mila at the hospital."

"When did this happen?" I asked.

"About thirty minutes ago," Kevin said, but worry pulled at his brows. "She has a head start."

"The concert traffic is going to snarl things up."

I nodded, letting them know I heard. "Car. I need to get out of here. Now."

"We'll stay. Do the media thing here," Hayden said, waving us off. He pressed a kiss to the side of Briar's head. Goddammit, I wanted to be doing that to Mila now myself.

Kevin and I jogged toward the exit, Jake talking to mum, a couple steps behind. Kevin grabbed a set of keys from the waiting roadie and hustled us into the car, keeping his body between us and the reporters who'd turned and started snapping pictures, yelling questions. Breathing was laborious, no way I'd be coherent. Not that I'd waste time on the media when Mila was in danger.

"Keep talking to me, Mum. Don't stop." Jake slid into the car first.

"Let me talk to her," I said. Jake handed me the phone.

"You'll get there in time, Murphy, love. Mila's smart." Mum sniffled into the phone. "She'll be 'right."

"What if she's not?" I whispered. My throat closed.

"Don't think that. Don't ever think that, son. Stay positive. For Mila."

I hissed out a breath. So much to say. I hadn't told Mila I loved her. She needed to know.

"What were you doing when Jake called?"

"Making lunch."

Strange to think Mum was seventeen hours ahead of me—living in the next day. A day when I hoped to hold Mila again. My knuckles whitened as I gripped the phone tighter, and my thigh jiggled, but I stayed on my mobile while she finished the drive to the police station. There, I talked to the officer and then to a detective, telling him what I knew. I gave them Mila's phone number, which she wasn't answering—I rang her number near constantly while I spoke to my mum.

As angry as I was that Mila left me after she'd promised to be there, waiting for me, I worried more about her surviving the next few hours. By the time we were on the open highway, another twenty minutes had passed, putting Mila nearly an hour closer to Jordan. To find and hurt her.

I handed Jake his phone, tilted my head back, and did something I'd never done before. Not when my dad beat my mum, not when house foreclosure was imminent. Not when Mila dumped me the first time.

I prayed.

CHAPTER TWENTY-SEVEN
Mila

Much as I wanted to silence my phone, I couldn't do that. I had to wait for the next set of instructions from Jordan. But each time Murphy's name popped up over the last twenty minutes, I inched closer to losing control.

I shoved my hand into the pocket of my cardigan once again, wishing Murphy didn't have my pills. Ever since Jordan's call, I was jittery, on edge. In desperate need of my Xanax, my escape and prison all in one.

Ironic that I'd finally started to see relief from the symptoms just to fall right back in, harder than before.

Much as I wanted to talk Noelle out of coming with me, I wasn't able to do so. Her presence next to me both added to and mitigated some of my worries. "I want you to go to the front desk and wait there," I said.

Noelle was stubbornly silent, but her white knuckles showed she was just as scared as I was. I gave in and texted Murphy. What if this was my last chance to say something to him?

Jordan called. He has Tanya. I had to come. I love you. Then, now. Always.

Not enough. I wasn't sure I'd ever finish telling Murphy everything.

I swallowed down the bile that threatening to spew forth so many times in the few hours. The cab pulled up in front of the hospital. I leaned forward and handed the cabbie my credit card.

"Go to the nearest police station," I begged Noelle.

"I'm not leaving you," she said. Her lips trembled before she tightened her jaw. "Though he probably wants to cap me, too."

I took her hands in mine, unsurprised hers were clammy, too. "Please? Let the dispatch know I went inside because Jordan threatened Tanya's life." Noelle's nod was reluctant, her face too pale.

"Lady, I can't let you walk in there knowing that mad man's trying to get you. It's been all over the news."

"There's a pregnant woman inside who's going to be shot if I don't respond in person in the next"—I glanced down at my phone—"ten minutes. You don't have a choice." I sucked in a breath as I watched his weathered face crumple. "And neither do I." I hugged Noelle hard. My chin wobbled. "Tell Murphy I love him. That he's all I think about."

I slid out of the car before either Noelle or the driver could say something else. I ran through the front door before my knees turned to mush. I shuddered, wondering if this would be my last chance. To run. To breathe. To love.

The front atrium's bright lights slammed against my night vision–sensitive eyes, the bustle of a normal hospital mind-numbing.

"I need to report a threat to a patient here," I said, my knees knocking. Please don't let me get Tanya and her baby killed. I cleared my throat and shoved my phone at the security guard. "He said he was in her room. That he'd kill her."

The guard's bushy white brows shot up, his thin lips flattening further, but he picked up the phone and dialed. Once he'd given the information to the police dispatcher, he looked up at me, his rheumy eyes filled with concern.

"Shelter in place, young lady. You don't do anything until the police show up."

The warning signal blared from the speakers. I startled hard.

Oh, God. What had I done? What if Jordan knew the signal? What if he hurt Tanya now because I'd called in the threat?

I sprinted away from the desk. The guard yelled at me to stop but I barreled into the elevator, slamming my hand against the Close button, before pressing the button for the third floor.

Stepping back from the control panel, I sagged against the wall. I gripped the metal bar in the elevator as I sailed upward to face one of my demons.

I would end this sick fascination of Jordan's. On my terms. No matter the outcome, I wasn't going to fear him again.

I'd left my phone at the guard's stand. Dammit. I'd wanted the connection to Murphy. I pulled his image up. Mentally, I traced his thick brows, the strong line of his nose. Those sharp cheekbones and stubborn jaw. His soft lips. With his image planted firmly in front of me, I took a deep breath. I would survive this to see Murphy again. If he still wanted me after my stunt tonight.

When Murphy was upset or angry, he mouthed off, acted out. He'd do something incredibly stupid—like talk to the media—and destroy our chance at a life together. Even with his spontaneous edge that teased the line of self-destruction, I loved him. I loved him because he couldn't quite control his emotions. Because he cared about *me* so much. If I made it out of here tonight, I'd tell him that in person.

Or I might die in this building tonight and Murphy would implode as well. I didn't like that option near as much.

The elevator chimed and the doors slid open.

The series of beeps—hospital code for credible threat and shelter in place—no longer sounded. My footfalls seemed achingly loud in the too-quiet space.

No one walked the halls. Most of the doors were shut. A hand slid onto my shoulder. I jumped and screamed.

"Jesus, Mila. You almost gave me a heart attack," Noelle's cheeks paled.

"What do you think happened to me? You were supposed to go to the police station. Please."

She swallowed as she scanned the waiting room nearby, noting, as I had, the strange quietness of the place. "ICU is under heavy lockdown, with additional police and security, emergency surgeries sent to other area hospitals, but the rest of the wards and here…" she spread her arms out to encompass the main hospital. "This is as barebones as the place can get."

"Noelle—"

"I called Sasha. She moved Tanya down to ICU. As soon as you jumped from the car. I told her why. She said she'd do it."

I closed my eyes against the fear trying to take over my mind. The need to flee was consuming. "Thank you. Now go home. *Please.*"

"Kevin called. He's asked some of his cop buddies to find you here."

"I have to go in there. I have to be sure he hasn't hurt Tanya or the baby."

The alarm sounded again. I tensed, expecting Jordan to pop out of one of the rooms. She tugged my shoulders and turned me to face her. "You don't, but I can't stop you. Just know you aren't doing this alone. Your job is to stay safe and get home with your sexalicious boyfriend." She hugged me hard and disappeared to the left—toward the stairs—before I managed to speak past the knot of emotion in my throat.

I stepped into the L and D ward hall, also silent.

I pulled out my badge and moved through the quiet, sterile hallway. Two more sets of doors and I was in Tanya's room, my heart pounding a million miles per second. Her bed lay empty, just as Noelle said it would. I bit my lip.

I prayed Jordan hadn't shot her as he'd threatened. The bed sheets were white, not stained in blood. I gripped the edge of the bed, my finger wound tight into the metal bar and hoped for Tanya's—her baby's—continued safety.

I opened my eyes, listening, waiting for Jordan to come out from his hiding place. One minute turned into ten, maybe more. Nothing. Jordan wasn't here.

Okay. Something was wrong.

I touched Tanya's pillow, the fetal monitor. "I'm so sorry," I whispered. "Be safe." Without my phone, I didn't know what to do next. I stepped out into the hall, moving slowly and with as much caution as I could muster.

The hall's bright lighting was a shock. I blinked a few times, trying to acclimate to the difference.

"Ms. Trask?"

Three men jogged toward me. I pushed my back against the wall.

"We're colleagues of Kevin Granger. He asked us to see you safely back to your hotel room."

I opened my mouth but no words came out. Instead, I watched, horror making my vision tunnel, as red blossomed across the man's chest. Another man—an innocent man—collapsed next to the first. The third pulled his gun from his holster but he, too, was shot. Before I could move, a hand gripped my wrist.

"So nice of you to join me," Jordan murmured. "I was beginning to worry you didn't care about the whiney bitch here as much as I'd anticipated."

The barrel of the gun dug into the back of my neck, which was slicked in sweat. Much as I wanted to see someone round the corner, I didn't doubt that Jordan would shoot another person without thinking twice. Especially Murphy, whom Jordan hated with an obsession bordering on mania.

The cold metal warmed against my skin; the heat transferring from my body up into the machine designed for destruction.

I'd missed my chance to run while he'd been shooting those men. Stupid. So stupid.

This time, I must break the cycle. Even though Murphy disagreed, this was my fight. While Jordan was bigger, stronger and probably faster, I was smarter, lighter and knew this building better. I wasn't the fearful, incompetent girl Jordan met all those years ago.

I just needed time to come up with another plan.

"Why are you doing this?" I asked.

"Your boyfriend flushed me out with his stupid media stunt. The police raided my motel room earlier today. Only sheer luck had me on the other side of the building."

I slowed my steps, not wanting to leave the bleeding men. Not wanting Jordan to touch me.

"Hurry up," he hissed, poking me in the back of the neck. The gun's barrel caught my vertebrae and I winced.

"You're hurting me," I whispered. Jordan liked it when I played the helpless damsel. For now, it was my best defense. "Guns scare me. Why did you have to bring a gun, Jordan?" I slowed my steps in time with my question, hoping to distract him long enough for someone to see us.

"You weren't paying attention. I told you, you are *mine*. Now, we'll finally live together with your mum. A family. Happy."

His delusions were beyond insane. I slowed my steps again, wracking my brain for a topic to keep him distracted.

"The laws here are different. Stalking carries harsher penalties here than in Australia." I crossed my fingers, hoping Jordan hadn't bothered to study the differences.

He snorted. "I'm not stalking you, Mila."

As I rounded the next corner, I caught a flash of movement, springy curls flying out behind a hot pink shirt. Noelle. She ducked back into a patient's room and settle behind the door, leaving it slightly ajar.

"You killed my chances at conceiving when you murdered my baby."

"I did no such thing, Mila. That was an accident. You shouldn't have tried to ride away from me. All this time, if you'd just done what you were supposed to, we could have avoided you being hurt. The police. This gun. But each time you need more incentive."

"You have to threaten the lives of the people I care about to make me stay in the same room as you. I will never, ever love you, Jordan."

"Stop lying," he hissed. He grabbed my arm, his fingers digging deep into my flesh. "You've always loved me. I saw it in your eyes, then, whilst you lived with your mother and me. You've become such a tease, Mila. I'm going to slap it out of you one of these days. No man likes to be challenged."

"It's a simple fact. I hate you. I'll always hate you. You destroyed the most important relationship in my life. You killed my baby."

"You weren't supposed to be hurt that day, but I'm not sorry

I destroyed the rock star's spawn. He's not meant to have you, Mila. You don't want a connection to that type of man."

"I loved my baby, and I love Murphy. I always will. You—you're just the sad, pathetic stalker who can't get the woman he wants without threats and weapons."

His hand moved from my arm to my hair. He yanked it, hard. My head fell back against his shoulder and my eyes filled with tears but I met his stare with my own, willing him to see all the loathing I felt for him.

"Go to the stairwell," Jordan said.

Much as I didn't want to respond, didn't want to look at him, my head hurt. "I can't walk like this."

He let go of my hair, and I started to pull away. He pressed his palm to my throat and kept the gun pressed to the base of my skull.

"You could just end this," I said, my eyes steady. Part of me wondered why I should stave off the inevitable. Jordan would kill me, eventually. At least if he did so now no one else would be hurt. "Pull the trigger. You know I don't want to go with you."

His eyes widened. "I don't want to kill you. I love you. I want to take care of you."

I stepped away, wincing at the pain in my neck and my tender scalp. I put up my arms, motioning around us. "This isn't love. This is psychotic."

His eyes narrowed as his nostrils flared. "Go down the stairs, Mila. Now."

I sped up so he wouldn't touch me again. But that just meant he kept pace and we were that much closer to leaving the building. If I did, if I got in a car with him, I wouldn't end this night alive.

Two flights of stairs to disarm him. Right. I sucked in air, trying to fill my lungs with as much oxygen as possible. Muscles needed more air to work optimally.

We came up on the door. If it was like many others, it would open with ponderous slowness and shut even more slowly. I couldn't try to slam it against his wrist and get him to drop the gun. I stood at the large metal door, unwilling to push it open. The stairwell, like the lot outside, was too far from the slim protection of the armed guards Kevin sent, the ones who were even now bleeding out. Jordan growled as he reached around me, impatient to get out of there.

I hadn't learned enough in my defense classes to beat Jordan in hand-to-hand combat, but I practiced using a man's bodyweight against him. It's a basic tenet of the form: unbalance the already unstable. Over and over again, I'd practiced these moves. Had I known then I'd need the training?

A siren screamed, bouncing off the high ceiling and the wide, empty hall. I flinched at the noise, as did Jordan. He turned his head toward the alarm. Noelle darted away from the red box, toward one of the doors. I shoved my left foot back between both of his and gripped his arm on the door. I used his body weight to carry him forward, over my left shoulder. His right hand—the one with the gun—flailed. Heat seared my ear as a bullet whizzed by my head. Jordan tumbled into the metal door, his head catching on the release bar.

He dropped the gun as he tried to break his fall, his body still careening forward into the stairwell. I spun out from under his body and shoved as hard as I could, trying to force him off the first step. My ears roared with the blood filling them. Hope built.

The more noise he made, the quicker someone would find us.

Get away as fast as you can. You may only have seconds. Make them count. My self-defense instructor's words filled my head, and I ran. I darted down the corridor, breathless from the adrenaline.

The gun! Why didn't I pick it up? My steps faltered but I pushed forward, unwilling to give up my small victory. Going back would be stupid.

Should I find a place to hide? I didn't want to get caught in a small, enclosed place without another exit, but I also didn't want to stay in the hall where I was easy to spot—and easy to pick off with that gun.

I swung round the corner and slammed into a much larger body. His arms slid up to my shoulders, steadying me as I glanced up. I met the concerned gaze of the heavyset security guard who'd warned me to shelter in place in the hospital's atrium.

"He's behind me." I wasn't sure how loud I'd spoken. My ears were buzzing and my head felt like it was stuffed with cotton. The man shoved me behind him. As I turned, a scream built in my throat. Jordan, head bloodied, raised his gun. I didn't see him pull the trigger or witness the flash, but the impact was instantaneous. The guard's thick body flinched as if struck by a hard blow. I screamed as he started to fall. Jordan walked forward and his voice was loud enough for me to hear over the din in my head.

"Don't hide from me."

He'd shot at least four people tonight. Plus Hank at the hotel pool. And those were just the people I knew about. He trained the gun on me, right in the middle of my chest. The barrel moved up, to the left. Every muscle in my body tightened to quivering urgency.

"I'll give you everything you ever wanted. I'll love you right," Jordan said, his face collapsing with grief. "Why isn't that enough for you?"

The ringing in my ears distorted his voice, but I was sure I'd heard Murphy scream my name. Jordan's facial features filled with loathing, and I could see in his eyes that he planned to shoot again. Shoot Murphy.

"Because you want to control my feelings. My body. My love. And you can't."

I lunged forward. Jordan's eyes widened as my body flew into motion. He wouldn't hurt Murphy. I'd lost our baby, but I would *not* lose Murphy, too. Even if… even if he didn't want me forever, even if I was just a passing fancy to him, Murphy deserved his chance at life, at happiness, and that meant ending this standoff. Now.

Whatever Jordan read in my face caused him to flinch back. The bullet hit, ripping through my skin, shattering bone.

I screamed, but the sound dulled as the pain hit. I looked at Jordan, eyes wide, mouth open as I gasped for air. He rushed toward me, arms outstretched as I fell to my knees. I reached for the gun, ignoring the searing heat against my palm as I ripped at the barrel.

He called my name as I pulled harder, adrenaline spiking as I needed it. "Mila!" he sobbed.

The gun. Get the gun away from him so he wouldn't shoot Murphy.

CHAPTER TWENTY-EIGHT
Murphy

Noelle's frantic call said Jordan planned to lead her from the building by the south entrance. I kept running. They'd last been up here. Thanks to Kevin's insane driving skills, we made it to the hospital in under twenty minutes, an impossible feat that nearly killed us half a dozen times. Not that I was complaining. Fast. She must know the odds of being found were low once she left the building. She'd figure out how to stay here.

Another shot. Shouts of alarm rippled through the ward like a wave cresting in the ocean only to be hushed by their own fear of discovery. My legs pumped faster.

He'd broken her before. He'd do it again in an effort to own her body.

Another corridor. I rounded the corner. She stood there, at the far end. Her back was to me, her beautiful hair floated wild around her head, her back straight. Jordan stood mere feet away, the gun pointed at her chest. One of the guards lay crumpled at her feet, too still.

"Mila!"

Her name ripped from my chest. Jordan raised the gun. He wanted to shoot at me, not her.

"I'll give you everything you ever wanted. I'll love you right," Jordan said, his face collapsing. "Why isn't that enough for you?"

"Because you want to control my feelings," Mila said, her voice steady. How could it be so steady? "My body. My love. And you can't."

I didn't take my eyes off Mila. I was still too far away. I couldn't wrap my arms around her and shield her. I ran faster, my lungs convulsing, needing air.

Her whole body quivered as if preparing for flight.

No.

She jumped forward. Jordan flinched. The gun's report was more menacing than anything I'd ever heard. Mila screamed, a high, thin sound that cut off as she sank to her knees. Her shoulders hunched. Bloody hell. He'd done it. He *shot* her.

Jordan reached forward. I ran closer. Mila grabbed at the gun. I vaulted over the prone guard and lowered my shoulder. I'd played rugby as a young boy, and tackling was one of the first skills I mastered. Mila struggled. Jordan held firm, reached his hand forward to touch her face. My shoulder caught him in his lower jaw. Bone hit bone and, thanks to my speed, his jaw snapped as I continued pummeling him, sending us both crashing to the ground.

Angling my body just so, I made sure Jordan's head hit the floor first. Unprotected, his head slammed into the linoleum with a rich *thunk*, as my chest slammed into his body, his head bounced and hit the ground again.

If I was lucky, he'd remain knocked out. On my knees, his body between my thighs, I searched for his gun. Where was it? Footsteps and shouts pounded around us.

"Step back! Mr. Etsam, get off the suspect."

"He's not a suspect. He's a bloody killer."

The police were here. I didn't care about the gun. Mila. He'd shot her. At such close range. I scrambled up and turned. She'd slumped down, cheek resting on her arm. Her face was so pale. Her lips white.

"Murphy," she whispered. I fell to my knees beside her. "Love you."

Two men in scrubs raced around the corner, pulling a gurney. Much as I wanted to push them away, I couldn't. The doctors here would save her. They *had* to.

A hand slid to my shoulder and I jerked.

"She's going into OR," Noelle said, her voice thick with tears. Clearing her throat, she continued. "One of our best surgeons is here. He'll do the surgery."

"I need her to be okay."

Noelle squeezed my shoulder. I'd gone on too long in my sentence. *I need her*.

That summed up everything, and the fear clawing through my gut told me I might not see her alive again.

"Come on. Best we can do is be in the waiting room when they come out."

"What about Jordan?" I asked.

We turned in time to see Jordan struggling against the officers holding him. His broken jaw hung slack. I smiled, thrilled he felt some of the pain he'd inflicted on Mila.

With an enraged howl, Jordan lurched toward me, grappling at the police man's belt for a weapon. I shoved Noelle behind me, pressing her tight against the wall. Jordan and the officer grappled as another officer yelled for him to stop. Their guns pointed at Jordan, who'd managed to unholster the weapon. His eyes glazed with hate, he yanked it from the belt. Immediately, multiple shots rang out. Jordan, like Mila, lurched, quivered.

He died before he hit the floor.

Noelle's hands gripped into the back of my shirt, and I eased forward so her nose no longer pressed so hard into my shoulder blade.

"You okay?" I asked.

"I don't want to see him."

I turned and wrapped my arms around her, keeping her face pressed against my chest. "He's dead, Noelle. He can't hurt you or Mila or anyone else again."

Her body shook but she nodded. One of the officers led us back down the hall the way we'd come, away from Jordan and the guard. Toward the waiting room, I hoped. I needed to be close to Mila. No, I needed to hold her, to know she was going to make it through being bloody shot.

One of Noelle's nursing friends was there, offering water as she shepherded us into a waiting room. We sat there until another man, hair tousled and eyes wide, ran into the room. He dropped to his knees in front of Noelle, touching her cheek. She opened her eyes and peeled her other cheek from my tear-dampened shirt. She wrapped her arms around the man and shivered. He held her as he stood, transferring his bum to the chair while Noelle curled into him.

"Kent," he said, his voice low.

"Murphy," I replied.

"Did you really step between Noelle and the gunman? That's what I heard the officers say as I came down the hall."

My brows drew low in a scowl. "Course, mate. I wasn't going to let him shoot her."

Kent swallowed hard, his eyes bright. "Thank you."

I nodded.

"Have they told you anything?" Kent asked.

"No," Noelle mumbled. "Murphy's been comforting me, and

I was too shaken to go ask. I should be better about this. I'm a nurse."

Kent slid his hand over Noelle's mass of wild curls. "You're in shock, darling. Nothing wrong with that after the last couple of hours. Sit here a second? I'll find out."

He was gone for a long time but neither Noelle nor I spoke. We stared at the entrance, both of us willing someone to walk in.

"What happened to Tanya?" I asked. Shame rippled over my skin. The poor girl. I'd only just remembered her.

Noelle started. "Oh! They moved her down to ICU. It's got better security. She's fine."

"You sure?"

Noelle nodded. "I talked to the nurse on call, had her make a big show of needing to move Tanya for testing. Jordan was in the room, then, and Sasha—the nurse—will have to give her statement to the police, too, I'm sure. They moved most of the women and babies from this floor to other sections of the hospital before the shelter in place took effect."

"Calm under pressure. You medical people amaze me."

Noelle snorted. "Pretty sure I just experienced an epic meltdown."

"Nah. You stayed with Mila." I gripped her hand. "Thank you for that. Thank you for letting us know where she was. Made the whole rescue possible." I swallowed hard. *If* we'd rescued Mila. Mum said to stay positive for Mila. I was trying, but it was bloody hard.

Kent returned and resettled Noelle in his lap once again. She snuggled in tight against him with a familiarity that bore out when he cupped her waist, his thumb rubbing in a soothing rhythm against her ribs.

"Mila's still in surgery. He shot her clavicle. The surgeons are working to rebuild it."

"But she's going to make it?" I asked—ok, more like choked. Bollocks. That couldn't be my voice.

"She lost a lot of blood, and the impact at such close range increases the severity of the trauma, but one of the nurses in OR stepped out long enough to tell me he hit her high, more in the muscle just above the bone. Granted, that means closer to her neck. As long as he didn't clip her carotid artery, she should be stable soon."

I closed my eyes and dropped my head to my hands. "And if it did hit her artery?" I managed to ask.

"That's a lot harder to fix," Kent said, his tone careful enough for me to realize he didn't want to talk about the possibility. "Not impossible, but hard."

"He didn't hit any nerves, right?" Noelle asked.

"I don't think so. I don't have any other information, but what Nancy told me is pretty good news. Let's run with that for now."

Hayden sped into the room, holding Briar's hand.

"Murphy!" She slammed into the chair next to me, her blue eyes searching mine. "The reports we've listened to on the way over have been confusing. What's happened? Is Mila okay?"

"Dunno how the sack of shit got into the building. Kevin texted that he's in the OR downstairs where they took his buddies. All three of them were shot trying to get Mila out of the building. Jordan shot Mila." The words felt wrong in my mouth, sounded worse as they met my ears.

"The number of media outlets outside is insane," Hayden said.

"The reports on the radio and Internet said multiple people were killed."

"Jordan downed at least four men. I don't know anything about their conditions yet. The police shot him. Jordan's dead."

Hayden dropped into the chair next to Briar's. "Holy hell. This is a bloody nightmare. Any word on Mila?"

"She's in surgery," Kent said.

"Hi, Kent," Briar said. "Sorry to see you here, like this."

He smiled as he pressed a kiss to Noelle's hair, who'd squeezed her eyes shut as we retold what we knew.

Two uniformed officers walked in, needing statements from Noelle and me. Kent wouldn't let her out of his lap, so we sat there, on those plastic chairs and told them our pieces of the story.

Briar stiffened as I talked, tears pooling in her eyes. Hayden took her hand and squeezed.

"This is Harry's fault, too. I can't believe he locked us in that room," Briar snapped.

I could see why Hayden was drawn to the woman. I hoped—one day—she and I could become friends. She'd make a great one to Mila, too.

"Don't worry, love," Hayden said. "Jake may have fired him, but I still plan to deal with Harry."

I nodded my head in thanks, my throat too clogged with my emotions. Where was Jake? I was nearly as worried about him as I was Mila.

Noelle told everyone about watching Mila walk by the room she was hiding in, of seeing the gun in Jordan's hand. Calling 911 with the exact location of the downed men and the route Jordan was taking from the building before she called me. I owed her another big thank-you. More than likely, her call saved Mila's life and hopefully that of the men sent here to help her.

God, I hoped it did.

"What about the other men?" I asked the officers.

"The three we found together are still in surgery. The doctors think they have a good chance. The security guard didn't make it to the operating room."

Silence descended, heavy with worry.

Jake bolted into the room, trailed by another uniformed officer. I wasn't sure if the policeman was following Jake for safety's sake or chasing him down. "Mum's straight. Rosemary Jones is being questioned, but Mum said all she'd done so far was whine about what a difficult child Mila was, how hard she tried to keep her safe." He slammed into a chair across from me, out of breath and red-faced. The officer hovered at the entrance to the room. "How's Mila?"

"Shot," I said.

Kent started talking, but I didn't bother to listen. I dropped my head into my shaking hands and tried to breathe. I wanted Mila. Beside me. I needed to touch her, hear her voice.

Tell her it wasn't pity or guilt that made me want to spend my life with her. It was her determination to help people, her intelligence, her love. No matter what happened, no matter how hurt she was, I would take care of her and love her the way she deserved to be loved. The way I should have anyway. As I'd promised her the day I put that platinum band on her finger.

The officers left and the wait continued.

CHAPTER TWENTY-NINE
Murphy

The woman encapsulated more stubbornness than three mules. "You are not going to the concert tonight. You were *shot* six days ago. You almost died." I tugged at my eyebrow ring, fiddled with my lip ring, anything to keep from breaking down.

She lifted her right hand, on her good side, grimacing a little as it jostled her other shoulder. "Before you come up with all the reasons I shouldn't go, I've been released with my doctor's blessing. Noelle's coming with me to the Showbox. She'll monitor me. And I want to see you play. I didn't get to see enough at the charity concert."

"I'm not going. I told you, I want to stay home with you." I glanced over at Alpie, who'd settled into Mila's other side. The cockatoo turned her head so her bright black eyes gleamed as she stared back at me. "Fu-'atoo!" she growled. She waddled over Mila's lap and rubbed her beak against my hand. "Love-oo."

I rubbed my forefinger under her chin. "You're glad I brought Mila home. I told you the trip to the hospital was a bad idea."

The bird dipped her head, her crest rising. "Mil! Love-oo. Shush."

"You two were so cute. I can't believe you snuck her in to see me."

"Bloody bird wouldn't stop calling your name."

She smiled as she raised my good arm and placed her palm on my chest. "Please, Murphy."

"Night," Alpie sang. She fluttered off toward her cage.

"Is this your way of exerting control?" I asked, annoyance and love flashing over my skin, heating me too much.

"Murphy," Mila said, her voice serious. "I want to come. Please."

"I want to manage the situation. You. So you can't ever leave me again."

Mila rolled her eyes as she giggled. "I understand that. Sort of. I don't want you to get away again either."

I studied her eyes. The one benefit of her surgery was Mila hadn't taken her Xanax in days—and better, no longer craved it. Her eyes were clear, her smile real. *My* Mila was shining through, and I couldn't be happier. Or more relieved.

I cupped her cheek. "I promise I won't try to force you to do things my way. Or control you. Or get in the way of your patients. I want you happy, Mil. Happy and healthy."

"It would make me happy to come to your concert tomorrow night."

Bollocks. Like I could deny her anything when she looked at me like that.

"On one condition," I said, wrapping my arm around her waist and pulling her closer to me in tiny increments. I searched her features, making sure I wasn't hurting her. She snuggled there, just where I wanted her, her head bobbing up and down eagerly. I pressed a kiss to those sweet lips. Touching her, kissing her thrilled me. Every time.

"What's that?"

I sucked on my tongue ring, considering. Was I ready? Was she? Was I pushing? Trying to control her? "Promise to take a nap."

Mila smirked. "Deal. As long as you nap with me."

I kissed her again. "You drive a hard bargain, Mila Trask, but I accept your terms."

———•———

Nerves skated through my belly. I didn't do nerves. But Mila was out there, watching, listening. I wanted to do her proud, not just of me tonight but to call this tune her own. I played the piece for Jake via Skype while Mila napped.

"You nailed it, mate," he said, smiling. "If that isn't a hit, I know nothing about music."

"You reckon?"

He nodded. "Wish I was there to see this," he sighed. "I wish I could have stayed."

"I'm glad you went home to keep an eye on Mum. This whole thing scared me pretty much shitless."

"Bloody right. Rosemary still whining to the police and the papers, but no one here's listening."

I huffed out a breath, trying to ease the ache in my chest and neck.

"Jake?"

"Yeah?"

"Thanks, mate. Your help with all this, what you did to save Mila and Mum… It means a lot."

"Anything for you, big brother."

"We'll talk tomorrow?"

"You know where to find me."

I smiled as he rung off.

Now, a few hours later, I swiped my palms on my jeans before

I walked out onto the stage. The wood boards creaked, giving under each step. The lights burned my eyes, heated my skin. I nodded at the audience, but my eyes sought hers. There, front row. Next to Noelle's bushy-bright hair.

"Thanks for that. Always nice to hear the love."

Hoots and hollers filled the room. "As many of you know, I'm here with a special lady. She's been through a rather spectacularly awesome week." I winked at Mila who shook her head at me, a sweet smile sliding over those pink lips. "But her stalker's dead and she gets me in the bargain, so I figure it's not a complete loss."

Most of the audience clapped, though some of the girls scowled at Mila.

"None of that now. She was shot protecting me. Not everyone can say their woman saved a bloke's life. I can. And that's heaps cool."

I strummed my guitar. "I've been asked more times than I can count about the impetus for 'She's So Bad.' I'm still not telling that, but I will tell you that I wrote this song for the lovely lady down there. Mila, this is for you, love. And I hope to write you many, many more songs."

The crowd *aw*ed. The same women wiping their eyes. I'd never understand that lot. I started the with a G-chord, strumming softly.

We'd saved this song for the last of the first set because I wanted to take Mila back after this, letting Asher, Hayden, Bill, and Carl play some of the songs they'd put together these past few weeks. I was shocked by how happy they'd been to play this one for me.

But perhaps I shouldn't have been surprised. Both Hayden and Asher found their loves during the past year, but this was a new song, a complicated melody that broke out of the standard four-chords to hit the minor fifth. Because there was nothing traditional about my relationship with Mila, and she deserved an exceptional song. The melody held all the yearning I felt as I'd sat at the dining table in our suite days ago, looking over at Mila and wishing to get back what we'd had.

Asher built the melody with his fast fret work. Bill slid out of a shadow, his guitar hitting the octave lower. They both grinned, pleased as I was with the three-part harmony. Hayden played an intricate series of chords along his keyboard. Carl brushed out some soft beats, his head bobbing.

I kept my focus centered on Mila as I stepped back to the microphone. A flash zinged up my spine. I'd missed her presence in the crowd. I didn't want to tour again without her. Hell, I didn't want to live without her again.

"There comes a time,
Somewhere, down the line
Where it's about what could've been.
But you know what, baby?
I don't worry
cuz I found you again.
Now let me hold you close
and keep you warm.
Pride ain't that mighty,
not when yours is the best love
I cannot lose,
So baby, I'm here, needing you—
If you stay,
Let me hold you close
and keep you warm.

Her lips parted, and her eyes darkened. If I was closer, those brown-green swirls would suck me in.

I sang the next verse as the music built up and crashed over me. Asher revved up, head bent over his guitar. One of the most awe-inspiring moments ever—standing on stage and watching him handle his instrument. I was playing with Asher Smith. He played the lead guitar on a song I wrote.

My eyes snapped back to Mila's. She stared, entranced, even when Noelle leaned over clasp her hand. I slid into the final chorus.

"So baby, shut the door—
Slip in close
and keep me warm."

The crowd went insane. It took five minutes for the fans to quiet enough for us to be heard through the sound system.

Hayden stepped forward, making the gesture to settle down. "You got the biggest treat. Ets wrote that song last week, and you're the only people who've heard it. Now, we have to break. We'll be back with some more excellent tunes in a few."

I slipped off my guitar, handing it to a waiting roadie. I turned to Hayden, and he gripped my hand, pulling me into a one-armed hug. "Bloody amazing! Best song we've ever performed."

"That's because I played the lead," Asher said. He smiled at me, slapped my back. "But Hayden's right. A great one tonight."

"Thanks to both of you, Bill and Carl. Playing with you, having Mila here, that meant everything." I shook their hands, hoping Hayden understood all that I was feeling.

"She's safe and she's yours, mate," Hayden said. "Go home. We'll talk soon."

"Sounds good. And Hayden?" I cleared my throat. "You've always been my best mate."

The corner of Hayden's mouth flipped up. "You have good taste."

CHAPTER THIRTY
Mila

"He wrote you a song, Mil. It's freaking beautiful." Noelle swiped her knuckle under her eye. "Holy hell. He made me cry."

Me, too. The lyrics were gorgeous and heartfelt. But it was the softening of his features, the Murphy I met over five years ago peeking through those shuttered eyes that took my breath away. He hopped off the stage, much to the fans' delight. They surged forward; everyone wanted a piece of him.

"Oi!" Hayden's voice poured out of the speakers. "Give the bloke enough air. He's got to get to his woman. She's recovering from being shot, remember. No jostling that precious merchandise unless you want to see Ets go thermal-nuclear. It's not pretty."

The crowd, even the overzealous women, laughed and stepped back.

He sauntered through the crowd because, hey, Murphy would always thrive on the adoration. But as he stepped close, his eyes sought mine. And I fell into his blue-gray gaze, falling in love with him all over again.

"You sang me a song," I whispered.

He pulled me into his arms with the most exquisite care. He kissed my eyelids, where tears trembled. Then he kissed my nose and I smiled. Finally, he placed his lips over mine. His lip ring was warm and I flicked it with my tongue, pulling his lip deeper into my mouth, just like he liked. We both moaned as need torched over our skin.

He pulled back, much more aware of our audience than I. "Sorry, folks. We're out."

I squeaked as his arm slid just under my bum and he lifted me off the ground. I rested my head against his shoulder, too caught up in Murphy's scent to care about the videos soon to be uploaded on every social media site.

An hour later, we lay facing each other in the hotel suite's bed. He ran his finger over my nose and lip. "I love you in bed with me."

"I love you," I replied.

His eyes lit up just before his teeth flashed white in the building darkness. He wrapped his arm around my waist but didn't pull me any closer. He worried about my wound. I inched toward him until I all our skin touched. He pressed a soft kiss to my forehead.

"I'm sorry, Mila."

"For what?" I murmured.

"Lots of things, really. For thinking I knew best. For the way I handled our breakup, for trying to get you to quit your meds before you were ready. But mostly, that Jordan took away your chance to have another baby. I wanted to see a little girl just like you running 'round our place, rocking some glittery pink princess shit."

I struggled not to laugh. Only Murphy. "I have something to tell you about that."

He ran his fingertip over my nose, across my lip, up my jawline, his eyes following his finger. In all my dreams about being touched like this, none felt as good as the real deal. I sighed.

"You tired?" he asked.

"A little." I paused, wondering if it was too soon. But, no, I should have told him days ago. Like he'd asked me before, *why did you wait?*

I didn't plan to wait, to hold secrets in, ever again.

"My doctor ran blood work after my surgery. A couple of times. Both times my hCG levels came back elevated. I'm going to see a specialist next week."

"Okay. So you need some more tests runs then? Are you going to be okay?" He sounded so worried. I loved how he worried about me.

"The hCG is the pregnancy hormones. It's still early days yet, but it's possible I'm pregnant."

"And you're just now telling me?" Murphy's brow pulled low and a scowl twisted across those gorgeous lips.

"I'm not sure if I am. It'll be another couple of weeks to know for sure." And you haven't told me you love me.

"But you *could* be?"

"Yes."

"And it is likely?"

"It's a strong possibility," I said, grinning up at him. He leaned down and kissed me, taking great care not to bump my shoulder. He pulled back and I hummed against his chest, feeling happier than I could ever remember.

He ran his fingers through my hair, each of us soaking up being near the other. "You're thinking hard in there. Spill it, love," he said.

I thrilled at the endearment, but I wanted the words.

"You start your next tour soon. I bet."

"About that. Flip wants some time off to enjoy his new family. Hayden's settling down into his new life with Briar. Jake wants to go back to uni and study more art history. He's applying to the program here, at Northwestern, where Briar is taking courses."

I giggled. "Jake's turning into a tweedy professor."

"That he is." Murphy's smile slid off, leaving him serious, nervous even. Why did I like him best just off balance? He seemed so much more human. "Mila, I—"

He stopped talking and my heart sank.

"You do have a new song to record," I said, trying to lighten the mood.

"Did that at the show tonight. It's on YouTube and the record label will release it as a live single."

"Thank you. For the song."

"If I'd been smart, I would have written it instead of 'She's So Bad.'" He continued to trace his fingers over my face and my lids grew heavier. "I love you, Mila. I even love your damn annoying bird, who I plan to build an entire room for once you pick out a house. And I have plans to marry you someday. Soon. No. When you're ready. Preferably before the little nipper shows up."

"Don't be silly," I scoffed. "You don't have to marry me."

"I'll propose as soon as you're feeling well enough."

"But it's so soon after we got back—"

"Mila? You need to fight less. With me, I mean. You're getting a big fucking ring and you're going to take my name, make the bub ours."

"Oh, am I?" My tone was dry. "What if that's not what I want?"

Murphy groaned. "Bollocks. I'm trying. I'll ask you right as soon as you feel well enough for the rest of your surprise evening."

"What if I don't want a surprise evening?"

"Go out, take on the rest of the world but let me give you this.

And you have to promise to stay safe whilst you save other people. Because I *need* you. And I love you. We're meant."

I pressed my lips to his throat, soaking in the words I'd desperately needed to hear. Pulling back, I looked up into his eyes. "I love you, too."

He smiled, brighter than I'd ever seen before, which made me smile.

"You think we were meant?" I asked.

"No." His finger traced my nose, lips, cheeks. "I know it."

ACKNOWLEDGMENTS

There are so many people I need to thank. This journey wasn't an easy one. First, my husband, Chris, and my parents. Your support made this possible.

Taylor, your thoughtful comments were insightful and so very helpful. I'm so glad we've had the opportunity to work together.

Juliette, thank you, thank you, THANK YOU for all the help with the Aussie-isms. And for reading such an early draft and giving me hope there was, indeed, something special in this story.

Shane and Susie, your knowledge of the criminal justice system allowed me to write an informed story. Thank you so, so much for sharing your expertise.

My LERA friends, thank you so much for your generosity and support.

Clarissa, thank you for an amazing cover. I love it.

Nicole, your thoughtful edits made this book shine (just like the ones before it!). I cannot thank you enough. I've so enjoyed getting to know you and now count you a dear friend as well as a kick-ass editor.

Erin, you amaze me with your ability to create such strong back cover copy. My books are stronger because of your efforts. Thank you.

And to my readers, thank you, thank you, thank you for reading. You're the best! Be sure to say hello on Facebook or Twitter. I'd love to "meet" you all.

ALSO BY ALEXA PADGETT

Sweet Solace (Book One of the Seattle Sound Series)

She Knew Him When

When they first met, she was far too young—seventeen, and already in love with the man who would break her heart. Asher Smith was an up-and-coming songwriter, but he knew better than to show his fascination. He wrote a song for Dahlia. And then he moved on. His whiskey-rough voice made him a star, even as fame extracted its price.

He Never Forgot Her

When she sees Asher next, Dahlia Dorsey is the widowed mother of a teenager, a reclusive writer. She's given up on happy endings—she can't even script them for her characters. But a moonlit beach and the touch of an old friend turn loose her pain and her desires, whether she's ready or not.

They're Risking It All

Dahlia's career is on the rocks. Asher's family is falling apart. Neither can chase a passing attraction. But for two souls wounded worse than they can admit, the connection between them is a balm too precious to refuse—and a thrill too exhilarating to resist...

BETWEEN BREATHS (Book Two of the Seattle Sound Series)

Grief brought them together

A hospice center is no place to fall in lust. But with his world cracking during his estranged mother's last days, Hayden Crewe needs something sweet to focus on. It doesn't matter that he's the backbone of Australia's hottest international rock group—here, watching his mother die, he's more alone than ever. So when he meets long-legged, clear-minded Briar Moore, he suddenly knows exactly what will fill the hole inside.

Fortune will drag them apart

Briar has just escaped a job and relationship that nearly crushed her. Crawling out of the wreckage of her previous life, she's done playing it safe. Sexy, vibrant Hayden is what she wants, and Briar is going to take him. For as long as she can...

Out of heartbreak comes hope

With their time short and the ghosts of their pasts haunting every moment, Briar and Hayden know they've fallen too deep. While those few, intense days changed them both forever, everyone knows a connection this intense should burn out as fast as it ignited...

Read on for a peak at Abbi's book, MANY SOUNDS OF SILENCE.

CHAPTER ONE
Clay

This was one of the last times I'd stand in this spot, ever.

Glancing around campus, inhaling the sharp tang of a late September morning, I reveled in it—that crackle of energy that always accompanied the first day of school. I'd looked forward to day one every year since kindergarten when I finally got to join my brother at "big school." For the first time, nostalgia warred with excitement.

In nine months, I'd have my degrees in music theory and finance. I wasn't going to be caught, as my father had been, without an understanding of the business side of the music industry. That's what really mattered—more than talent or stage presence.

With my contacts in the music scene, Kai, Dane, and I were sitting in a mighty prime spot. Just where we wanted. Because next year, we were…My thoughts skidded to a halt. Why was that guy taking pictures?

We hadn't blown up big enough to warrant paps on campus. His camera wasn't pointed at me…there. Long, dark red hair bobbing away from me. Yep, the photographer was snapping shots of that girl.

I tracked her as she walked across the Quad, near the fountain. Her hair glowed in the sunlight, whipping out behind her before sweeping forward across her face. She brushed it back with an absent-minded hand as she cast a furtive glance back at the photographer. She knew he was there, and if the tiny frown was any indication, she wasn't happy about his invasion of her privacy.

I totally got that.

She wore gray Toms and jeans, cuffs rolled up to show off a hint of slender calves and slim ankles. Her top was gray, elbow-length. A kind of don't-notice-me outfit that blended into the crowd.

Except she didn't blend. Part of it was the way she held herself—tight, tense, waiting for the next blow. I knew that stance because it was my mother's since she sat my brother Colten and I down to tell us our baby sister Cassidy had cancer.

The photographer was *still* taking pictures of her. Maybe she was a model or actress. I moved forward, trying to catch a glimpse of her face as a niggling feeling of recognition built. Her messenger bag's strap cut between her breasts, emphasizing them. She didn't look at anyone; she moved with purpose toward her goal.

Because she was alone, I assumed she was a freshman or a transfer student. Finally, I was close enough to catch a glimpse of her profile. She didn't have the wide-eyed wonder of a first-timer, which made the transfer option more likely. I tracked her until a group of girls passed between us.

I blew out a breath, trying to push aside my annoyance and need. Annoyance *because of* the need.

I wanted to know her, tell her I understood her frustration. But that wasn't the worst of my ridiculousness. Already, I dreamt about the breathy way she'd say my name when I gripped her chin, tilted her lips up to meet mine.

A man stopped in front of her, and she stepped back when he touched her arm. Her body tensed, as it would with a stranger invading personal space, mirroring my own stiffening muscles. The pap moved in closer, the predator scenting blood.

Oh, fuck no. Before I realized it, I was once again moving across the open area.

I'd already picture my fist in the guy's face when she brushed passed him. The photographer set aside his camera, clearly annoyed the shot wasn't a money one.

A big group of students moved between me and the girl, laughing and joking, clearly glad to be back on campus. If I went after her, the photographer would stick around. Craning my neck, I watched her open the door to the Bagley Hall. The girl was into chemistry.

I smiled, feeling like a cat given a bowl of cream, especially when the photographer packed up his equipment. Good riddance.

"You're that glad to see me, Clay?"

I glanced down at Bethany, quickly arranging my features. She was our version of Mel from *Flight of the Conchords* except Bethany was shorter, way clingier and pretty much not someone I wanted to see. Ever. She reminded me of those pixies my little sister used to watch. A bothersome one.

I spun about and started walking toward the Music Building. She fell in next to me. I tried hard not to sigh. And failed.

"What's that about?" she asked.

You. Not getting the hint. "Just tired."

"That's too bad. You should take better care of yourself."

I grunted. She kept trotting next to me.

"I missed you guys. I even stayed on campus, hoping you'd do some shows."

"Nope. We went home for a while. You know, to see family."

Which is what you should've done, too.

"I took a couple of classes. In fashion design? Oh, and my cousin came to visit. We went to a couple of gigs. Not as good as yours."

She batted her stubby eyelashes at me. Batted. Them.

I shied away, unsuccessfully suppressing a shudder. Whatever she was thinking wasn't going happen.

"Glad you got to spend some quality family time. So I have to go. I'm late."

"But it's 8:30. Next classes don't stay until nine. We should grab a coffee. Catch up."

She put her small hand on my arm, and I suppressed the urge to shake her off. Bethany's expression collapsed into one of hurt. I gritted my teeth against the good manners so ingrained in me by my mother. There was only one woman I wanted touching me. The one with the beautiful hair and intent, haunted expression.

"Meeting with my advisor."

"Then I'll see you at lunch?" Another hopeful, puppy-dog look.

God, I hoped not. "Got some stuff to take care of." A blatant lie I hated to give. No way I was eating on campus now. So much for first-day excitement "Bye."

I trotted into the music building and headed toward one of the empty practice rooms. Sure, Northern U wasn't Berklee School of Music, but turning down that spot worked out pretty well because I was still getting an excellent education with state-of-the-art equipment and the chance to double major in finance. Meeting Dane and Kai that first week of school solidified the rightness of sticking close to home. We'd just gotten Cassidy's Hodgkin's diagnosis, and there was no way I could be on the East Coast worrying about my baby sister. In fact, I would've traded anything—including my band's successes—to make sure Cassidy regained her health.

I hadn't brought my guitar, but I could work on scales on one of the grand pianos.

I should be more patient with Bethany—her rabid interest in our band really helped get us off the ground three years ago when we were just starting out. She'd dated Dane then, much to his embarrassment.

I'd never understood his attraction. She was tiny, perky, more than willing to help out. Dane said she was fun in bed, willing to try anything, always open to his ideas. Which was a place I would *never* go. Bethany loved to flash those soulful eyes. Eyes that held sharp interest and dark secrets.

I hated secrets and lies. I'd lived with both for years from my peers and it was the fastest way out of my circle. Much as I wanted to kick Bethany out, I couldn't tell a girl who was barely tall enough to ride a rollercoaster to get out of my space.

I had, though, when she climbed naked into my bed after a party. Kicking her out had been a no-brainer—getting her to actually leave had been difficult. But I hadn't fought her territorial growling too hard because the rest of the females on campus kept their distance. I liked the ability to walk around again without a mob of groupies following me—that had gotten old within weeks of playing our first gig our freshman year. As had the offers for just about anything sexual I could imagine. Not that I didn't like sex. With the right person, sex was fantastic.

I just wasn't interested in a long-term relationship. Nor was I interested in a one-night stand. Limited my choices.

Maybe I'd taken my celibacy too far, especially if I was panting after one glimpse of that mahogany hair and pert ass. I dropped my bag and shut the door. Setting the alarm on my phone, I sat down and began to play.

I'd worked through all the minor scales and had nearly finished one of my favorite Prokofiev's etudes when I realized whom that girl was.

My fingers collapsed onto the keys. "Holy shit."

"I agree that was a really shitty ending."

I turned on the bench. "Kai." I fist bumped him. "Good seeing you, man."

"So what was that about? You were rocking that piece then you got this surprised look on your face and lost your concentration. I've never seen you do that before. Well, I don't see you play the piano often either."

"I saw Abigail Dorsey this morning. By the fountain. She walked into the science building."

My frown deepened. I hadn't liked that dude touching her. That bothered me more than the paparazzi. Kai raised his eyebrow. His arms were crossed and his gray tee shirt rode up his biceps, flashing his tattoos. One was some Celtic design. The one on the other side was Hebrew. He'd told me what they both meant right after he got them our freshman year, but I'd forgotten.

"And we care about some chick because?"

"She's Asher Smith's stepdaughter."

Kai dropped his hands to his sides and his eyes lit up. "Really? Think she can get me an autograph? Maybe a guitar lesson? That guy is amazing."

I shook my head and picked up my phone and bag. "You don't play the guitar. You play the bass. And as the son of a rocker, I can tell you that's the last thing she's going to want. After you hitting on her, of course. She flattened a guy's ego this morning in under ten seconds."

"Aw, stop being a dick. I could learn to rip the chords, especially if a rock legend was teaching me."

"No, Kai. Don't do that. Actually, don't even talk to her. You'd just ask her for sex and then be mad when she turned you down."

"Didn't you see those pics of her? When she was at some school in Cali. Dude, she likes to party. Maybe Asher Smith brought her back to Seattle to get her to buckle down. He sure has since he met her mom. I'd be pissed if his music wasn't so amazing." Kai shook his head. "Maybe love can help with creativity. Cuz the Supernaturals are hitting a second wave of awesome I've never seen before."

"Don't count on it."

The familiar flush of heat creeping over my skin at the L-word. People went searching for it like it was the holy grail of youth and perfection. It wasn't. My parents loved each other, and it was hard work for both of them. I was glad they were still together. Most of the time, anyway.

"Asher's just hit his stride, found some creative juice in the tank. I'm surprised Abbi's here. I heard they didn't get along," I said, picking up my pack before turning off the lights, stepping out of the room and shutting the door.

"Why are we talking about Asher Smith and some girl? Didn't he get married?" Dane asked. He was shorter than me, thin, with a shaggy mop of blond hair. Both his eyebrows were pierced and he had a tattoo crawling up his neck. Some Manga character I figured he'd hate when he was thirty.

270

My mom was old-fashioned. With a capital O. She'd made my brother and me promise not to get body art, and because my mom didn't ask a lot, I was cool with her request.

"Saw your ex already," I said, letting my lip curl with disgust. "She was lying in wait for me. Expected a lunch invite. Because, you know, super fan."

Dane leaned his head back and closed his eyes. "We broke up years ago. And she's more of a stalker than a super fan."

"Now she's got her sights set on Mr. Banjo-player here," Kai chuckled. "Thanks to Mumford and Sons and The Avett Brothers, the banjo is sexy. The new guitar and all that."

"If that was true, we would have traded you in for a cellist," I said without any heat.

Kai loved to tease me about the banjo, but when we'd started featuring it in our songs, our songs—and following—took off. I could play it and the kick drum at the same time, a trick I'd practiced from the time I was seven and my dad let me start playing on his old set down in the basement.

"Bethany can look all she wants," I said. "From a distance. She just can't touch. And I wish she wouldn't talk to me. She's creepy."

"Dude, she's like a third your size," Dane said.

"That's part of the problem. We can't be from the same species."

"She claims to love you," Kai said.

My shoulders tensed and I glared at him. "Love and rock-and-roll don't mix. Like pickles and chocolate—two great tastes that are much worse together."

Kai snickered while Dane scratched his head, considering. "Not buying that. Nessa's pretty awesome. Your parents are tight. Why don't you follow that example?"

"Clay thinks he saw Asher Smith's stepdaughter here," Kai said to ease my building tension. I never spoke to anyone about my dad's affairs because that was the family line, and Kai and Dane assumed the long list of names linked to my father's were to sell more magazines and website clicks. But Kai also knew how sensitive I was about the topic. I shot him a glance filled with thanks.

"I've seen her. She lives across from Ness and Jenna. From what they've seen so far, she seems fairly quiet and serious." Dane shrugged. "Maybe she pulled her shit together. Kinda would have to after those pics went live, right? I mean, she was a mess in those."

"What?" Kai rolled his eyes. "Now's the time to live it up, baby. It's not like Asher's going to ride her about it. He did crazy shit when he was her age. Part of why he's my hero."

"I don't think she's a partier," Dane said. If Nessa told him that, he'd run with it. This was another reason why I was against long-term relationships. Dane couldn't have his own thoughts anymore. "I read an article about him—did you see it? Went live last week. He talked about how he was hurt and did lots of stupid stunts because the girl he wanted was with someone else. The girl turned out to be Abbi's mom. They're all settled in, playing family."

"She's hot," I said. "Abigail. Cool name, all old-fashioned. Probably why she's such a partier."

"Invite her to our show next week," Kai said. "Maybe she can talk Asher into coming."

I shook my head again. "If my folks find out she's here, they'll ask me to befriend her."

"Something crawled up your ass. So you have to be nice? It'll get you closer to Asher." Kai asked. "And to Abigail."

"Naw, man, I don't want to use her like that." Mainly because I didn't want to get too close. My reaction to her—from a distance—had been electrifying. What if I actually met her? I could already see the headlines: *Local rocker screwing school party girl. Both go up in flames.*

Nope. Not happening. Famous people couldn't stick it out. Look at Brangelina. If that paradise blew, then I didn't stand a chance at dating some chick with her own famous people problems and hang-ups.

"It's like you have feelings," Kai mocked.

I shrugged. "I feel just fine. For the right people."

"Hookups don't count." Kai snorted, thinking, no doubt, about my lack of dating the past year and a half.

"Yeah. All three of 'em last year. What are you up to, man-whore?" I responded with more rancor than any of us expected.

"Did you get Abbi's number?" Dane asked as he pushed between us. Both Kai and I had some inches on him, but Dane was quick. Plus, he'd studied ten different kinds of martial arts growing up so he knew all kinds ways to break me into pieces, fast. "You did that at least. Right?"

"I didn't get her number because I didn't talk to her. And you guys aren't going to bother her either. She's a hot mess." A beautiful, famous hot mess. "We don't need that shit in our orbit."

I glared at both of them until Dane threw his hands up in the air.

"I'm not dirty macking your girl. Got my own. Chill, dude."

"She's not my girl. Look, we've got to make this semester shine. We've been working hard for that contract. We're not screwing ourselves over because of some chick."

We entered the classroom. Each of us studied various aspects of

music, and this was our only course together this year. I missed
hanging out with Dane and Kai on campus more often but I
was glad to see the light at the end of this slog. Double majoring
wasn't the easiest of choices.

"Whatever you say, bucko. But I can tell. You like her," Kai said.

"I don't," I said, scowling.

"Yet," Kai said. He stretched out in his seat, eyes wondering to
the few females already in their seats. Dismissing them, he turned
back to me. "I've never seen you wound so tight about one before. And you didn't even talk to her."

"Yet." Dane smirked.

"Drop it. Both of you. I don't want to talk about her anymore."

The instructor came in, and I was glad for the interruption. But
Kai made a point, much as I hated to admit it. Something about
Abigail had gotten to me. And I didn't like it—not one bit.

———◆———

Footsteps pounded down the stairs. I braced myself at the
bottom, legs spread and arms open. Cassidy hurled herself into
my arms as she'd done every time I came home. She seemed even
lighter than she had the last time I'd held her in my arms two
weeks ago.

I rubbed her back, counting each of her vertebrae on the
way down. I hated the physical manifestation of her illness. I
squeezed my eyes shut, heart aching, as I held my baby sister for
a long moment.

"Missed you, ladybug."

She wiggled free from my arms and set her fists on her little hips. "I told you not to call me that anymore. I'm fourteen. Do you want to embarrass me in front of my friends?"

"Course not, Cassidy. Just, you know, it's hard for big brothers to remember you're growing up." Sort of. Though I was beyond thankful she was home for her fifteenth birthday next week. Four years ago, Cassidy was healthy and even bubblier than she was now.

"How are you feeling?" I asked.

"You sound like Mom. All she did after our appointment yesterday was cry." Cassidy rolled her eyes. Like me, Cassidy had inherited our mom's green eyes. But Cassidy's were darker than mine, more uniform in color, and looked way too large for her thin face. The second round of chemotherapy had been so hard on her, but her hair was finally growing back and she looked cute with the dark fluff swirling around her head. I was still trying to get used to the color—Cassidy used to have dirty blond hair.

Like so many details of our lives, her hair color was pretty much a nonissue.

I opened my mouth, but the words wouldn't come. Clearing my throat, I tried again. "So that means the doctors were wrong and you're not in remission?"

Cassidy frowned at me. "It means I'm not dead yet, and I'd really like it if someone would remember that I have a life to live."

I swallowed down my follow up question, knowing it would irritate her more. As soon as possible, I'd ask about the appointment. Right now, Cassidy needed normalcy.

"That you do, Cassie. How about we hit the pool?"

"Now you're talking! Be right back." Cassidy ran up the stairs. Sometimes, like now, she seemed so unaffected by her illness, it was hard to remember just how touch-and-go her prognosis had been.

"Hey, honey," Mom said, sliding an arm around my waist.

"Cassidy said you cried after her appointment yesterday. Everything okay?"

Mom's eyes, so like Cassie's, filled with tears again. She'd aged a lot these past few years as Cassidy sank deeper into the disease. I bit the inside of my cheek, hating the secret I'd kept from her. Seeing her now, vulnerable, I knew I'd made the right decision. For her.

I hugged her tighter, wishing these past few years were different.

"The PET scan was clean."

"That's great." I grinned. Damn, that was the best news I'd heard in ages. "Excellent. So why the tears?"

Mom cleared her throat. "It's just…we didn't expect her to make it during the last round. I'm so happy."

I wrapped my arms around her again and let her cry. After a moment, she patted my chest. "You're a good man, Clay. Thanks. I needed that. Your dad's trying, but…" she sighed, looking away. "Nearly losing Cassie changed him."

More than my mom knew. The anger swelled again. We'd all been to counseling when Cassie was sick, and Dr. Thomas suggested I talk to my dad about the situation. I'd been too hurt, then too angry to broach the subject.

With Mom and Dad stable and Cassie improving, it seemed like the wrong time to bring up Dad's affair. Correction. His last affair that I knew about. I didn't want to shatter my mom's happiness. She, like Cassie, deserved the best of everything. I bent and kissed her cheek.

"Anything for the prettiest lady I know."

Mom chuckled as she wiped away her tears. "You are such a flirt. Just like your father."

"Nah." Horror and frustration built in my throat, clinging there. If I didn't keep my feelings buried, my mom would notice. I looked away, pretending to be searching for Dad. "Where is he, by the way?"

"In the hot tub with Colten."

"Let's head that way, then."

"You go. I'm still too weepy to be much fun. I'll join you in a bit."

I gave her a final squeeze before heading out the pool. It was indoors, taking up what would've been the basement if we'd had one. Seattle was really too cold for an outdoor pool most of the year, but Mom had insisted we put one in when Colten and I were young. We'd had too much energy for her to run off.

Once Dad finally figured out how to get and keep the money he'd earned from his record label, he'd hired the workers as a gift to Mom, and the natatorium turned out to be the most-used room in the house.

My brother and Dad were there, leaning back and enjoying the hot bubbles.

"Clay. Glad you could come."

Dad smiled at me. I'd searched his eyes and smile for months to see if he looked different, acted differently. He didn't, and that led me to wonder how many times he'd cheated on my mom over the years. Had our pool been a gift to assuage his guilt?

I cleared my throat, forcing the word *asshole* back down.

"Sorry I'm late. Slept in. Cassidy told me the good news. I'm sure you're relieved."

A shadow crossed Dad's face. "Yeah, now Cassidy can enjoy being a girl again."

There was more to that statement, but I didn't push it. I'm not sure I could handle another one of his secrets.